THE
ENDS
OF
THINGS

THE ENDS OF

A Novel

THINGS

Sandra Chwialkowska

BLACK STONE
PUBLISHING

Copyright © 2025 by Sandra Chwialkowska
Published in 2025 by Blackstone Publishing
Cover and book design by Alenka Vdovič Linaschke

All rights reserved. This book or any portion
thereof may not be reproduced or used in any manner
whatsoever without the express written permission
of the publisher except for the use of brief quotations
in a book review.

The characters and events in this book are fictitious.
Any similarity to real persons, living or dead, is coincidental
and not intended by the author.

Printed in the United States of America

First edition: 2025
ISBN 979-8-212-98527-7
Fiction / Psychological

Version 1

Blackstone Publishing
31 Mistletoe Rd.
Ashland, OR 97520

www.BlackstonePublishing.com

To Jeff, who, long ago, convinced me this should be a book.

And to Dad, with all my love.

Absence, the highest form of presence.

—James Joyce

North Eleuthera Airport

Glass Window Bridge

The Pink Sands

Gregory Town

Governor's Harbour Airport

GREAT
BAHAMA
BANK

Eleuthera

ATLANTIC
OCEAN

CHAPTER ONE

From Laura's window on the plane, it seemed like the only thing keeping the cobalt waves of the Atlantic Ocean from spilling into the turquoise shallows of the Great Bahama Bank was the long, pencil-thin island. The waters pressed against Eleuthera's shores, threatening to swallow it whole, but the island managed to keep itself intact and the two massive bodies of water apart, in eternal parallel.

Laura had read on the resort's website that at its skinniest point, the island tapered to an isthmus that spanned only thirty feet across, giving Eleuthera the nickname *the Narrowest Place on Earth*. At that juncture, a strip of rock had once formed a natural arch called the Glass Window Bridge. Winslow Homer had been so moved by the ethereal sight that he'd painted its likeness during his trip to the Bahamas in 1885.

As the plane made its descent, the beach resorts that dotted the coastline came into view, and Laura pointed them out to Dave. He peered out her window, his face close to hers, but he didn't seem as dazzled by the sight as she, presumably because he'd been to the Caribbean before.

"I'm so glad we're doing this. You're going to love it," he said and squeezed her hand.

Laura smiled and gazed out the window as the topography of the island revealed itself in more detail. She felt giddy. Their vacation was very sudden, booked impulsively on short notice, and yet she felt like she had been waiting for this trip all her life.

Laura squinted in the bright sunlight as she and Dave stepped onto the tarmac. Perspiration instantly collected under her breasts and dripped down her back, and she couldn't pull off her jacket fast enough. The man in the Hawaiian shirt and sandals who'd looked stupid at their gate at JFK seemed wise now, and she wished she had worn her flip-flops on the plane instead of her sneakers, but they were buried at the bottom of Dave's suitcase.

After they claimed their bags and emerged from the tiny airport onto the street, Dave placed his hand on Laura's lower back and ferried her toward the nearest taxi.

"Where can I take you?" the driver asked, leaning languorously against his cab.

"The Pink Sands," Dave said.

"How long is the drive?" Laura asked. She couldn't wait to see the resort, to swim in the sea, to drink a cocktail. She felt an impatient yearning for her entire vacation to happen all at once.

"Relax, miss. You're on Bahamian time now." The driver smiled, revealing a row of teeth as white as his short-sleeved shirt, and loaded their bags into the trunk.

No one here seemed to be in a great rush to get anywhere. Even time itself seemed to move more slowly, as though it were filtered through the humid air that hung heavily, like wet laundry, over everything.

The cabbie shut the trunk and slid into the driver's seat, which Laura was surprised to find was on the right side of the car, but then she remembered the resort's website had also said that the Bahamas was a former British colony and people still drove on the left side of the road, a vestige of imperial rule.

They sped along Queen's Highway, which spanned the length of the island and connected all the villages that were scattered across the western coast. The road was mostly empty, save the occasional pickup truck that roared past them blasting percussive Junkanoo music.

"What's goin' on, you two? All is well?" the driver asked, smiling at them in the rearview mirror. "Here on our little island for a vacation?"

"We are. Just for a few days," Dave said.

"You're gonna have a nice time."

"How long have you been driving a taxi?" Dave was always asking people how long they'd been doing their jobs. He always seemed genuinely interested in the people he met, and because he asked questions that endeared him to them, Laura found she could participate in conversations without having to engage directly. The driver, whose name was Tafari, told him he'd been driving for two years, that he and his brother had saved up to buy the car, and once they paid off their loan, they planned to build a house in the hills. As Tafari described his plans to Dave, Laura listened passively and gazed out the window at the Caribbean Sea, which unfolded, sparkling and blue, all the way to the horizon. It was early June, and after a long New York winter and a gray, drizzly spring, the vibrancy of the color was astonishing, and all she could do was sit and stare.

The vacation was Dave's idea.

"What's this?" he asked, one night two weeks prior, when he turned her laptop around, revealing an Excel file on the screen entitled *vacations.xlsx*. Laura froze. They'd been dating for six weeks and had shared many things—food, her bed, his maroon hoodie—but her spreadsheet was something she had never intended anyone to see. To have this relic of her single life in his hands embarrassed her.

"It's just something I work on sometimes," she said lamely, walking over to take her laptop from him. But he held it out of her reach.

"Bora Bora. Tuscany. Are these places you've been to?" he asked, arching an eyebrow.

Laura couldn't tell if his tone was playful or mocking, and she felt her cheeks grow warm.

She had never been to either of those places. She had dreamed of traveling the world ever since she was a girl but was discouraged by her mother, by her friends, by society itself, it seemed, from traveling alone.

Her mother had cautioned her that traveling alone as a woman was dangerous. Threats, she was warned, lurked around every corner. Men could backpack across Europe without fearing unwanted advances or rapes, but not women. Still, Laura yearned to traipse through open-air markets, swim in cerulean waters, and lie under palm trees while drinking colorful cocktails garnished with tropical fruit.

She had faded childhood memories of family vacations—long, hot car trips with her crayons melting on the back dash—and an awkward recollection of a high school exchange trip to France with a Parisian girl who chain-smoked cigarettes and ignored Laura completely. But she yearned to experience the world outside the constraints of a familial or collegiate itinerary. College loans, however, left her too broke to travel, and law school saddled her with even more debt. Not that it mattered—during her first few years as an attorney at Reinhart, Mader & Stern, vacations were discouraged, and she felt an unspoken pressure to put in long hours at the firm. Five sweltering New York summers came and went with her locked away in her office, wrapped in her black cardigan with the tortoiseshell buttons to combat the AC that blasted at corporate freeze levels.

She contented herself with watching a TV show on Netflix that followed two jet-setting hosts who visited exclusive destinations around the world. Every episode featured a different resort, each one more luxurious than the last, outfitted with high-end amenities like private plunge pools and tree-house-style suites located in lush rainforests. Laura would watch the show after work while eating takeout and drinking wine, and whenever a particular resort appealed to her, she'd enter its details into her Excel file. Among her favorite entries were a rustic Italian villa that had sweeping views of the Tuscan countryside and an overwater bungalow on Bora Bora that overlooked a blue lagoon. Whenever she added a new place to the Excel file, she felt a little thrill of adventure, but it was always followed by a twinge of sadness because she knew she'd never have the courage to travel alone. She dreamed that maybe one day she'd meet someone who would want to travel with her, but since she was perpetually single, she didn't see how that could come to pass.

The previous year, her fifth as an associate, Laura had decided that she'd finally paid her dues and was overdue for a weeklong getaway. The thought of vacationing alone still made her anxious, though, and traveling as part of a group of singles made her squirm. She wanted to travel with someone she already knew. In her long-held fantasy of adulthood, in which her life was fully activated with a career and disposable income, there was a boyfriend in the picture. But she didn't have a boyfriend at the time. Her mother had said it was Laura's own fault that she hadn't "found someone" because she hadn't really "made the effort," hadn't "put herself out there." She didn't even have an online dating profile. The idea of revealing intimate aspects of herself to strangers on the internet terrified and repulsed her. Besides, she wanted to meet someone in real life. In college, she had been surrounded by guys her age, but the few relationships she'd had had been short lived, and now she found it nearly impossible to meet people outside work.

So when her colleague Jasmine Chaudhry complained of burnout, Laura had suggested they take a girls' trip. Over a lunch of boxed salad, while flipping through the latest issue of *Vogue* and analyzing the resort wear on display, she had proposed that they decamp for a few nights to some Caribbean island.

"I would love to," Jasmine had said, "but Brian would never forgive me."

Brian was Jasmine's boyfriend, and on the rare occasion that she did take time off work, she spent her precious vacation days with him. Laura knew for a fact that Jasmine and Brian had taken a zip-lining trip to Costa Rica with another couple, and she had wondered if Jasmine would have taken her up on her offer had Laura been in a relationship at the time. She'd considered inviting Brian to come along but decided against it because she didn't want to be a third wheel. So she abandoned the idea.

Until, months later, Dave broached it.

"We should go," he said, handing back her laptop.

"To Bora Bora?" Laura was skeptical.

"That might be a little rich for my blood, but I bet we could get a discount at one of Marcus Lowry's resorts."

Marcus Lowry was the owner of The Sands International, a global chain of luxury beach resorts. And Dave, who was also a lawyer at Reinhart, Mader & Stern, handled Lowry's account.

"He's got a place in the Bahamas, on Eleuthera. I think it's called the Pink Sands. He's offered me a friends-and-family discount. Why don't we go there?" Dave said it so simply. Laura marveled at how easy it was for him to just decide to go somewhere, like it was no big deal.

She had always been intrigued by the Bahamas, those seven hundred islands floating in turquoise waters, but she had never heard of Eleuthera. It sounded exotic and remote, so she was surprised to discover there were direct flights from JFK to Nassau, followed by a short connecting flight to the island on a much smaller plane.

As Laura scrolled through the Pink Sands' website, studying the photos of attractive couples lounging in infinity pools and enjoying candlelit dinners, she could not imagine herself staying there alone, but she could definitely see herself there with Dave.

Dave was most excited about the Seahorse, the resort's open-air restaurant. Not only did it boast an impressive seafood menu, but Marcus Lowry had apparently lured Aito Nakamura, a famous sushi chef who had been formally trained in Japan, away from the Nobu Miami with the promise that in the Bahamas he could spear his own bluefin tuna.

Dave was a foodie and often sought out restaurants owned by celebrity chefs. Every weekend since they'd started dating, he'd taken Laura to a different spot, and because he was a much more adventurous eater than she, he'd introduced her to dishes she'd never heard of before. Shakshuka and bouillabaisse and fideuà. Laura accepted his invites gamely but never told him about the digestive issues that ensued, as her stomach was not as strong as his. Though she didn't always care for the food, she loved hearing him talk about it. His face was never more animated than when he described a dish he loved. The way he grabbed at life was exciting, and she found his spontaneity among his most attractive qualities.

So when he suggested they stay at the Pink Sands, she took the plunge and called the reservation line. She was informed that the resort's twelve luxury cabins were all booked up with a six-month waiting list.

There had been one cancellation, however, for the Tuesday after next. It was short notice, and the cabin was only available for a three-night stay, and it was pricey, even with the 20 percent off friends-and-family discount, but Dave suggested they split the cost and book it. At first, Laura balked at this impulsive move. She had no time to shop for travel clothes or plan an itinerary. Dave shrugged and said they'd figure it out when they got there. The going, he said, was the important thing. Though she was anxious, she couldn't help but also feel a little thrill. There was no time to prepare or worry, no time to stage-manage every detail. All she could do was pack and go.

Three miles past a village called Gregory Town, they saw a sign for the Pink Sands. The driver pulled up to a twenty-foot white metal gate flanked on both sides by dense foliage. A security guard carrying a clipboard emerged from a hut next to the gate and asked to see their passports. Laura and Dave handed them over, and after cross-referencing their names with the photocopies of their passports Laura had been asked to send when she made the booking online, the guard returned to his hut and pushed a button to open the gate. He waved them through, and they drove down a narrow road under a dense canopy of trees.

"Here we are," the driver said, stopping in front of a white gazebo. Dave paid him, and they both climbed out. A woman emerged from the gazebo with a tray in her hands. She wore a white silk blouse and a white pencil skirt, and her black hair was pulled back into an elegant bun at the nape of her neck. On her tray were two rolled hand towels and two pink cocktails garnished with paper umbrellas.

"Good afternoon and welcome to the Pink Sands," she said and offered them each a towel that was cool to the touch. "Would you care for some rum punch?" She gestured at the glasses on her tray. They thanked her and both took a glass. The punch smacked the back of Laura's throat, cold and sweet and surprisingly strong.

"My name is Priscilla." She pointed with a manicured finger to the name tag pinned to her blouse. "I'm the concierge, and I will help you with anything you need during your stay with us, Mr. and Mrs. Mitchell."

Hearing her name merged with Dave's reminded Laura of how whenever her old friend Chloe Shipman had a crush on a boy in high school, she would write her first name and the boy's last name over and over in her notebook, practicing her signature for some imaginary future in which she and the boy would be married.

Laura and Dave were not married, and this was their first vacation as a couple, but instead of correcting Priscilla, Laura took another sip of her drink.

Dave didn't notice Priscilla's gaffe, or if he did, he didn't seem to mind. Laura would have made a joke about it, but she didn't think they were far enough along in their relationship for her to do so. Besides, she didn't want to come off as one of those women who planned out their entire lives with their boyfriends. She hadn't even decided whether she would keep her last name, Phillips, if she ever got married, because she'd never been engaged or even in a relationship long enough to make it worth thinking about.

Laura followed Dave into the gazebo, where Priscilla checked them in on her computer.

"It's too bad you'll be leaving before the Pineapple Festival starts on Saturday. People fly in from all over."

"What's the Pineapple Festival?" Dave asked.

"It's a celebration of Eleuthera's history of pineapple farming. There's lots of dancing and eating and a beauty pageant and a big concert." Priscilla smiled proudly as she described the festivities.

"And pineapple," Dave said.

"Yes, and lots of pineapple." Priscilla smiled again. It wasn't her professional smile but a more natural, unguarded smile. Dave had this effect on people. He wasn't flirting exactly, more like actively listening. His innate curiosity about people was part of what made him good at his job. The partners at the firm were always inviting him to signing meetings so he could charm prospective clients. Not in a slick way but in a way that made people want to tell him their life stories. Even at the end of their cab ride to the resort, Tafari had given Dave his card and offered him a discount if he ever needed another ride.

"Well, we'll just have to come back then," he said to Priscilla and smiled. She returned the smile, and because she had warmed to him, she smiled at Laura too. One of the advantages of being with Dave was that the little courtesies extended to him were also extended to her.

Priscilla handed them keys to their cabin along with a map of the resort, on which she circled the gym, the spa, and the Wi-Fi password. She ushered them back outside to a golf cart, where a porter in a white uniform had transferred their bags from the taxi and was waiting to take them to their cabin.

Cocktails in hand, they climbed into the back of the golf cart and were whisked down the road. They drove through a grove of palm trees and over a small hill, and then the view opened up, revealing the resort's lush grounds. Everything here—the open-air restaurant, the row of oceanfront cabins, the lounge chairs and beach umbrellas, even the hammocks that swayed between the palm trees—was white. The homogeneity of the color palette made everything look luxe and sophisticated. She couldn't believe they were here. She couldn't believe they were like one of those couples in the photos who actually went to places like this.

"Welcome to your new home," the porter said as they pulled up in front of cabin five. Laura and Dave climbed out and carried their drinks inside.

The cabin was spacious and airy with white walls and a vaulted ceiling, teak armchairs with white cushions, white orchids arranged on a coffee table, and a king-size canopy bed made up with white linens. The air conditioner had been turned on in advance of their arrival, so stepping inside gave instant relief from the humid air.

The porter set their bags on the tile floor, and Dave handed him some folded bills. Witnessing this transaction, Laura became acutely aware that their luxurious vacation could not happen without legions of local workers doting on their every need, and this jarring truth embarrassed her. She didn't know what exactly to say, so she hid in the bathroom while Dave spoke to the porter. She admired the double vanity sinks and the walk-in shower with the rainforest showerhead.

Then, when the porter left, she emerged from the bathroom and flopped down next to Dave on the massive bed. She ran her fingers over the sheets, trying to gauge their thread count. Eight hundred? Maybe twelve hundred?

"This place is spectacular," Dave said.

"It really is," Laura said.

She stared up at the ceiling fan overhead (acacia wood, she guessed) and felt something she had not anticipated. Maybe it was the all-white decor, or maybe it was the fact that every detail had been painstakingly taken care of, but she felt her stomach unclench and was overcome with a deep sense of calm.

"Come here," Dave said and pulled her to him. They kissed and lay there, luxuriating in the immaculate quiet.

As Dave lay beside her, Laura propped herself up on her elbows and gazed out the sliding glass door at the far end of the cabin that looked out over the private beach and beyond, to the sea.

"Holy shit. I can see the ocean from our bed."

She had not anticipated this either. She jumped out of bed, ran across the tile floor, and pulled open the sliding glass door. She stepped out onto a little porch and looked out at the beach. A handful of couples were lying on the lounge chairs under the umbrellas that were positioned at evenly spaced intervals in the sand. Beyond them, the sea glittered invitingly.

The sunbathing women were lean and toned, and they were wearing bikinis in shades of blue or pink or white. They looked like the grown-up versions of the girls Laura remembered from high school, the beautiful girls who had boyfriends and toe rings and thighs made taut from field hockey practice. They were in no rush, these women. Every movement they made was graceful and deliberate: the way they pulled their hair into buns on the tops of their heads, carefully, not a wisp out of place, before wading slowly, arms bent at the elbows, into the gently lapping waves.

Seeing them now, up close and in detail, Laura felt a sudden jolt. It was not unlike the jolt she had experienced on her first day of high school, when she had walked into a changing room full of beautiful girls strutting around confidently in their underwear. She had felt like an interloper then, unwanted and out of place, and had sneaked into a stall to get changed for gym class. Even though she had as much a right to be at the resort as the beautiful women did, she couldn't help but feel like an interloper now too.

Laura headed back inside the cabin, unzipped her carry-on bag, and pulled out the only bathing suit she owned, a plain black one-piece, which she wore when she swam laps at the Fourteenth Street Y. Since she hadn't had time to go shopping, it would have to do. She had never been very good at shopping anyway, but she was very good at packing. Her point of pride was that she had managed to fit a vacation's worth of tank tops, maxi dresses, and toiletries into a carry-on bag, which made it unnecessary to check any luggage. The only items that hadn't fit in her bag were her flip-flops, which she'd stuffed into Dave's suitcase. He pulled them out and handed them to her with a smile.

Laura knew that having a boyfriend meant having a date every weekend and having someone to share inside jokes with, but it was these small details—the commingling of their belongings in a shared suitcase, having someone to wait with her luggage while she went to the bathroom—that surprised her about being in a couple. These were perks she didn't want to take for granted. After all, it all felt so tenuous. She and Dave were still in the first blush of their relationship, and this was all still a delicate house of cards that, she was certain, could topple at any moment, so she felt the need to be performative around him, always on her best behavior.

After they both changed, Laura tossed sunscreen and a magazine into her beach bag, Dave grabbed the two towels that were neatly rolled at the foot of their bed, and they headed out the sliding glass doors and down to the beach.

They draped their towels across the backs of two unoccupied lounge chairs and collapsed. It was so quiet here. The only sound Laura could hear was the water lapping gently on the shore. It was surreal to her that only two weeks ago, she had never even heard of

Eleuthera, and now here she was, on this private pink-sand beach. She had never seen pink sand before. It was fine and powdery and the color of cotton candy. She felt protected by the security guards who stood sentry on either edge of the crescent-shaped cove and by the limestone cliffs that towered overhead. It felt safe and peaceful here, like nothing bad could ever happen.

One of the lean and toned women, who was using architectural logic to position her lounge chair in relation to the angle of the sun, stopped what she was doing and looked at Dave. He was one of the better-looking men at the resort, and the fact that she was ogling him now made Laura feel a kind of proprietary pride she had never experienced before. There was something sculptural about Dave's body, like a statue come to life.

Though neither of them would ever admit it, Laura was not as objectively good looking as Dave, and this awareness made her feel a little inadequate, especially since he had never told her what it was about her that he found attractive. Dave had also been in more relationships than she, and it didn't help that she had seen some of his ex-girlfriends, all of them lean and toned. Picturing them now, Laura couldn't help but feel like she was dating a little above her station. Nevertheless, she told herself, she was here now. With him.

She looked at Dave, but his eyes were closed behind his sunglasses. She heard her mother's words reverberate in her head: *The world is built for couples, not singles.* As long as she could remember, her mother had said this. Laura's father died when she was little, and she believed her mother's worldview was largely shaped by his absence. For years, Laura had assumed this warning was an excuse for her mother to call her nightly out of feigned maternal concern while masking her true desire, which was for conversation. It wasn't until one night three months ago, when Laura was washing her Riedel wineglass in the sink, her phone wedged between her shoulder and her ear, that she came to fear her mother was right.

Laura had indulged in the Riedel wineglass—glass*es*, actually; she'd bought two because who bought a single wineglass?—not only because she liked the delicate feel of the thinly blown glass against her lips but also because it seemed like a purchase a successful person might make. Years earlier, after she had graduated from law school and moved into her first rental, a shabby little one-bedroom in Queens, the contents of her cramped galley kitchen had consisted of hand-me-down pots from her mother and a starter dish set from IKEA. She had told herself then that this setup was only temporary, that she was on a path, and if she put in the work and paid her dues, in time she would graduate to a nicer apartment with a better view and a pair of Riedel wineglasses.

She would peruse the aisles of Williams Sonoma on Seventh Avenue, fantasizing about the kind of life she would lead one day, the kind in which she could afford to shop at the overpriced kitchenware store, and she would examine the wineglasses with delicate hands. Her mother had deemed them a ridiculous purchase. *Why pay so much for something that will break in no time?* Laura had ignored her mother and promised herself that when she bought her first apartment, she would celebrate by buying the wineglasses too. She had assumed that by the time the day came to purchase them, she would be in a committed relationship with an upwardly mobile man whose handsome face was still a vague blur. In her fantasy, they would move in together, and in the dim but ambient light of their new, as-yet-unpacked home, he would surprise her with takeout from their favorite restaurant, she would pour wine into their new Riedel glasses, and they would toast their future together.

But none of that had come to pass. Laura's thirtieth birthday had come and gone, and she was still single. She had, however, saved up enough money for a down payment on an apartment while devoting herself to her career at the firm. So after viewing two dozen condos and losing three bidding wars, she'd bought a one-bedroom in the East Village. It was small, only seven hundred square feet, but it had an open layout that made it seem larger. When move-in day arrived, Laura took the subway to the Williams Sonoma on Seventh Avenue and ceremoniously purchased the Riedel glasses (even though it would have been more convenient to buy them online). But when she'd come home—to her *own* home—wineglasses in hand, she'd felt a familiar sad twinge, like she was still waiting for something to happen. During the day, she was preoccupied with work, but at night the twinge would return, as it did that night when she was on the phone with her mother.

"Have you met anyone interesting?" her mother asked. It was her favorite question.

"No," Laura said, squeezing dish soap onto a yellow sponge. But her answer didn't stop her mother from pushing the subject.

"What about that man in Corporate Compliance? What's his name?"

"Mark. And I already told you, he's gay." Their names were always Mark or John or Steve, and they always had girlfriends or boyfriends or were otherwise unavailable.

"I don't understand. You're smart and you're beautiful."

Laura knew her mother meant this as a compliment, but she found the baffled tone of her voice insulting, as though it were Laura's fault that her life had not panned out as they had both anticipated. In that moment, Laura felt the familiar twinge of sadness morph into anger, but she didn't know whom she was angrier with: her mother for her incessant lecturing, or the quiet voice inside Laura's own head that agreed with her mother, that despite all her quantifiable success, she was still, somehow, a failure. Laura's simmering rage caused her to thrust the soapy yellow sponge into the wineglass a little too forcefully, which caused the thinly blown glass to shatter, and at the exact point where the pinkie finger of her right hand joined her palm, the broken glass sliced a deep gash into her flesh.

There was a sudden gush of red in the sink. A throb of pain followed, and then her phone clattered to the floor.

"Laura? Are you still there?"

Blood streamed down Laura's forearm and spattered on the tile floor, surprising her with its dark-red, almost black color.

"I have to call you back, Mom." Laura ended the call, and yanking paper towels from the dispenser she had installed under the cabinets, she swaddled her right hand. But no matter how much pressure she applied to the wound, blood seeped through, crimson and relentless. She fumbled for a Band-Aid in the drawer next to the stove but was unable to tear open the waxy envelope, as her right hand was her dominant hand. She needed help, a second set of hands. But there was no one. No roommate. No boyfriend. No one. She couldn't even call Chloe. Even though they had been best friends as children, in high school, and even though Laura still looked at Chloe's Facebook photos and kept up to date with her life developments (wedding, birth of son, new house, new dog), they hadn't been on speaking terms in years. Laura didn't know any of her neighbors either, even though her mother had advised her to befriend the old Russian woman who lived down the hall.

"You might need to borrow a cup of sugar one day," her mother had said.

Laura had only rolled her eyes.

She sank to the floor and, ignoring her mother's repeated phone calls, applied more pressure to her hand, making sure to keep it elevated above her heart with the hope that it would slow the bleeding. It occurred to her then that knowing one of her neighbors would have been useful. If she had made the effort to befriend the old Russian woman down the hall, she could have knocked on her door, and the kindly old lady would have ushered her in and, making a great maternal fuss, fixed her a cup of tea while attending to her wound. But it was too late for that. There, on the floor, surrounded by the soggy red blooms of discarded paper towels, Laura became overwhelmed by a new feeling. Maybe her mother was right. Not about the wineglasses, though she had been right about them too—such a large expense for something that would break in no time. No, this was something else. What Laura felt was a creeping dread that maybe the world was indeed built for couples, not singles, and that she would always be alone. She felt a familiar twinge of sadness that told her nothing in her life would ever change.

Until the next day, when everything did.

Years later, after the incident, after the police investigation, after all of it, Laura would think back, trying to pinpoint when it was exactly that everything changed, and she determined that it all started the day Dave Mitchell started working at the firm.

"Dave?"

He'd fallen asleep, his lips slightly parted. Over the two months of their relationship, Laura had discovered he had the enviable ability to fall asleep anywhere. She, on the other hand, couldn't sleep unless she was in her own bed. She was slightly annoyed that he had drifted off but couldn't really fault him. Before they left, he'd been working endless hours on a complicated acquisition, and he was entitled to his rest. And now the trancelike effect of the resort, the gentle ebb and flow of the waves, the rustle of the palm trees overhead, had taken hold. Laura felt like she was in some kind of tropical womb, only her toes felt unpleasantly hot. The sun had shifted its position in the sky, and her feet were no longer protected by the shade of the big umbrella. She stood up, adjusted the straps of her bathing suit, and headed across the pink sand down to the shore.

The water was crystal clear and surprisingly warm, and she felt no seaweed or pebbles or sharp shells underfoot. She waded to the depth of her shoulders. Despite the heat, no one else was swimming. The other couples were lying in tandem on the white lounge chairs, their faces upturned to the sky, unsmiling but calm, their sunglasses reflecting the dazzling sunlight. They looked so comfortable in their repose, so entitled to their vacations, like they belonged here, these beautiful people at this beautiful resort. Only one woman seemed out of place.

She was the only other woman besides Laura who was wearing a one-piece bathing suit, which also happened to be black. She wasn't lying in her lounge chair but was sitting up, arms hugging her knees, her sunglasses folded in her hands. Her wavy brown hair was cut to her chin, frizzed by the salty breeze, and she was gazing into the distance with a cryptic smile on her face. Most notable to Laura was the fact that no man was lying next to her in board shorts. No beach towel was draped on the chair next to hers indicating the presence of a companion. The woman was alone.

Once Laura caught sight of the woman, she couldn't look away.

There was something odd about her, something out of place. Up until that point, everything about the Pink Sands had filled Laura with a profound sense of safety, but seeing the woman sitting alone on a beach chair at this romantic couples' resort, smiling strangely to herself, filled Laura with unease.

The woman must have felt Laura looking at her, because she turned her head slowly and stared directly at her. The woman's gaze was so piercing that, despite the bath-warm water, Laura felt goose bumps prickle her skin. She looked away but felt the woman continue to stare at her, so she looked back, and their eyes met again. The woman had an impish expression on her face, as if she knew some dark secret about Laura. Partly to avoid the woman's intense gaze and partly out of embarrassment from being caught staring, Laura ducked under the water and swam away.

CHAPTER TWO

When they first met, what had stood out to Laura about Dave was not that he was good looking, though he was. His ruddy cheeks—the result of a mild case of rosacea, she assumed—were in stark contrast to his dark hair, which fell in tousled waves around his face, giving him a perpetually windswept look, as though he'd just stepped off a yacht. No, what struck Laura was that she knew Dave. Well, perhaps *knew* was too strong a word. It was more accurate to say that she recognized him. Years earlier, they had taken the same Modern American Poetry seminar while undergraduates at Yale. Every Thursday morning during the spring semester of Laura's sophomore year, between 10:30 and 11:20 a.m., they had both sat at the large oak table in room 201 of Linsly-Chittenden Hall.

Laura had been surprised that Dave had elected to take the seminar, not only because it was populated mostly by sophomores and he was a senior, but because he did not seem like the type of guy who would voluntarily attend a poetry class. There was something jock-like about Dave, so Laura had assumed he needed the credit to graduate.

On the first day of class, she watched him pull a little black Moleskine notebook from his backpack, along with a copy of the poetry anthology required for the class, which she couldn't help but notice he had purchased new from the campus bookstore, unlike the dog-eared used edition she had bought online at half price.

While the other students were keen to have their opinions known, Dave never spoke in class. Instead, he'd sit quietly but attentively, really listening, it seemed, as their professor, a rotund little man, read a poem aloud and then lectured at length about a particular stanza's significance. As Dave watched the professor, Laura watched Dave. Every now and then, he made notes in his little black notebook, and Laura wondered what those notes said. And because he listened so intently, more intently than she, she also wondered if she had made a miscalculation about him. Even though Dave had the kind of good looks that allowed him to coast through life without having to cultivate a personality or a sense of humor, let alone develop educated opinions about poetry, perhaps, Laura thought, she had pegged him all wrong.

There was only one thing she knew for sure: even though she had come to memorize Dave's face, his mannerisms, and his wardrobe—mostly flannel shirts and fleece pullovers in rotation—he definitely had no clue who Laura was. So naturally, it surprised her when, one Thursday morning toward the end of the semester, Dave entered the room, and rather than sitting in his usual seat across the table from Laura, he sat down in the empty chair directly adjacent to hers. He slipped his backpack from his shoulders, and as he pulled out his poetry anthology and his little black notebook, he glanced briefly at Laura and smiled a wordless hello. She smiled back. This was their first point of contact.

Though his move across the table was silent, it felt extremely loud to Laura, loaded with meaning. Why had he chosen this day of all days to change seats? She waited expectantly for him to say something, anything, to explain his actions, but when the professor started reading a William Carlos Williams poem, Dave opened his little black notebook and gave his full attention. Laura, however, found it impossible to focus on the professor's analysis of the plums in the icebox and instead stared at Dave. Fortunately, he was seated between her and the professor, so she was able to study him discreetly. She spent the duration of the class memorizing his hair, how it curled adorably around his left ear, as well as the small mole near his temple and his eyelashes, which were surprisingly long. Most fortuitously, she was finally able to get a peek at what he was writing in his notebook. The first thing she noticed was how neat his penmanship was, rare for a guy and much appreciated during her act of espionage. She had expected some thoughtful notes about the poem du jour, but instead, across the middle of an empty page, he wrote, *I am always pretending. Why am I always pretending?*

She read it again to make sure she had read it correctly. What did he mean by *pretending*? Was all his nodding and note-taking some kind of performance? Did he feel like an impostor at this Ivy League school? The idea that Dave might feel out of place surprised her because he of all people looked like the kind of person she had imagined would end up at a place like this. But the notion that Dave, with his good looks, could feel uncomfortable in his own skin endeared him to her. She wondered what had happened in his life to make him feel so inadequate. What great tragedy had struck? She felt strangely close to him then, as if she had stolen a rare glimpse of his most vulnerable self.

Dave did not speak to Laura that day, and the following Thursday he resumed sitting in his usual seat across the table from her. They did not speak for the remainder of the semester, and then he graduated, and Laura thought she would never see him again.

She had forgotten about that incident, but the day Dave started working at Reinhart, Mader & Stern and Laura watched him make his way through the receiving line of associates that had formed in the bullpen, the little note he had written to himself all those years ago floated up from the depths of her subconscious. The last time she had seen Dave, he'd worn a fleece pullover and jeans, but as he approached her in the receiving line, he wore an immaculately tailored blue suit, a white shirt, and brown dress shoes. His outfit projected an aura of confident professionalism, but his relaxed smile and his hair, which he still wore in tousled waves, emanated a sense of casualness. The combined effect suggested he was a man to be taken seriously even if he didn't take himself too seriously.

Laura marveled at how quickly life could change. Only the night before, she had been sitting on her kitchen floor surrounded by shards of the broken wineglass, clutching her bleeding hand and feeling utterly alone. Laura was not a religious person, but in that moment she felt as though events were conspiring in some kind of cosmic alignment, as though the universe was winking at her, like sunlight through trees, letting her know that while life could be randomly cruel at times, there was reason to believe she was part of some grand design.

As she mentally prepared herself for the imminent reunion with Dave, she felt her palms moisten and panicked momentarily at the thought of their clamminess, until she remembered that her freshly bandaged right hand gave her a good excuse not to shake his at all. When he finally stepped in front of her, she held up her wounded hand and smiled apologetically. He returned the smile, and she searched his face for a flash of recognition, but his eyes, while friendly, remained vacant.

"Nice to meet you," he said. "I'm Dave."

Laura was struck dumb. She opened her mouth to return the greeting, but no words came out. He didn't recognize her. Though his face was permanently etched in her memory, he didn't have the foggiest clue who she was. Was she really that forgettable? Laura considered telling him that they had gone to college together, but she feared that even with this reminder, he would only shrug apologetically and admit that he didn't remember her.

So she simply said, "I'm Laura."

As Dave moved on and shook the hand of the associate next to her, Laura's flush of nervousness was replaced by a wave of resentment. *Well, fuck him then.* And truth be told, it gave her an edge that, even though he had no idea who she was, she knew a little something about him. She wondered if, as he was getting dressed that morning, picking out his bespoke suit and tousling his hair just so, did he, all these years later, still feel like a pretender?

During Dave's first week at the firm, while Jasmine Chaudhry and the other associates invited him to lunch and coffee and drinks, Laura kept her distance. She loved watching him stride through the office in his suits—his body was made for suits, the double vents of his tailored jackets flapping gently, showing off his ass. Then she would feel ashamed of how petty she'd been, feeling affronted when he didn't recognize her on his first day. Partly because of these conflicting emotions and partly out of embarrassment, she gave him a wide berth, to the point where she wondered if she was being rude. Then, three weeks into his employ at the firm, Dave stopped by Laura's office.

"Did you go to Yale?" he asked, leaning casually in her doorway. He was always leaning, in doorways, in elevators, even against the boardroom's floor-to-ceiling windows during staff meetings, which seemed to Laura sexy but also a little bit dangerous.

"I did," she said, assuming he had finally recalled their shared history.

He stepped into her office and picked up the small plush bulldog that sat on the corner of her desk. Outfitted in a blue sweater embroidered with a white *Y*, the toy had been a graduation gift from her mother. She had debated whether or not it was appropriate to keep a stuffed mascot on her desk at work, but it was small and served as a reminder of how hard she had worked to get to where she was.

Dave tossed the bulldog in the air like a football.

"What college were you in?" It was the standard question all alumni asked each other upon meeting. He was referring to the residential colleges that made up the undergraduate campus. They were like the houses at Hogwarts, each with its own name, courtyard, and (some would argue) personality.

"Branford."

"Trumbull." Dave pointed at his chest, his voice taking on a warmer tone, as if he finally recognized her (though he still hadn't). Laura realized she now had another opportunity to inform him that they had actually met before, but she hesitated. Telling him, three weeks after they'd been introduced, would be awkward in a different way. What was the statute of limitations for this kind of thing? The last thing she wanted was for him to think she was weird. Still, she wanted to get it out there, to clear the air, as it were—but before she could get the words out, Dave said, "Cute."

Wait, who was cute—she or the bulldog? He placed the stuffed animal back on her desk.

Ah. The dog.

"Well, see ya." And then he was gone.

With that brief conversation, their relationship changed. Dave started waving hello whenever he passed her office and nodding good night on his way home. When the vending machine spat out two bags of Doritos by mistake, he offered one to her. He even learned how she liked her coffee: black, two sugars.

Though their relationship in college had been virtually nonexistent, here in this glassy downtown law firm, their semblance of a shared history took on new value. They were becoming, of all things, friends.

Dave specialized in mergers and acquisitions, and when he was assigned to a rather large case, he stopped by her office one morning and asked if she had enough bandwidth (his words) to help him out.

"The hotel my client's acquiring has a valuable manager that he wants to put under contract. But when the manager's contract is up, we need to make sure he won't go out and open up a competing hotel," Dave said.

"So you need an ironclad noncompete."

"Right."

"And a nonsolicit. You don't want him to raid your client's employees if and when he leaves."

"Exactly. So, you wanna work with me on this one?" he asked, leaning in her doorway. She loved his leans.

Over her tenure at the firm, Laura had developed a reputation for being a diligent lawyer who wrote immaculate contracts, so she assumed he wanted her on his team for this reason. But Dave had a glint in his eye when he asked, and it seemed conspiratorial, this glint, as if he were inviting her to join him in a top-secret plot. She was excited but didn't want to seem too eager. After all, she was a professional with a heavy workload of her own. This wasn't college.

"I'm in back-to-back meetings all day, but I think I can make the time."

"Cool," Dave said and stepped inside her office. He tossed her stuffed bulldog in the air and caught it, which had become his go-to mode of behavior during his little office visits.

"How about we go over the contracts tonight?"

"Sure," she said.

He smiled, placed the dog back on her desk, and left.

He reappeared in her doorway that evening, after most of the other associates had gone home. This was Laura's favorite time of day. When the hum of the office subsided, she would gaze out her window, Manhattan a sea of glittering lights.

"Now a good time?"

The sleeves of Dave's blue oxford shirt were rolled to his elbows, exposing his elegant forearms. She often caught herself in staff meetings staring at his forearms and wondering how it would feel to have them wrapped around her body.

She looked up from her computer and stared at him quizzically, as though trying to remember why he was visiting her now, even though, ten minutes prior, she had reapplied deodorant and lip balm in preparation for his arrival.

"Oh, right. Sure thing," she said, feigning distraction. "Show me what you got."

He set a stack of contracts on her desk, pulled up a chair, and sat down next to her. The last time she had been in such close proximity to his face was during their poetry seminar all those years ago, and it gave her a heady rush to inhale his scent, pine needles and sandalwood, and stare at his mouth, which back in college she had on more than one occasion fantasized about kissing. Only a few things were different: tiny laugh lines had formed around his mouth, and some crow's-feet were visible at the corners of his eyes. As he walked her through the details of the acquisition, she initially found it difficult to concentrate, but soon her work muscle kicked in and she became engrossed. Sometime later, she glanced at her watch and balked. It was nearly 9:00 p.m. Dave was equally surprised.

"Wow, it's late. I'm starving. You wanna grab a bite?"

"Sure." She was famished.

"You like sushi?"

Laura did like sushi, so much so that she had taken to ordering takeout from the restaurant down the block from the office two to three times a week. "I love sushi. You been to Shunoko? It's my favorite place and only a block from here. I've always wanted to try their tuna tataki."

Dave looked at her, a crease appearing between his eyebrows. "It's your favorite place, but you've never tried their tataki?"

Laura didn't know how to respond. The tuna tataki was only available as a dine-in option, but the anxiety she felt when she imagined herself eating alone in a restaurant filled with couples on romantic dates made her chest feel tight. So she invariably ended up ordering from the (limited) takeout menu instead.

Dave stared at Laura expectantly.

"Well," she managed, haltingly, "it's just . . . it's only available if you eat there, and I usually get takeout, so." She stared hard at a coffee ring on her desk. Her answer hung in the air for what felt like an excruciatingly long time, but when she finally summoned the courage to look him in the eye, she was surprised to find him smiling. Flirtatiously.

"I guess we'll be dining in, then," he said.

CHAPTER THREE

Laura squeezed the water from her hair as she waded back to shore. Her dip in the sea had refreshed her, and she was eager to explore the resort grounds. It was thrilling to finally be here, and she couldn't wait to see every inch of the island. She walked down the beach, past the beautiful couples sunning themselves on the loungers, past an employee who was raking the sand, and kept walking all the way to the resort's property line, where the sand met a precipitous wall of craggy rock that was covered in shrubs and Caribbean pine. The sun was warm on her face, and it occurred to her that she hadn't applied any sunscreen. One errand she had managed to accomplish before leaving New York was buying sunscreen. She had indulged in the expensive kind that was a spray, not a cream, even though she had read somewhere that aerosols were bad for you or bad for the environment or both, but she liked the scent and how luxurious it felt when she sprayed it on her arms and legs. The sunscreen was in her bag, at the far end of the beach, but she figured going without it a little while longer probably wouldn't hurt.

She'd also managed to get a mani-pedi. Normally, she chose neutral shades like pale pink or taupe, what Jasmine called *power nudes*. There was something powerful about those muted colors, something confident in their restraint, but for the occasion of her vacation, she had selected a bright fruit-punch red and had paid extra to have the gel polish cured under a blue UV light, which she had read somewhere was potentially carcinogenic but according to the nail technician would make her manicure last longer.

Whether it was sunscreen or nail polish, it seemed to Laura that the trade-off for quality was accepting a certain degree of risk.

The wind picked up then and blew sand across the shore, and Laura watched as the beautiful couples started gathering their things, shaking sand from their towels, and heading back to their cabins, presumably to get changed for dinner. Only the woman in the black bathing suit stayed where she was. The gusty wind didn't seem to bother her, even as it blew her hair to one side. She just sat in her lounge chair and stared out to sea.

Laura turned back and felt a sharp stab on the ball of her right foot that made her wince. She crouched to examine the corkscrew-shaped offender that was half-buried in the sand. She dug at its contours with her fingertips until she excavated what turned out to be a conch shell. She had seen conchs for sale in souvenir shops, but finding one in the wild was thrilling.

"If you see two of them together, they be juicin'."

Laura squinted up at the man. The sun was behind his right shoulder, and his face was obscured by shadow, so Laura stood up to see him more clearly. It was the employee who had been raking the sand. His name tag said *Javarro*.

"Juicin'?" Laura asked.

"Yeah. Juicin'. Matin'. Conchs always be matin'." Javarro laughed and headed down the beach, dragging his rake behind him.

She walked across the beach back to her lounge chair, examining the conch with both hands. Its outer layer was coated with brown, flaky scales, but its inner curves were smooth and shockingly pink, vaginal. Then again, everything here, it seemed, was suggestive of sex. The long row of loungers, paired two by two under the white umbrellas, encouraged coupling. As did the extra-wide hammocks, swaying in the breeze. Even the dragonflies flew in tandem here, one on top of another, in a blatant carnal display. Sex seemed to hang in the air, thick like humidity, but that was the point, she supposed, of a beach resort that advertised itself as a couples' getaway.

Dave claimed he had chosen the Pink Sands because of Marcus Lowry's discount, but now that they were here, Laura was surprised that he had suggested this resort for their first vacation. They were, after all, still in the early stages of their relationship, and the Pink Sands was the kind of place where rose petals were sprinkled on their bed upon request; where a bottle of champagne would greet them at the door, chilling in an ice bucket, with two flutes nearby. She had even spotted a couple, likely newlyweds, wearing matching T-shirts that said *Wifey* and *Hubs*, respectively. The whole place felt indulgently romantic, which made it even stranger that the woman in the black bathing suit had come here alone.

Before Laura and Dave started dating, she had felt like she was floating on the outside of life, like a ghost, watching meaningful relationships happen to other people. She had been invited to her friends' weddings, more and more each year, it seemed, and while observing the vows, she'd wondered if love would ever happen to her. At some point, she made peace with the fact that it probably wouldn't and decided to be satisfied with her career instead. But the night Dave asked Laura out for sushi, she had wondered if love was finally starting to happen to her.

That fateful night, inside the restaurant, she gazed out the windows at the passing pedestrians and realized that she and Dave were now one of the dining couples she used to glance at when she walked past. This realization created in her a feeling of inversion, as though she had stepped through a looking glass and were living on the inside of a life that previously she was only ever able to peer at from the outside. They ordered tuna tataki, and it was as delicious as Laura had hoped it would be. Two bottles of sake later, their bellies full of expanding rice, Dave walked her to the subway, even though her station was only a block away. He rationalized that since he was going in her direction anyway, it made sense to take the subway together and walk her home. Laura agreed, claiming it was probably safer that way, even though she had walked home from her station alone at night countless times before and had never once felt unsafe.

When they reached her building, she invited him up for a nightcap. She didn't know what a nightcap was exactly—did it have to be liquor, or could it be wine?—but it seemed like the appropriate thing to suggest, even though she only had half a bottle of red wine in her apartment and no liquor. Inside her apartment, she offered to give him a tour, but since most of it was visible at a glance, she followed that up by offering him a glass of wine. But as the words left her mouth, she realized that while this would be an ideal time to pull out her Riedel wineglasses, she was now only in possession of one of them, and though the accident had happened a month before, she had not yet purchased a replacement glass. She cringed at what the optics of being a single woman in possession of a single wineglass said about her, but thankfully, instead of accepting her offer, Dave leaned over and kissed her on the mouth.

Laura had often wondered what it would feel like to kiss Dave Mitchell, and she was pleasantly surprised to discover that though his face was very familiar to her, the experience was entirely new. His lips were softer than she expected, and his mouth, which she assumed would taste like sushi, tasted like peppermint, which meant he must have, at some point, in anticipation of this moment perhaps, discreetly popped a mint into his mouth.

As they wordlessly pulled off their coats and sank onto her sofa, it occurred to Laura that this was her last opportunity to divulge the truth—that she and Dave had met before, back in college—but she was enjoying what was happening way too much to interrupt it. As they removed their clothes, she determined that this was really and truly the point of no return because if she didn't tell him now, she likely never would, and their relationship, or whatever this was or would evolve into, would be built on a lie. A lie of omission, but a lie nonetheless. And yet, in the headiness of the moment, it seemed to Laura a small point, insignificant in the wake of the very significant act that was about to happen.

Laura still hadn't told Dave the truth and had accepted that she probably never would. She had made peace with the fact that she would probably carry the secret to her grave because the longer she withheld it, the harder it would be, ultimately, to tell him, and if and when she finally would divulge the truth, it could have weighty implications beyond her current understanding.

Lies were like that. She had seen in her work at the firm how they always started out so small and innocuous but had the potential to grow into dangerous, even lethal threats. Her lie of omission was not unlike a warped metal washer that, when affixed to the fuselage of a massive space shuttle, was seemingly inconsequential, but when enough pressure was exerted on such a tiny thing, the friction created could be so overwhelming in its magnitude that it had the power to destroy the entire machine.

Laura found Dave in his lounge chair, awake. She set the conch on the little wooden table that was attached to the white umbrella.

"Hey, babe," he said and stretched. "Where were you?"

"I went for a swim and then a walk."

"Nice find," he said, examining the conch.

"Cool, right?"

He nodded and kissed her.

"I missed you. Wanna go back inside?"

"Sure."

Laura shouldered her bag, Dave grabbed both of their towels, and they headed back up the beach.

When they stepped inside the cabin, Laura dropped her bag on the floor and kicked off her flip-flops next to the sliding glass door so as not to track sand across the tiles. Dave tossed the towels onto an armchair and pulled Laura into a hug.

"I like you in Eleuthera," he said and kissed her.

"But nowhere else?" she asked playfully.

"No, silly. You're just different here."

Laura was suddenly self-conscious. "Different how?"

"I dunno. When I met you, you just seemed a bit . . . aloof?"

"Aloof?"

She had never thought of herself as aloof. Shy, maybe. Formal, sometimes. But aloof?

"Not in a bad way. That's not the right word." He studied her face, searching. "Inaccessible. You were a bit inaccessible."

"Inaccessible?"

This seemed worse, somehow.

"Yeah. When I asked the guys about you—"

"What guys?"

"At the firm. They said you didn't really seem to date."

Laura felt her heart quicken. She couldn't fathom being a topic of conversation between The Guys.

"Why inaccessible?"

"I mean, you did avoid me for like three weeks. I thought you hated me."

Laura bit the inside of her lip. He had a point. She had avoided him. But that was because she'd been embarrassed that he hadn't remembered her from college.

"I didn't hate you."

"Well, good. I didn't hate you either. I wanted to get to know you. You seemed so mysterious."

"Mysterious?" She almost laughed. The idea that she was perceived by him in this way thrilled her. She kissed him. "And are you getting to know me?"

"A little bit."

He smiled and gently pulled the straps of her bathing suit down to her waist so that she was topless before him. Ordinarily, this would have made her shy, but for some reason she didn't feel shy now. Maybe it was because Dave seemed to regard her as an elusive challenge. Maybe it was because the sun and the wind and the salt air made everything seem so wild, or maybe it was because everyone here walked around in some state of undress, including Dave, who was shirtless now, even though he rarely was at home. Or maybe it was because she was away from the office and its accompanying stress, and her mind felt empty of everything except basic, primal desire. Whatever the reason, she felt like she was outside her own body, like she was someone else, like one of those beautiful women from the beach, unconstrained and carefree. She watched herself run her hands over his shoulders and down his back. She watched him gently push her down onto the bed and remove her bathing suit completely. She watched him remove his own shorts, and then he was inside her.

"You're so gorgeous," he said and kissed her neck.

Laura did not usually feel gorgeous—in fact, she often took to scrutinizing her body's every flaw—but she liked how it felt when he gazed at her now. *This is what it feels like to belong to someone*, she thought. Soon, Dave let out a moan and it was over, and they both lay on their backs, staring at the ceiling, satisfied, their bodies slick with sweat despite the air-conditioning. Laura looked up at the ceiling fan rotating slowly overhead. *Juicin'*, she thought to herself and smiled.

They lay like that for a few minutes, until Laura finally got up to take a shower. She didn't grab a towel to cover herself. She didn't even grab one of the complimentary white bathrobes that hung in the standing wardrobe next to the bed. Instead, she walked naked into the bathroom. Normally, she took quick, efficient showers, but now she let the hot water drum on her back, washing the salt and sweat off her skin, until the steam fogged up the glass door, making it opaque.

Laura hadn't packed her blow-dryer because its bulk would have precluded anything else from fitting into her carry-on, and she assumed the resort would provide her with one, which it did, in an elegant wicker basket under the bathroom sink. She felt refreshed as she toweled her wet hair, but as soon as she turned on the blow-dryer and directed the blast of hot air at her head, she felt new rivulets of sweat drip down her neck and back. She turned it off, stuffed it back into the basket, and pulled her damp hair into a bun.

She emerged from the bathroom, and Dave headed in to take his shower. While she waited for him, she dug through her beach bag, pulled out an issue of *Cosmopolitan* magazine, and flopped back on the bed. She hadn't read *Cosmo* in years, but seeing it at the Hudson News in the airport had reminded her of Chloe, and she'd felt a pang of nostalgia for all the hours of girlish fun they'd had years ago, turning the pages of the magazine.

Laura had first met Chloe in seventh grade, when Chloe's family moved to town halfway through the school year. While other new kids struggled to be accepted into a social group, Chloe did not have that problem, because she was beautiful. Her hair was long and black, and her eyes were dark and enigmatic, and her eyelashes were so lush and so thick that the other girls assumed she wore mascara every day even though she didn't. Chloe didn't speak much in class and often wore overalls, but instead of being labeled shy or weird or a tomboy, she was considered a conquest. To the boys, she brimmed with the promise of discovery, like an unknown continent.

As luck would have it, or perhaps it was the random cruelty of the universe—Laura's opinion on the matter would change in the years that followed—Chloe was assigned the desk next to Laura's, and as bonds at that age often formed out of proximity, the two of them became friends.

Laura's mother didn't like Chloe from the moment she met her. *That girl is dangerous*, she used to say. There *was* something dangerous about Chloe, but Laura couldn't put her finger on what exactly it was. Maybe it was her beauty. Laura had often found beautiful things to be a bit dangerous.

When Chloe invited Laura over for a sleepover, they hid under the covers of Chloe's queen-size bed and flipped through her book of Greek myths, a large hardcover volume that had illustrations of all twelve major gods in the pantheon. Chloe's favorite myth was about Actaeon, who wandered through the woods one day and came upon Artemis bathing in the nude. He was taken aback by her beauty, but when she caught him staring, she turned him into a stag, and he was subsequently torn to pieces and eaten by his own hounds. Chloe loved Artemis's raw, vengeful power, and she loved how inciting her wrath could lead to a man's destruction. She also loved that Artemis never married and that she traveled the world alone.

"When I grow up, I'm never getting married," Chloe announced with confidence. "I'm just going to travel the world." Laura echoed that she too would never marry and would also travel the world. Chloe laughed then, her deep, throaty man laugh, and Laura laughed, too, and it was understood in that moment, without either of them needing to say it out loud, that they were best friends. Every day, they would compose letters to each other on lined, three-hole paper, fold them into little triangular footballs, and swap them in the halls at school. Laura didn't know it then, but what she was experiencing in those daily handoffs was love in its purest form. Unconditional, untested, all-encompassing love. It was as though, in finding Chloe, she had found a part of herself that she had lost at birth and was reclaiming, piece by triangular piece.

Back then, Laura imagined herself and Chloe growing old together, two best friends who would never marry and would instead travel the world together. She never told Chloe about these fantasies, but she planned imaginary trips they would take together in the future, to faraway places like Reykjavík and Buenos Aires and Marrakesh. Laura's vision of their future as two unmarried, well-traveled women faded, however, when they entered high school and Chloe used her allowance to buy a subscription to *Cosmopolitan* magazine. Every month, a new issue of *Cosmo* would arrive in the mail, thick and shiny and covered in plastic wrap, and Chloe would mark the occasion by inviting Laura over for a sleepover. Her book about Greek mythology was shelved, and they would lie awake at night filling out quizzes to ascertain their love matches and reading makeup tutorials that detailed the precise execution of a smoky eye. *Cosmo* was Chloe's favorite magazine because it was more risqué than the others. Not only did it offer tips on how to make oneself attractive to men, but it also offered graphic explainers on sex, which had become her favorite topic of discussion. Together, they would study blow job techniques delineated in the magazine, learning how best to pleasure their nonexistent boyfriends. Laura didn't realize it at the time, but their friendship underwent a subtle shift then. Its basis was no longer how they, as individuals, related to each other but rather how they, as girls, related to boys.

Laura glanced at the magazine in her lap. She hadn't read *Cosmo* in years, but every time she saw an issue on a rack in a bodega, she thought of Chloe. She had remembered the magazine as being sophisticated and, well, cosmopolitan, but flipping through it now, it seemed juvenile, and she felt stupid for having bought it. She peeled the magazine off her thighs and tossed it back into her beach bag.

"Wanna get dinner?" Dave asked as he emerged from the bathroom. He had changed into a navy button-down shirt and black pants and looked smart and fresh.

"Definitely," Laura said. She pulled a jersey maxi dress out of her bag. It was creased in places because she had left it folded in her carry-on rather than hanging it in the standing wardrobe when they'd first arrived, but there was nothing she could do about that now.

"I'm ready to go," she said as she slid her feet into her sandals.

He surveyed her, and she noticed a flicker of disappointment cross his face.

"You're not going to wear your hair down? It looks so good down."

As far back as Laura could remember, everyone in her life—her mother, Chloe, even *Cosmo* magazine—had told her that she looked best with her hair down. It had been drilled into her from a young age that wearing her hair down softened her features and elongated her face, and for years, her mother had told her that the cost of having long hair was putting in the work to show it off. Faced with such unanimity of opinion, Laura felt she had no choice but to invest in an expensive blow-dryer and styling products, and she took great pains to blow-dry her hair every morning before work. It made her wrists ache, and it added a lot of time to her already busy schedule, but she did it anyway. Still, as soon as she left her apartment, she felt an urgent desire to pull her hair off her face. Wearing her hair up was how she felt most comfortable, most like herself, and when she was alone in her apartment, she would pull it into a bun, and no one could say a word about it. But she had come to understand that this was a version of herself no one else wanted to see. Apparently, not even Dave.

"Give me twenty minutes," she said and headed into the steamy bathroom. This was their first romantic dinner at the Pink Sands, she told herself as she pulled the blow-dryer out of the wicker basket. She ought to look her best. So she ignored the rivulets of sweat that dripped down her back and blow-dried her hair until it was silky and smooth.

The Seahorse was situated right on the sand at the far edge of the beach under a large thatched roof. Waiters came and went from the circular bar, placing drink orders with the bartenders and delivering cocktails to the guests, who sat at tables that all faced the water, enabling everyone to enjoy an oceanfront dining experience. Most of the other couples had already been seated by the time Laura and Dave arrived, and wine was being poured. The tables were outfitted with votive candles that, against the backdrop of the darkening sky, gave the restaurant a romantic ambience, and the tinkle of cutlery, the lapping of the waves, and the aroma of grilling meat mingling with the sea breeze made all of Laura's senses feel heightened.

"Welcome to the Seahorse; my name is Sadie," the hostess announced, pressing a pink acrylic fingernail to her name tag. "Is this your first evening dining with us?"

"It is," Laura said. "We're in cabin five."

Sadie nodded and checked their names off on a clipboard. "Welcome, Laura and Dave. Follow me."

They followed Sadie past the other couples who sipped their chilled wines and spoke in hushed tones, murmuring approval and delight as their entrées were ceremoniously brought to their tables.

When they were seated, Sadie handed them menus. "Can I get you something from the bar?"

Dave ordered a beer and Laura a piña colada, which was a drink she didn't usually order, but there was something about the sweetness of the coconut milk and the tartness of the pineapple that tasted to her like vacation. As Sadie poured their ice water, she encouraged them to try the conch salad, which, she explained, was a local delicacy. Laura listened politely, thinking of the conch shell she'd stumbled upon earlier, but the idea of eating its slimy innards disgusted her. She had no desire to ingest what was, let's face it, a snail from the sea. Dave, however, eternally seeking culinary novelty, was intrigued.

When Sadie left to fetch their drinks, Dave perused the menu, trying to decide between the whole grilled grouper, which he had previously been considering, and the conch salad. Laura glanced at the other women dining at the adjacent tables. They had also blow-dried their hair but had gone further, applying makeup and changing into gauzy, flowing evening dresses, which they accessorized with tiny purses that dangled from their wrists. Laura hadn't thought to bring an evening purse to dinner since the Pink Sands was all-inclusive, and sitting there, looking around, she felt underdressed.

Some women, it seemed, intrinsically understood the world and their place in it and knew how to use clothes and hair and makeup to communicate a sense of confidence and poise and self-control. Laura was not one of these women. She admired them, and though she now had the resources to emulate their style, she never managed to pull off the desired effect.

As Laura took mental snapshots of the beautiful women at the other tables, collecting inspiration on how to dress the next time she and Dave dined at a place like this, one particular woman caught her eye. It was the woman she'd seen earlier at the beach, the one with the black bathing suit. She was the only woman at the restaurant who wasn't wearing a dress. Instead, she wore an oversize linen shirt with denim cutoffs and sipped a glass of white wine while she read a book. Once again, she was alone.

One of the beautiful women stole a glance at the woman in cutoffs and arched an eyebrow at her own male companion, but the woman either didn't care that she was being looked at or didn't notice because she was so consumed by her book. Only when her entrée arrived—she'd chosen the conch salad—did she put down her book and dig into her meal. Laura couldn't fathom dining alone at a romantic restaurant like the Seahorse, but somehow, the woman eating by herself did not seem remotely concerned by the optics of the situation.

"What are you looking at?" Dave noticed Laura's distracted gaze.

"It's that woman." Laura nodded at the table behind him. "I think she came here alone."

Dave stole a discreet glance over his shoulder. "Why would she do that?"

"I don't know, but I saw her earlier at the beach. She was alone then too."

"Guess she didn't get the memo about the dress code," Dave said.

Laura hadn't known there was an actual dress code and felt relieved that after blow-drying her hair, she'd changed out of her casual maxi dress and into her nicer maxi dress. But if she was honest with herself, the woman eating alone looked more comfortable than anyone else in the restaurant.

Their entrées arrived. Dave had decided on the conch salad; Laura, the sashimi sampler. She popped a piece of albacore in her mouth and felt it melt on her tongue.

"So. What do you want to do while we're here?" Dave asked.

Laura swallowed quickly and grinned, excited by the question. Though there hadn't been time to plan an itinerary before they'd left, she had found a few spare moments at work to google Eleuthera and put together a list of points of interest.

"I definitely want to see the Glass Window Bridge, and there's a hike I read about on the resort's website that sounds cool. And snorkeling, obviously."

Dave laughed.

"What?" she asked.

"Nothing. I just love how excited you are."

She *was* excited. Was she too excited? She pinched a piece of salmon with her chopsticks and stuffed it in her mouth.

"And it's nice having dinner with someone who actually likes to eat," Dave said.

She assumed he meant this as a compliment, but when it came to eating, she, like many women, had been trained from girlhood in the art of restraint, so she felt momentarily derailed. Was his comment actually a dig? She didn't know how to respond, so she took a sip of her piña colada, which was now mostly watery ice.

When they finished their meals, their waitress cleared their plates and brought them the dessert menu. Crème brûlée was listed, Laura's favorite. She glanced at the other women. Most of them had finished their meals. The woman on her honeymoon, whom Laura mentally nicknamed Wifey, was taking a selfie. None of them had ordered dessert. None except for the woman who was dining alone. She had finished her conch salad, had ordered another glass of wine and a slice of chocolate cake, and was eating it slowly while she turned the pages of her book. Though Laura had spent the previous two weeks trying to shed a pound or two in anticipation of this trip, during which she would be mostly wearing her bathing suit, she was here now, so she decided to indulge in the crème brûlée. It was vacation, after all.

When Laura and Dave returned to their cabin, they discovered that while they were at dinner, their bed had been freshly made up as part of the resort's complimentary turndown service.

Individually wrapped chocolates had been placed on their newly fluffed pillows, and even though they were both full, they unwrapped the chocolates and ate them.

They pulled off their clothes and slid under the cool sheets. Laura loved how massive the bed was, both longer and wider than the one she had at home. Did other people have beds like this in real life? she wondered. They must. It concerned her how quickly she was getting used to the luxury here and how hard it would be to readjust to her lumpy mattress back home.

Sometime later, Laura awoke with a start. She didn't know where she was or what time it was, and it took a few minutes before her eyes adjusted to the darkness. Only when she glanced at Dave, who was a shadowy mass on the far side of the bed, did the memories of the previous day come rushing back. She fumbled on her nightstand for the cool, sleek contours of her iPhone, and when she held it up to her face, the screen came to life, glowing so brightly in the darkness that she was forced to squint in order to make out the time: 1:47 a.m.

She was wide awake, but there was no discernible reason why. She couldn't blame her insomnia on jet lag because she was in the same time zone as New York, and though she had forgotten to insert her earplugs before she fell asleep, Dave wasn't even snoring. Apparently, no matter how lavish her accommodations were, she could never sleep well in someone else's bed. Ordinarily, she would make herself a cup of tea and watch some late-night TV to lull herself back to sleep, but she didn't want to disturb Dave, so she climbed out of bed, pulled on one of the complimentary bathrobes, and slipped out the sliding glass door.

The sound of the waves lapping on the shore was muffled inside the cabin, but out on the porch, it was loud. The trade winds had picked up over the course of the night, causing the palm trees to thrash overhead and blow hair into her eyes. She was struck by how quickly the weather conditions had changed, as though the island's true nature had been unleashed while the guests slept. She pulled her hair into a bun and secured it with the elastic she kept around her wrist. It felt good to finally have it off her face.

She stepped down from the porch and walked across the cold sand, tightening the bathrobe's sash around her waist. Had she known the nights here would be so windy, she would have brought some kind of wrap, but once again, she hadn't packed anything appropriate, so she decided she would visit the gift shop in the morning to see if they had any suitable cover-ups she could buy.

Laura reached the shore and dipped her toes into the inky water, which was much colder than it had been that afternoon. The horizon was no longer visible in the darkness, but when Laura tilted her head back and took in the night sky, she was dazzled by the vast number of stars. She rarely got to see stars in New York, as the city's light pollution rendered them invisible, but there were so many of them here, thousands upon thousands of tiny pinpricks of light. Laura tried to wrap her mind around the idea that each one of those stars was actually a massive, blazing orb of gas, light-years away, but the concept was so dizzying it made her feel weak in the knees, so she lowered her gaze and focused on the water instead.

"Can't sleep either, huh?"

The voice startled Laura. A woman was standing a few feet away in the darkness. It was the woman from the restaurant, the woman who had dined alone.

"You spend so much money to come to a place like this, but at the end of the day, you still can't sleep." Her voice was pleasant if surprisingly deep, and Laura felt herself nodding in agreement.

"I can never sleep in a strange bed," Laura said.

"These might help." The woman held out a small, decorative tin containing a dozen white pills. "I'm just waiting for mine to kick in. Takes about an hour, but they're magic."

From girlhood, it had been ingrained in Laura never to take anything, least of all a pill, from a stranger, and in college, she had learned how to hold her hand over her glass in such a way as to prevent men from slipping drugs into her drink. So much of womanhood was preoccupied with fending off potential attacks from strange men. But this was not a strange man.

"Are those sleeping pills?" Laura asked.

The woman nodded. "No grogginess, I swear."

Laura rationalized that if she didn't get a few more hours of sleep, tomorrow would be a wasted day, and since her vacation was so short, each day took on precious value.

"Thanks." She took a pill and dry swallowed it. It left a chalky aftertaste in her mouth.

"No problem. If you need more, I'm in cabin twelve." The woman snapped the tin shut and pocketed it.

They both stared at the water for what felt like a long time. The woman didn't seem to mind the silence and just stared straight ahead, letting the wind ruffle her hair. But as the quiet dragged on, Laura felt a growing desire to ask her name and where she was from and, more importantly, why she had come to the resort alone. This seemed like the perfect opportunity to satisfy her curiosity, but Laura froze. It was one thing to observe the woman from a distance, but here, now, so up close, she felt intimidated. She didn't want to offend her, so she tried to formulate a question in a polite, unintrusive way, but before she could get the words out, the woman said, "Your hair looks good like that, by the way. You had it down at the restaurant, but it looks better pulled back."

She said it simply, like it was a fact, without taking her eyes off the water. Laura was struck, not only by the woman's bluntness but also because it was the first time in her life anyone had told her they preferred her hair pulled back. It surprised Laura that the woman, who at the restaurant had seemed so wrapped up in the pleasure of her own company, had noticed her enough to register how she had worn her hair. Apparently, while Laura had been discreetly observing the woman, the woman had been discreetly observing her too.

"Thanks," Laura said.

But her words were met with silence because the woman was already walking back up the beach to her cabin.

CHAPTER FOUR

Laura awoke and stretched out like a starfish in the massive bed. It was Wednesday.

"Dave?"

There was no answer. She glanced out the sliding glass doors, through which the ocean was visible, a long blue bar. Seeing the water filled Laura with a bubbling excitement. She was here now, her spreadsheet had come to life, and her first full day of vacation lay ahead with absolutely no demands. She climbed out of bed and noticed how refreshed she felt, how deeply she had slept. The woman was right—she didn't feel remotely groggy. Laura made a mental note to thank her for the sleeping pill.

Dave was not in the bathroom, but when Laura poked her head out the sliding glass door, she found him sitting in one of the chairs on the little porch, reading something on his laptop.

"Hey, you," she said.

He looked up at her and shielded his eyes with his hand. "Hey, you're finally up. If you hurry, we can still get breakfast."

Laura checked the time on her phone. It was 9:32 a.m., and according to their welcome packet, breakfast was served until ten. Dave seemed happy to see her but also a little annoyed that he was being made to wait. When he didn't stand up to kiss her, she leaned over and kissed him.

"Give me five minutes," she said and hurried back inside to shower and change.

The Seahorse had a very different vibe that morning than it had the night before. The little votive candles had been removed from the tables, and the dappled sunlight filtering through the thatched roof and the breeze coming off the water made everything feel airy and bright. The tables were occupied by couples finishing their breakfasts and lingering over coffee. Laura and Dave were seated, and while the waiter poured coffee, they looked over the menu, which consisted of several American dishes like bacon and eggs but also a few Caribbean specialties like salt fish, fried plantain, and something called johnnycakes.

"Everything looks good," Laura said, smiling.

"Someone slept well." Dave was not used to seeing Laura so upbeat before she'd had her morning coffee.

"I think it's because of the pill."

"What pill?"

"Remember the woman who came here alone? I couldn't sleep last night, so I went for a walk, and I saw her by the water, and she gave me a sleeping pill."

"You took a pill from a stranger?" Dave seemed more concerned than surprised.

"Yeah. And I'm glad I did because I'm not even a little bit groggy."

Dave looked at Laura in a way that made her feel self-conscious.

"What?"

"Nothing. It's just weird."

Laura supposed it was a bit weird in retrospect, but last night, she'd simply felt grateful to the woman who had gifted her the kind of restful sleep that would have otherwise evaded her. Still, she was surprised that she had blurted this detail to Dave. Up until now, she had been so careful around him, meticulously curating a perception that she was normal and socially acceptable. But had his opinion of her just changed? Did he now think she was *weird*? She felt anxiety simmering but forced herself to relax.

"I think it's fine," Laura said. "She's nice."

She glanced at the woman, who was sitting a few tables away, wearing cutoffs and the same oversize linen shirt she had worn the night before. Dave followed her gaze.

"I guess I'm not surprised that she's here alone," he said.

"Why?" she asked.

"Well, I mean, look at her."

"Yeah, and?"

"She's not exactly beautiful. You're way prettier."

Laura knew Dave meant this to be a compliment, and she liked that he didn't ogle the other women at the resort, but she found it disturbing that he attributed the woman's aloneness to a lack of attractiveness. Chloe had once claimed that dining solo was relegated to ugly losers, and Laura had always feared this might be true, and now Dave's comment confirmed it.

"You don't think she's beautiful?" Laura asked.

"You know what I mean."

She did know. He didn't mean *beautiful*. He meant *fuckable*.

Laura had first heard the word *fuckable* uttered in the ninth grade because it was the name of a game the boys played in the schoolyard at lunch. Whenever a girl walked by, they would categorize her as either "fuckable" or "unfuckable." Back then, the boys were always trying to categorize the girls.

Up until that point, Laura had largely felt invisible in the presence of the boys and had assumed that if and when she ever was noticed by them, she would like being looked at, but what surprised her was how uncomfortable it made her feel to have the boys' eyes roam across her body, silently appraising her breasts and hips. Being the subject of their gaze did not feel emboldening to Laura. Rather, it made her feel naked and vulnerable, reduced to her anatomical parts. Chloe, however, loved being looked at. It was as if she gained power from the gaze of other people. She was always keenly aware of where attention was in a room and how to redirect it toward herself. Whenever Laura was in Chloe's presence, she felt as though Chloe were the sun, emanating a brilliant light, and she were the moon, reflecting Chloe's glow.

One day, Laura and Chloe walked past the boys in the schoolyard, and Laura overheard them classify Chloe as fuckable and Laura as decidedly not. Laura never asked them to explain what criteria determined their decision, but she privately concluded that there must be some intangible quality that Chloe possessed and that Laura clearly lacked.

As that word, *unfuckable*, rang in her ears now, Laura felt demoralized.

"I think she's beautiful," she said.

"Really?" Dave arched an eyebrow.

She nodded, indignant. She felt oddly protective of the woman. And Laura did think she was beautiful. Not in the way the other women at the resort were beautiful, but there was something striking about her. With her slender frame and gamine bearing, she exuded a dignified elegance, like a wild deer that didn't have to prove anything to anybody.

"You think she's here alone because something bad happened?" Laura asked. "Like maybe this was supposed to be her honeymoon, but she got stood up at the altar or something?"

It was possible. The resort's website had said bookings were nonrefundable within twenty-four hours of the arrival date, so if the woman had been abandoned by her fiancé at the last minute, her only options would have been to cancel and lose her money or travel on her own.

"Or maybe she's a travel writer. You know how some magazines pay writers to come to fancy places and write about them? What do you think?" She looked at Dave expectantly.

"I dunno, Laura."

Whenever Dave used her name as punctuation, it added a degree of formality that she took as a sign of his irritation, so she dropped the topic, and they studied their menus in silence.

Laura craved waffles, but there weren't any on the menu, and when she glanced at the other tables, the beautiful women were picking at plates of sliced melon. Wifey was eating a bowl of yogurt and berries. The fact that they had all ordered fruit made Laura feel an unspoken pressure to order fruit as well.

The only woman who hadn't ordered fruit was the woman who was alone. Laura watched as a waiter brought her breakfast, a stack of pancakes that were made of some kind of yellow substance, which Laura guessed was cornmeal. The woman thanked the waiter and took a bite. Then she rose from her table and crossed to the bar, where she poured herself a glass of mango juice from a large dispenser.

"I'll be right back," Laura said and stood up. She wanted to thank the woman for the sleeping pill, but as she made her way between the tables, she felt a little nervous. After all, the woman was still technically a stranger. Laura didn't even know her name.

She arrived at the bar, but the woman's back was to her, so she said, "Morning," a little too loudly to get her attention. The woman turned.

"Hey," she said.

"Hi. I just wanted to thank you for the sleeping pill," Laura said. "It really worked."

The woman smiled. "Told you it would."

Up close in the morning light, Laura was struck by how much the woman's short hair flattered the shape of her face. For years, she had been of the opinion that short hair made women look mannish and unattractive, and yet the woman looked anything but. Her loose waves complemented her cheekbones, and though the waves were unruly, they looked purposefully unruly, which made Laura wonder if she had woken up looking like that or if she'd used styling products to obtain such a carefree effect.

The woman looked appraisingly at Laura, absorbing the details of her face. Laura, who was not used to being looked at so intently, especially not by another woman, froze. She tried to think of something else to say but could think of nothing, and then the woman said, "Have a good one," and carried her mango juice away.

Laura poured a glass of mango juice for herself and one for Dave and returned to their table, where a waiter was taking Dave's breakfast order, which was salt fish and fried plantain. Dave glanced at Laura and asked, "Do you want bacon and eggs or a fruit plate?"

"Actually, I'll have the pancakes," Laura said.

The waiter looked at her quizzically. She nodded at the woman sitting a few tables away. The waiter followed her gaze and smiled with recognition.

"Ah, johnnycakes. Good choice." He made a note in his pad and walked away. Dave glanced at the woman, and if he registered that Laura was copying her breakfast order, he said nothing about it and instead said, "I think she's a spy."

"What?"

"That's my theory. Why she's here alone." Dave nodded in the woman's direction. "I think she's here on a job."

Laura felt a sudden urge to lean across the table and kiss Dave.

"I think you're right," she said conspiratorially. "She's probably carb-loading before she heads out to execute a hit."

Dave smiled. "It's too bad her archnemesis is in town."

Laura nodded. "You know how that's going to end."

"They've always been so competitive."

"I know. I wish they could get over themselves and admit they're in love with each other."

"They'd make a great couple. They have so much in common."

"True. They both know about spying."

"And killing."

"Common interests are important in a relationship." This made Dave laugh.

Their food arrived. Laura's short stack was garnished with strawberries and a pat of melting butter. She poured maple syrup over all of it and took a bite. The johnnycakes were fluffy and gritty, like cornbread, and tastier than she expected.

"Do you want a bite?" Dave held up a slice of his fried plantain.

She ate it off his fork. It was crispy and caramelized and deliciously sweet. She offered him a bite of her johnnycakes, and when he nodded, she forked some into his mouth.

"Really good," he said.

She felt an acute pleasure feeding him, doing this intimate thing she'd seen other couples do. It still astonished her that they were in a relationship. Even though ten years had passed since their college poetry seminar and many things had changed, she struggled with her new identity as Dave Mitchell's Girlfriend. She felt like she was in possession of something others secretly desired, an art object that reflected her status. In college, Dave had always seemed so unattainable, so categorically out of her league, that there was no way the two of them would have ever dated. Back then, though Laura didn't know Dave personally, she was aware of him and would occasionally spot him on campus with one of his girlfriends. Dave's college girlfriends defied Laura's paradigm of beauty. In high school, girls had existed on a binary: they were either beautiful or smart but never both. Chloe was beautiful and Laura was smart, and there was a certain fairness to this. Dave's college girlfriends, however, did not exist in a binary. They were beautiful *and* smart. And often also rich. They were tall and thin with tiny perfect features, and they articulated thoughtful insights about their assigned readings. Laura did not have tiny perfect features. Her face was rounder than she'd like, her nose more convex than ski slope, and her frame was too large to ever allow her to feel small and cute. Yet here she was with Dave, and they were feeding breakfast to each other.

"What do you want to do today?" he asked.

Laura smiled, excited. "I was thinking we could go for a hike before it gets too hot, then maybe come back for a swim? I want to try out the infinity pool. Then, after lunch, maybe take a tour of the island?"

Dave nodded. "Oh, before I forget, I want to drop by the management office and introduce myself to Carl Reyes. He's the guy I dealt with on the tax-compliance stuff a few weeks ago. I let him know we were coming, and he said to come by and say hi."

"Cool," she said, sipping her mango juice.

"Probably a good idea to put a face to the name," he said.

It was a good idea. Still, she was a bit annoyed that he wanted to take time out of their short vacation to meet with a client. But being part of a couple, she had come to learn, meant every decision had to be negotiated. Quotidian decisions she was used to making on her own, like deciding what to watch on Netflix, became lively conversations. While she liked aspirational travel shows, he preferred gritty cable dramas about male antiheroes who were in over their heads. Compromise, she found, was key. For Dave to watch an aspirational travel show, the host had to be a celebrity chef who sampled food in various exotic locales. For Laura to watch a gritty cable drama, there had to be at least one compelling female character who had some degree of agency and wasn't always taking off her clothes.

"OK, new plan," she said. "How about we do some pool time this morning and then drop by the office later and say hi real quick and then go for a hike in the afternoon?"

Dave smiled. "Love it."

She finished what was left of her mango juice, and they got up from the table and headed back to their cabin to get changed for the pool.

Despite the extra negotiation, Laura loved that she and Dave were a team. It was how she had always hoped being in a relationship would feel—the two of them against the world. What she'd been unprepared for when they first started dating was the profound impact her relationship had on the way she was treated by other lawyers at the firm. When she and Dave first came out officially as a couple, colleagues she had worked with for years but whom she didn't actually know very well looked at her in a new way. Men smiled at her more. Women too. In fact, Jasmine, who previously had never seemed all that interested in Laura's personal life, stopped by her office on Monday mornings and asked how her weekend was. Or, more precisely, how *their* weekend was. Because what Laura discovered was that she was now a *we*. As in, *We tried that new Thai place in Brooklyn last night.* Jasmine would then volunteer anecdotes about the trip she'd taken with Brian to the farmers' market in Union Square, where they'd found absolutely amazing heirloom tomatoes, and she would describe a movie they'd seen and elaborate in great detail about whether or not they had agreed with the review in the *New York Times*.

Laura started receiving invitations for her and Dave to attend dinner parties and baseball games, and those gestures made her feel like she was living a new life, a real life, not the monastic existence she had been enduring up until that point. In this new, real life, everything felt kinetic in a way it hadn't before, even though, in all other respects, her life was exactly the same. She was still the same person who lived in the same apartment and who went to work every day at the same job. Only the behavior of everyone else around her suggested that something fundamental had changed. It was not unlike standing on the deck of a giant ship and being told that it had set sail. Even though the ship's motion was undetectable, it was the well-wishers waving to her from shore and receding into the distance that indicated the ship was actually moving and that she was finally on her way to somewhere.

While it thrilled Laura to gain entrée into this new social world, it made her wonder how many engagements she had been excluded from when she had been single. Many, she assumed. Most. And this made her sad for her former self. Her mother had been right—the world was indeed built for couples, not singles—and realizing this, Laura was gripped by a new fear, one she had never really experienced before: the fear of having something to lose. While her single life had felt familiar and routine, she didn't want to return to it. She never wanted to be alone again.

"Ready for a swim?" Dave asked after they commandeered a pair of loungers on the pool deck.

Laura inspected her arms. Brown freckles had popped up all over them, as though the melanin in her skin had emerged in the night, like mushrooms after a storm. Otherwise, she was pale as ever, save the tops of her shoulders, which were pink. Compared to the beautiful women who were sunning themselves nearby, she looked like a piece of unevenly cooked meat. Wifey's skin, in particular, glowed with an even, golden tone, and Laura wondered if she'd gotten a spray tan before she arrived, and if that was something one was supposed to do before coming to a place like this.

"I should probably put on some sunscreen first," she said.

He grabbed her arm playfully. "Come on. You can do that later."

He led her over to the deep end, then let go of her hand and dove in. He was gone for a long time before he surfaced at the other end of the pool. He raked his fingers through his wet hair and beckoned Laura to join him. She walked over to the stairs at the shallow end and waded in. When she reached him, he gathered her up in his arms and kissed her. Then he lifted her out of the water and flung her back in. She shrieked as she plunged underwater, chlorine shooting up her nose. When she surfaced, she splashed him, and they both laughed.

No one else was in the pool, and when she glanced at the pool deck, she noticed that some of the beautiful women were staring at her. Under their gaze, Laura felt ridiculous, like one of those woo girls she'd gone to college with who always felt the need to shriek and giggle, broadcasting how much fun they were having in any given situation. But this was why she was here, wasn't it? To shriek and giggle and be thrown around in the water. This was what she'd fantasized about for years. This was what it felt like to be a couple on vacation. She turned her back on the beautiful women and dunked Dave's head under the water.

They played like that all morning, tossing each other around and splashing.

At one point, the woman in the black bathing suit waded into the pool to the depth of her shoulders and bobbed quietly in Laura's periphery. Spotting her, Laura was overcome by a strange feeling she couldn't immediately identify. She felt an affinity with the woman, was grateful to her for the sleeping pill, and had felt protective of her at breakfast. But now, seeing her alone in the water, Laura felt a sharp stab in her gut. Was it jealousy? she wondered. Eating alone in a romantic restaurant required a degree of confidence Laura lacked, and that was something to be jealous of. But no, it wasn't jealousy, she decided. It was something else.

"I want to get some laps in," Dave said. "Want to swim with me?"

He looked at Laura expectantly. But she didn't feel like swimming. It was as if some spell had broken. She wanted to get out of the water.

"You go ahead," she said.

"You sure?"

"Yeah. I should put some sunscreen on, anyway."

"OK," Dave said. He turned and swam to the deep end with the steady strokes of a practiced swimmer.

Laura climbed out of the pool and dried herself off. She dug in her beach bag for her sunscreen and sprayed it liberally on her arms and legs. She glanced at the woman in the black bathing suit. She was floating face up in the shallow end and looked serene. Utterly content. It irked Laura. It didn't seem fair that the woman had come to this couples' resort alone. It was as if she had defied some unspoken rule. After all, Laura had fantasized about coming to a place like this for years, but she'd known it would have been inappropriate to come by herself. Didn't the woman know that she shouldn't be here alone? Didn't she know she was making everyone else uncomfortable? Who did she think she was?

Laura felt her feelings morph into a simmering anger. She didn't want to see the woman anymore, so she lay back on her lounger and squeezed her eyes shut. She kept them shut until she felt drops of water sprinkle her arm. She opened her eyes. Dave was standing over her, toweling off.

"I saw your doppelgänger in the water, and for a second I thought it was you," he said.

Laura glanced at the woman floating in the pool. "Why'd you think it was me?"

"I dunno. She kind of looks like you."

At breakfast, Dave had described the woman as "not exactly beautiful," so was he now implying that Laura was not exactly beautiful either?

"I don't think she looks like me."

Dave shrugged. "Same bathing suit, I guess."

He dropped his towel on his lounge chair.

"What time is it?" he asked.

Laura glanced at her phone. "Eleven fifteen."

"I think I'll go say hi to Carl Reyes. Want to come to the management office?"

Laura did not want to go to the management office. She did not want to make nice with Carl Reyes. She felt annoyed but didn't want Dave to know, as she was still on her best behavior.

"I was actually thinking of checking out the gift shop," she said. "I forgot to bring a cover-up."

"Oh. OK. You sure?" Dave seemed disappointed.

She nodded. "How about we meet back at the cabin in a bit?"

"Sure. I'll text you when I'm done."

"Great. Tell Carl hi for me."

Laura stood up and pulled on her maxi dress, which was warm from sitting out in the sun all morning. She slid into her flip-flops and grabbed her beach bag, and she and Dave headed down the paved path together. They parted ways at the gift shop, and Dave continued to the management office, which was at the far end of the grounds.

It was a relief to step inside the air-conditioned store. Laura nodded hello to the cashier, who was reading a paperback by the register, and she roamed the aisles filled with trinkets and jewelry. She flicked through a rack of sundresses and gauzy cover-ups in shades of cream and beige and paused to consider a romper. Laura didn't own a romper, had never even tried one on, but this one was bright pink with spaghetti straps, and it reminded her of a tank top Chloe had given her in ninth grade.

Chloe always looked stylish and put together in high school, and though Laura secretly coveted her stylish tops and skirts, she never had the confidence to buy any for herself. But when Chloe's favorite trendy knockoff store, Jayleen's, had a buy-one-get-one-free sale, she bought a pink spaghetti-strap tank top and gave a second one to Laura. They decided to debut their matching tops the following day at school. As they walked down the halls in lockstep, Laura loved that they looked so similar as to be interchangeable, one beginning where the other ended, and felt that that moment was the true high point of their friendship.

But soon after, Chloe was labeled fuckable by the boys, and Laura watched her ascend into the annals of popularity. Many tenth graders and even some eleventh graders became aware of her new status, and because of her growing social exposure, she wore increasingly tight-fitting outfits and started reapplying her lip gloss at her locker between every class.

"Doesn't it bother you that they call you fuckable?" Laura once asked Chloe.

"No, why?" Chloe said.

"Don't you think it means they think you're slutty?"

"You're just jealous."

Laura stared at Chloe, confused. "I heard people talking about you behind your back."

Chloe's nostrils flared then. "You don't know what you're talking about. And who are you to judge, anyway? You can't even pull *that* off."

By *that*, Chloe meant the pink spaghetti-strap tank top Laura was wearing. Laura had never given a thought to whether a pink spaghetti-strap tank top was something she could or could not pull off. She simply wore it because Chloe had gifted it to her and because it was, to Laura, a treasured token of their friendship. But in that moment, Laura absorbed two profound truths that would stay with her for the rest of her life. The first was that she was not innately stylish and never would be. The second was that she and Chloe were no longer best friends.

When Laura got home that night, she stared at herself in her bedroom mirror. She had never noticed it before, but her shoulders were broad, like a man's, and the spaghetti-strap tank top only accentuated their breadth. She pulled off the tank top, threw it in the trash, and pulled on an oversize hoodie. She didn't fully understand what had happened. All she knew was that she had felt invincible when she'd worn the tank top at school and strode down the halls with Chloe, but now she felt ugly and weak.

Laura stood there by the rack, staring at the pink romper for an indeterminate amount of time before a voice said, "You should try it on."

She looked up. It was the woman from the beach. Her short hair was wet, and she was wearing the same linen shirt she'd worn at breakfast. Laura hadn't noticed her enter the gift shop and wondered how long she had been standing there.

"It's not really my style," Laura said.

"How do you know if you don't try it on?" the woman asked.

A romper was one of those risky garments that tended to only look good on women who were rail thin or preternaturally confident, and Laura did not feel like she was either of those things.

When it came to fashion, she had become inured to her limitations. As an adult, she no longer tried to emulate trends but instead educated herself in the architecture of well-cut suits and the structural benefits of tailored jackets. Buying clothes was no longer about showing off her body but about camouflaging its flaws. It was sad, in a way, how in adulthood shopping for clothes had become a defensive act.

Laura felt an acute anger toward the romper then. It felt like something that was being dangled in front of her while simultaneously held out of her reach. Laura glanced at the woman, annoyed that she was challenging her in this way.

"I could never pull it off." Laura shoved the romper back on the rack with such hostility that the metal hanger screeched, causing the cashier to look up from her book. She flicked through the other dresses quickly, not even really looking at them, but the woman pulled the romper off the rack and handed it back to Laura.

"Just try it."

Laura was irritated by the woman's pushiness. Who was she to insinuate herself so forcefully into Laura's life, to have such a strong opinion about something that was none of her business? Why must she invade Laura's personal space and insist upon herself, first in the pool and now here in the shop? What was her problem?

And yet there was something about the way she was smiling and holding up the romper. It was like a dare, but a friendly dare, and for a moment, Laura felt like she was back in high school again, shopping with Chloe at Jayleen's.

"Fine," she said.

In the dressing room, Laura pulled the romper on over her bathing suit and studied herself in the mirror. Perhaps it was one of those skinny mirrors that made her look thinner than she was, but the romper did actually look pretty good on her. She emerged from the dressing room, and the woman nodded approvingly.

"You look good. You should get it."

The woman smiled, and Laura felt a wave of validation come over her. She did look good. She should get it.

Then Laura felt awash with shame. She had judged the woman earlier, but of course she had every right to come to the resort alone. She could do whatever she damn well pleased. Laura was no better than Jasmine and all the other associates at the firm who had undoubtedly judged and excluded her when she'd been single. In fact, Laura admired the woman for having the courage, or at least the indifference to judgment, to come here on her own.

Laura returned to the dressing room and changed back into her maxi dress. She hadn't even looked at the price tag. The romper cost ninety-eight dollars, which was a lot to spend on something so impractical, especially because it wasn't even what she had come here to shop for in the first place, but she watched herself pull her credit card out of her wallet and hand it to the cashier, who wrapped the romper in tissue paper and slid it into a paper bag that was stamped with the logo of the resort.

"Have a nice day," the cashier said.

"Thank you. You too," Laura said and took the bag.

For years, Laura never would have been caught dead in a romper, but now, suddenly, she owned one. A pink one with spaghetti straps, no less. It took her breath away how quickly it had happened, how quickly she had abandoned an idea about herself that she had held so deeply for so long. All because of a conversation with a woman whose name she didn't even know.

Laura knew that this feeling—this bright, sparkly surge of confidence that accompanied the purchase of new clothes—was finite, that it would pass, and that the romper, which felt foreign to her now but full of potential, would soon become familiar and eventually forgotten at the back of her closet at home, so it was important to savor this electric feeling of boundless possibility that was presently coursing through her veins. It was important to make it last. She wanted to celebrate. At home, Laura rarely drank alcohol during the day, least of all in the morning, but now, at 11:38 a.m., she wanted a cocktail. Still, she knew that she would feel self-conscious drinking alone, so she looked over at the woman and said, "Do you want to get a drink?"

The woman shrugged and said, "Sure," as if it were nothing, as if they were friends already.

There was something so freeing about that moment—her new purchase, their easy exchange—that as they exited the gift shop, Laura laughed out loud and swung the paper bag. It was so light in her hand, as weightless as she.

CHAPTER FIVE

The drink menus at the Seahorse bar were different from the breakfast menus, not folded cards but single sheets of laminated paper upon which a dozen cocktails were listed, with names like Caribbean Sunset and Bahama Mama and the Painkiller. Laura skimmed the list, then glanced at the bartender, who was waiting expectantly, and said, "I'll have a piña colada, please." The bartender nodded and turned to the woman, who studied the menu more closely and said, finally, "Caribbean Sunset, please." The bartender nodded again and headed to the far side of the bar to make their drinks.

"I'm Laura, by the way."

"Diana. Nice to meet you."

Laura recited the woman's name in her head. *Diana*. It was not the name she'd expected, but it was startling that she had a name at all. It seemed to tether her to the earth somehow.

Now that Laura was sitting next to Diana, she took the opportunity to observe her in more detail. She looked for obvious signs of a significant other, but her ring finger was bare.

"Is this your first time in Eleuthera?" Laura asked.

"It is. You?"

Laura nodded. "A few weeks ago, I didn't even know this place existed."

"That's why I like it here. I really needed to get away."

"Work's been stressful?" she ventured.

Diana sighed. "No offense, but I really don't want to talk about work on my vacation."

Laura nodded, relenting, even as Diana's deflection piqued her curiosity.

The bartender returned with their drinks. Diana's slushy cocktail was pink on the bottom and yellow on top, and it blended into a peachy orange in the middle that did indeed resemble a Caribbean sunset. Both drinks were garnished with cherries and paper umbrellas.

Laura held up her glass in a toast. "To not talking about work."

"Cheers to that," Diana said.

They clinked their glasses and each took a sip. The coldness of Laura's piña colada hit her hard, an acute punch in her chest.

"What do you think?" Diana asked.

Laura pressed her hand to her sternum, as if that would somehow attenuate the pain.

"I like it," she managed.

"Brain freeze?"

Laura nodded.

Diana smiled, sympathetic. "Isn't it funny how we say we like things even when they cause us pain?"

Laura had never thought about this before, but it was true in a way.

"I guess we're all just masochists," Diana said.

At the far side of the bar, Wifey and Hubs were eating a platter of nachos. Wifey was holding up her cocktail while Hubs took a photo with her phone. Wifey smiled widely when he took it, but when he handed back the phone, her smile vanished as she scrutinized the photo before telling him to take another.

"I think they're on their honeymoon," Laura said.

Diana followed her gaze, and together they watched as Hubs kept taking photos, Wifey rejecting each one, until finally he refused to take any more, dropped the phone on the bar with a clatter of frustration, and resumed eating the nachos. Wifey said nothing, picked up the phone, and flicked through the photos, presumably trying to pick out the least bad of the bunch.

"Are you married?" Laura asked.

"No. You?"

Laura shook her head, then looked back at Wifey. "She's probably taking pics for her Insta."

"Is that Instagram?"

Laura looked at Diana curiously. "Yeah. Are you not on social media?"

"Not anymore. Deleted all my socials last week. I was just over it, you know?"

Laura did not know. Even her mother was on Instagram.

Diana checked the time on her phone, and Laura noticed that her lock screen was not a photo of her family, child, or pet but a generic blue. This choice—not to personalize her phone's lock screen—intrigued her. There was something about Diana that seemed paradoxical: the more details Laura absorbed about her, the more mysterious she became.

"Don't you miss it?" Laura asked.

"Not at all."

Diana stirred her drink until the pink and yellow blended into a uniform peach. She did not seem self-conscious about her absence from social media, which made Laura embarrassed about the amount of time she spent scrolling through her various feeds. She used social media the way some people used cigarettes, as a palate cleanser after a long meeting or as a treat after finishing an assignment. Most of the time, she would scroll passively, not looking at anything in particular, and after a few minutes she would come away with a vague awareness that the kid of someone she knew from high school had had a birthday party or that someone who used to work at the firm got a new cat. But sometimes, if she was feeling angry or sad or wistful, she would look up someone with whom she had unfinished business, like Chloe, and study how their profile pictures had changed over the years. The pictures of Chloe at clubs with drinks in hand that showed off how great her single life was became pictures of her with boyfriends hiking in forests that showed off how great her dating life was became pictures of her in a wedding dress that showed off how great her married life was, and now her feed was filled with pictures of her hoisting her young son like a trophy. Laura knew that these photos, the ones that emanated extreme happiness and the sense of a life well lived, were carefully curated by Chloe and not necessarily representative of reality, and yet Laura allowed herself to believe that they were real and that Chloe's life was far superior to her own. She recognized this habit as a form of self-harm, yet she scrolled through the photos anyway. She concluded that Diana might be right: she probably was a masochist.

"Why'd you do it?" Laura asked.

Diana gazed out at the horizon. "I just hated the feeling of being watched, you know?"

Laura noticed that her face seemed to darken then.

"In that case, I should probably mention that I'm a lurker, not a poster," Laura said.

"A lurker?"

"I don't post a lot of pictures, but I look at my friends' pictures a lot."

"Have you posted any pictures from this trip?"

Laura hadn't. There was something performative about the way people posted photos from their vacations, a way of bragging under the guise of "sharing." She'd roll her eyes at these posts, even as she clicked through them, absorbing countless snapshots of other people's memories. A part of her wanted to post pictures of the resort, the view from the cabin, selfies of her and Dave, to broadcast to everyone she knew that her life was, if only for these few days, as fabulous as theirs. But something held her back. She figured it would look odd if she posted vacation photos when she hadn't even updated her profile picture in five years. It was still the same headshot from when she had been hired at Reinhart, Mader & Stern. But perhaps, she began to think, her failure to update her own online presence was just as performative as Chloe's careful curation of hers.

"No, I haven't even taken any," she said.

"How come?"

"I don't know."

The truth of the matter was that she didn't like having her picture taken. She never had, not even when she was a child. When her adult teeth had come in, her jaw was too small to accommodate them all, so they grew in crooked. Her dentist told her that as her jaw grew, her teeth would straighten out, and over time it had and they did, but by then she had stopped smiling in photographs. But it never failed to surprise her how often she was encouraged, prodded—by her mother, by her friends, by men on the street—to smile. Strangely, though, Chloe, who was very photogenic and had been blessed with perfect teeth, never smiled in photographs either. She didn't pout the way the other pretty girls did, trying to uglify their beauty, thereby amplifying it. There was nothing defiant or sarcastic in Chloe's refusal to smile. She would just stare neutrally into the camera lens, comfortable in her own skin.

"I want another drink. Do you want another round?" Diana asked suddenly, fidgeting with the clasp of her bracelet. The delicate silver chain featured a single ceramic bead painted with three concentric rings of blue and white, which Laura recognized as the Greek symbol of the evil eye.

Laura looked down at her drink and was surprised to find that her glass was nearly empty. She hadn't realized how quickly she had drunk her cocktail.

"Sure. I'll have another piña colada."

Diana signaled the bartender. "Why don't you try something else? This place is all-inclusive, right? Might as well," she said.

Laura glanced from Diana to the bartender, both of whom were looking at her expectantly, and she felt a sudden pressure. Was she a boring drink orderer? She had never considered this possibility, but she supposed Diana had a point. The drinks were free—or not free, per se, but included in the cost of her stay—so it was a good opportunity to try new things. Besides, she didn't want to be thought of as someone who always made safe choices, even if she apparently was. She skimmed the menu and picked the first cocktail that caught her eye.

"I'll have a Bahama Mama."

"Sounds fun. I'll have the same," Diana said, then looked back out to sea. Her face took on a pensive, faraway expression, and it occurred to Laura that this mystique she exuded was the same quality Chloe had emanated when they were kids.

"You remind me of someone," Laura said.

"Oh. Who?" Diana asked.

"Chloe. My best friend. Well, former best friend."

Diana focused her gaze back on Laura. "Former? What happened?"

"Jake Hollinger happened," Laura said.

"Who's he?"

Jake Hollinger was the only boy in the ninth grade who didn't play "fuckable" in the schoolyard at lunch. He was popular but quiet, a jock who got straight A's, and his ability to evade easy classification made him intriguing to both Laura and Chloe. With his blond curls and green eyes, he was widely considered to be the best-looking boy in their grade, so it was unsurprising that they both chose him as their ideal boyfriend. They weren't territorial, though, because fantasizing about dating him was like fantasizing about dating a celebrity. Naturally then, Laura was surprised when Jake Hollinger called her one night to ask about their homework. They stayed on the phone for hours, talking about wide-ranging topics like their classes, TV shows they liked, and even his parents' divorce. They talked until Laura's mother poked her head in the door and told her to go to bed. The following night, he called her again, and he proceeded to call her every night for an entire month. On these nocturnal calls, they were reduced to two disembodied voices, and in this liminal space, Laura felt an acute pleasure uncovering the vulnerable underbelly of such a beautiful, popular person. She never told anyone about these calls, not even Chloe. She felt guilty withholding the truth but feared that divulging this secret would cause the calls to cease.

One night, in a quiet, serious voice, Jake said, "There's someone I like. And I'm going to ask her out tomorrow." Laura didn't sleep that night. The following morning, she took extra care in selecting her outfit. When she arrived at school, she searched for Chloe to tell her the news, but Chloe found her first and blurted, "Jake Hollinger asked me out."

The rest of the day passed by in a nauseating blur. Laura stared into space, stung and utterly baffled. If it was Chloe he liked all along, why had he called Laura every night for a month? It didn't make sense. After that day, Jake Hollinger never called Laura again.

"What a dick," Diana said now.

Their Bahama Mamas arrived, bright red and garnished with pineapple wedges.

Diana raised her glass. "To surviving high school boys."

Laura took a sip and, surprised by how much she liked it, briefly wondered how many other things she had missed out on in life due to her tendency to make safe choices. She took another sip. The alcohol made her feel loose in the limbs, slightly outside her body, but it was a nice feeling. With the sea breeze on her face, she felt confident suddenly, like nothing could faze her.

"Why did you come to a couples' resort alone?" she asked. "I mean, I'm assuming you came here alone. I haven't seen you with anyone. Sorry if that's a rude question." Laura was aware that she might have come off too probing, so she wrapped her lips around her straw to stop herself from saying any more.

But Diana didn't seem offended. She laughed as she pulled the pineapple wedge from the rim of her glass and bit into it. "I don't think you're the only person here who's wondering about that. The staff is always asking me if I want an extra towel for my husband or a drink for my boyfriend."

"What do you tell them?"

"Put it this way: There are a lot of extra beach towels in my cabin. And I've gotten a lot of extra drinks."

Laura waited for Diana to answer her question, but she said nothing more as she placed the pineapple rind on her napkin. Laura couldn't understand why Diana was being so evasive, but before she could formulate another question, Diana said, "Have you seen much of the island?"

"No, not yet," Laura said. "I want to check out the Glass Window Bridge."

"I'm meeting someone here for dinner later, but I was planning on going for a hike."

So there *was* someone. It wasn't clear to Laura if this someone was a romantic partner or not, but she was intrigued.

"Do you want to come?" Diana asked.

Maybe it was because she was buzzed, or maybe it was because she was feeling spontaneous after buying a ninety-eight-dollar romper, but going on a hike with Diana sounded like a great idea.

"Sure," she said.

Then she remembered Dave. They had planned to go on a hike in the afternoon. She wasn't sure if he was still with Carl Reyes at the management office or if he'd gone back to their cabin. She hadn't texted him since they parted ways at the gift shop, but then again, he hadn't texted her either.

"I should check in with my boyfriend."

"He can come, too, if he wants," Diana said.

Laura texted Dave:

> Where r u?

He texted back a few seconds later:

> Hey, still with Carl.

She wrote back:

> Want to go on a hike?

Three dots flashed for what felt like a long time before his response finally appeared:

> We're going over some M&A stuff and it's taking longer than I thought. Rain check?

Laura chewed on her straw. Rain check? They were leaving the day after tomorrow. She didn't want to spend the whole day waiting for him.

She wanted to go on a hike. She considered telling him she was going with Diana but figured it would need a lot of explanation and she'd probably be back before he was done with Carl anyway, so she wrote back:

> OK, text me when u r back at the cabin.

Dave responded with a thumbs-up emoji, which irked Laura. In her mind, the thumbs-up emoji was reserved for professional correspondence, not shorthand between lovers. She pocketed her phone.

"He's not coming," she said.

Diana looked up from her phone, where she'd been scanning a map. "Oh well. His loss. So, the trailhead for Castaway Point is about ten minutes from the main gate. It says the loop takes about an hour, and apparently the view from the cliffs is 'panoramic and breathtaking.'"

"Let's do it," Laura said and downed what was left of her cocktail.

They left the bar and headed across the beach. The sun was high in the sky, and the pink sand was hot underfoot. Laura glanced at Diana's outfit—cutoffs, white shirt, and running shoes—and decided her maxi dress was not appropriate for a hike.

"I'm going to change real quick. I'll be right back," she said and, leaving Diana by the white umbrellas, headed up the beach.

When she stepped inside the cabin, she was instantly cooled by the air-conditioning. She took off her maxi dress and pulled her new romper on over her bathing suit. It wasn't a hiking outfit exactly, but it was more hike appropriate at least. She swapped her flip-flops for her running shoes and headed back outside, sliding the glass door shut behind her.

"Time to break it in?" Diana asked, nodding at Laura's new romper.

Laura nodded. She felt a little self-conscious in it, as she didn't normally wear bright shades of pink, but Diana's encouraging smile gave her a boost of confidence.

They headed down the paved path that led across the grounds.

"Is everything OK between you and your boyfriend?" Diana asked.

"Yeah. Why?" Laura asked.

"Because he's not coming on the hike, so I just wondered."

"Oh. Yeah, it's fine. He had to do a work thing, say hi to some clients."

"Clients?"

"We're both lawyers, and our firm represents the owner of the resort."

"Ah," Diana said. "Makes sense."

"Dave's great with the clients. Very popular."

"He sounds a bit like Jake Hollinger."

Hearing Diana make this comparison threw her a little. It was a strangely forward comment for a stranger to make.

"How's that?" she asked.

Diana shrugged. "Am I wrong?"

She wasn't wrong—there was a similarity. Laura hadn't made the connection before, and it made her wonder if she was with Dave vicariously, dating the adult version of the hot, popular, cool boy she'd never had access to before. But the thought made her uncomfortable, so she pushed it out of her mind.

"Maybe it's for the best that Chloe's not in your life anymore," Diana said.

"Why?" Laura asked.

"I mean, back then, she was clearly OK dating a guy she knew you liked. That's a little cold."

Laura felt herself getting defensive. "Everybody liked Jake."

As jealous as she'd been back then, it had made sense to her that Chloe and Jake were a couple. Like Jake, Chloe was beautiful and popular, and in Laura's mind, this gave her an inherent right to date whomever she wanted. The sun always outshone the moon.

She once asked Chloe what she and Jake Hollinger talked about when they hung out, and Chloe shrugged and said, "We mostly just hook up." Upon learning their relationship was predominantly physical, Laura felt emboldened by a strange new power. She didn't have access to Jake Hollinger's body, but she did have access to his mind, and it felt good knowing things about him that Chloe didn't. This newfound power made her feel like she was a member of a clandestine group that wielded great influence while hiding in plain sight, an intelligentsia composed of girls who knew the secrets of the boys they loved who didn't love them back.

"Have you ever considered that maybe Chloe was the one who betrayed you?" Diana asked.

"It wasn't like that," Laura said. She didn't like how Diana was twisting the story. It was Jake who'd betrayed her, not Chloe.

They reached the white gazebo, passed a rack of complimentary white bicycles, and headed through the main gate, emerging onto Queen's Highway. Compared to the resort's manicured grounds, the bushes and scrubby trees by the side of the road looked messy and unkempt. Ordinarily, Laura would have felt unsafe leaving the resort on foot, but the alcohol coursing through her veins made her less concerned about the unfamiliarity of her surroundings.

"Why did you stop being friends?" Diana asked as they made their way toward the trailhead.

"I think it was because of the contract," Laura said.

"What contract?"

Laura had never told anyone about the contract and was reluctant to now, but the way Diana was looking at her, with genuine interest, was disinhibiting.

After Jake Hollinger asked Chloe out, she was endowed with a newfound status that manifested in the form of invitations to exclusive events, like Hugh Keller's house parties, which was significant because he was a senior. Laura was stung when Chloe decided to forgo their monthly sleepover in favor of attending one of his parties. But the following Monday at school, a vicious rumor circulated that Chloe had given Jake Hollinger a blow job in Hugh Keller's laundry room. At first, Laura wondered if Chloe had employed the techniques they had studied in *Cosmo*. Had she knelt during the act? Had Jake Hollinger been sitting or standing? Were anyone's clothes being laundered at the time? Then she grew angry when she witnessed Jake Hollinger being lionized for his sexual prowess while Chloe was labeled a slut. She couldn't bear to see Chloe publicly humiliated, so she approached her at her locker after school.

"It's not fair that he gets what he wants and you get nothing," she said. "You should get something too."

"Like what?" Chloe asked.

"What do you want?" Laura asked.

Chloe thought about it, then said, "I want to be his girlfriend. Officially."

Laura suggested Chloe propose that arrangement to Jake, but Chloe was skeptical.

"He'll never go for that. But if he does, I want proof."

"What kind of proof?" Laura asked.

"I want to see it in writing."

It took Laura a moment before she realized what Chloe was proposing was a contract.

Laura was uncomfortable with the idea of drafting one, but Chloe was adamant. And when Jake realized that, in exchange for publicly acknowledging Chloe as his girlfriend, he could have his sexual needs met anywhere he wanted, he was game. Laura wanted nothing to do with the contract, but when she saw that Chloe was willing to agree to all of Jake's terms, she saw the best way to protect her friend was to negotiate a more favorable arrangement on her behalf. So she reluctantly agreed to broker the deal. She fought for things she knew were important to Chloe: gifts on her birthday and Valentine's Day, Candygrams delivered to her desk during the holiday season, and arrival at school dances as a couple rather than separately. Laura didn't know it then, but that contract was the first of many she would write in her lifetime. She would come to know that particular kind of contract as a bilateral agreement, arranged by two parties that had reciprocal obligations.

Laura drafted the contract on a page of lined, three-hole paper and folded it into a little triangular football. Chloe reviewed it during her third-period biology class, and since she would only agree to sign it under conditions of total secrecy, Jake skipped his after-school basketball practice, and the three of them met in the basement hallway to carry out the solemn affair. Chloe signed it with her signature pink gel pen, then handed it to Jake Hollinger, who countersigned it. Laura observed as witness. Since discretion was paramount, it was decided that Laura would be the keeper of the contract, and she swore never to disclose its contents to anyone.

Laura marveled at the contract, at the elegant formality of its language. She'd learned that sex was a form of currency one could trade on and that words written down had power, but she was unprepared for the impact the contract would have in the years that followed. Had she known it would cause Chloe to end their friendship, abruptly and with a kind of exquisite brutality, she never would have agreed to draft it in the first place.

"A blow job contract?" Diana said. "Yikes."

"I guess it was pretty yikes," Laura conceded as they made their way along the dusty highway, the hot sun beating down on them. She was ashamed now of how she had inadvertently participated in the objectification of her best friend. But at the time it had felt to Laura the only way for Chloe to retain any control in her relationship.

Up ahead, a man was sitting in the flatbed of a pale-blue pickup truck.

"Hello, sexy ladies," he said.

He smiled leeringly, and Laura noticed how yellow his teeth were and that one of them was missing. The state of his teeth agitated Laura, and she felt a sudden sense of alarm that she and Diana were outside the boundaries of the resort and no longer under its protection.

"Would you like to buy a T-shirt?" He gestured at a stack of folded T-shirts next to him.

"No, thank you." Diana's voice had a firm edge to it, not the shrill singsong quality Laura's voice had when she said no to people.

"Come on, ladies. I bet you'll like what I have." The man smiled again and jumped down from his truck. Laura was caught off guard by his speed and agility.

The man held up a large blue T-shirt that said *Eleuthera* across the front in white letters.

"Look at this one. Great color. It's the last one."

Laura told herself that the man was probably just trying to sell his T-shirts to tourists, but a lifetime of being warned about what happened to women who were lured into trucks by strange men had conditioned her to fear situations like this. Still, she felt guilty assuming he had unsavory intentions, so she repressed her fear.

"How much?" she asked politely and approached his truck. Diana hung back, looking at something on her phone.

Encouraged, the man walked over to Laura, holding up the blue T-shirt for her to see. "Twenty dollars," he said. He was standing close to her now, too close, and she felt stupid for having agreed to go on a hike without considering all the risks involved. She had changed into her running shoes, but she hadn't brought anything else, not even a bottle of water. Not to mention the fact that she was buzzed and not totally in control of her faculties. She felt like a stupid tourist, the kind she'd read about in *People* magazine, the kind who got attacked by strange men on vacation.

Diana walked over and handed the man a twenty-dollar bill. "Here," she said.

He gave her the T-shirt. "Thank you, pretty lady."

Diana grabbed Laura by the arm and pulled her away from the truck. She didn't let go of Laura until they were out of the man's earshot.

"I thought you didn't want it," Laura said.

Diana shrugged and draped the T-shirt around her neck like a towel. "He would have kept us there all day. Sometimes it's easier to give people what they want."

Laura nodded, a little shaken. As guilty as she felt for assuming the worst about the man, she was glad Diana had pulled her away. She was reminded of how unpredictable people could be, how abruptly situations could change, and how few things in life were actually within her control. She felt herself sobering quickly.

"You OK?" Diana asked.

"Yeah, it's just, that guy was sort of creepy."

Diana looked back at the man and shrugged. "He's fine. Come on." Diana didn't seem creeped out so much as annoyed, but Laura couldn't shake the eeriness of the encounter.

"Just so you know, if something were to happen to us, I don't think the resort would be liable for damages, since we're not technically on the property," Laura said.

Diana laughed. Laura looked at her, confused. "What?"

"Were you always like this?"

"Like what?"

"A lawyer."

"What do you mean?"

"'Liable.' 'Damages.' You even wrote a contract when you were in high school."

"That contract didn't exactly work out, though," Laura said defensively. She regretted telling Diana about it now. All these years later, it still felt like an open wound that had never fully healed.

After the contract was signed, the three of them vowed never to speak of it again. So three weeks later, when Laura heard a rumor about its existence circulating the halls at school, she and Chloe determined Jake Hollinger must have broken the terms of their deal. It enraged Laura, but there was nothing she could do. She couldn't sue or seek damages. There was no judicial body to enforce it because this wasn't the real world. This was high school. And in high school, popular boys were above the law.

"I never should have signed that thing," Chloe said when she confronted Laura at her locker after school. "This is *your* fault."

Laura was confused. Why was Chloe blaming her for the leak?

"I was just trying to protect you," she said.

Chloe, though, would have none of it. "Just leave me alone. I'm serious."

But Laura didn't leave her alone, and Chloe, perhaps to physically distance herself, said, "Why are you so *obsessed* with me?" and shoved her hard in the chest. As Laura staggered back, the wind knocked out of her, she saw a steely glint in Chloe's eyes, and it scared her.

Out of fear or perhaps self-preservation, Laura shoved her back, which caused Chloe to lose her balance, and her hand, which she used to cushion her fall, made contact with the ground in an unusual way. What happened next remained to Laura, even years later, a complete blur. All she remembered was blood and bone and paramedics pushing her out of the way. That afternoon, teachers asked Laura why Chloe was not in class, but she just stared at her open textbook until the words swam across the page. That night, Laura called Chloe's house, but her mother said she couldn't come to the phone. The next day, Chloe returned to school with a pink cast on her arm, and when Laura caught her eye, Chloe didn't look at Laura so much as through her, like she was air. In that moment, Laura knew their friendship was over. When she came home, she cried into her pillow. Her mother rubbed her back but offered only cold comfort. *I told you that girl was dangerous.*

"That's really sad," Diana said. "But it wasn't your fault."

Laura glanced at Diana. She had never told anyone the details of what had transpired between her and Chloe. She had told Dave a bit about their friendship, but not very much, mostly just that she'd had a complicated friendship in her youth that had ended painfully. She didn't know why she was being so forthcoming with Diana now. The only reasons she could surmise were that the alcohol had made her chatty and sometimes it was easier to tell intimate things to a stranger. Then again, Diana did seem to have an uncanny ability to pull information out of her, diverting focus from herself.

"I feel like I've been hogging the conversation," Laura said, wanting to change the subject. "You still haven't told me why you came here."

Diana shrugged. "I told you. I just needed to get off the grid."

It seemed odd to Laura that Diana was evading her question yet again, especially after she had just told her so much about herself.

Diana pointed at a faded sign by the side of the road that said *Castaway Point Trail*. "There it is."

They turned off the highway and headed up the trail, which wound through a grove of trees. The leaf canopy overhead was so dense it blocked out most of the sunlight and cast them in shadow. The trail was narrow, forcing them to walk in single file, Diana in front and Laura following behind. At one point, Laura looked over her shoulder and saw that the man from the truck had followed them and was standing at the entrance to the trail, blocking their only way back to the highway. He smiled his leering smile, and Laura felt a jolt of fear. The shade provided by the leaf canopy had initially felt like relief from the hot sun, but now it felt clammy, and she shivered, quickening her pace. She felt a strong urge to be with Dave in that moment and pulled out her phone to text him but found she had no reception. Her battery was down to 20 percent, and she regretted not having charged it earlier, but rather than sticking it back in her pocket, she clutched it in her hand as she hiked. They kept walking like that, single file, at what Laura assumed was an incline because she felt herself becoming increasingly short of breath. She looked back one more time, but the trail had curved, and the man was no longer in sight. She turned back, and to distract herself, she focused on Diana, who was a sure-footed hiker, nimbly dodging protruding roots and potholes.

"Did you talk to her again after that?" Diana asked, over her shoulder.

"No," Laura said. "After that, we weren't friends anymore. I was just The Girl Who Broke Chloe Shipman's Wrist."

Back then, Laura wanted to contain the rumors that were spreading about her, but she knew that trying to defend herself would backfire. So instead, she found solace in the cool dispassion of facts. She sought refuge in the library, the only place where gossip was forbidden because silence was mandatory, and she did her homework in advance of it being assigned. She did *anticipatory* homework, the hallmark of true loserdom. But she saw her focused study as the means by which she would escape the social hellscape that high school had become. In her senior year, the week Chloe was voted Biggest Flirt in the senior class poll was the same week Laura received her acceptance package from Yale.

The last time Laura saw Chloe was at senior prom. By then, she and Jake Hollinger had broken up. Laura caught her eye across the dance floor, and Chloe stared at her intently. In that moment, Laura was reminded of how dark her eyes were and how long her eyelashes were, so lush that she didn't need mascara even though she had taken to wearing quite a lot of it. At the thought of all the experiences they would never share because they were about to graduate and would probably never see each other again, Laura felt a tightness grip her chest.

"Have you reached out to her since?" Diana asked.

Laura looked up and almost collided with Diana, who had stopped walking on the trail.

"No," Laura said. "We're not in touch anymore. We're just Facebook friends."

"Maybe you should call her. Life is short."

They emerged suddenly onto a sandy plateau. The view was, as the internet had promised, panoramic and breathtaking. They were at a high enough elevation that Laura could see the gentle curve of the island and could make out the Pink Sands down below. She was struck by how small the resort looked, a little bubble of safety surrounded by craggy rock. The cove was so perfectly crescent shaped that, from this height, it looked incongruous with the rest of the island's ragged coastline. It occurred to Laura that the cove looked so perfect because it was probably man made, blasted out of the limestone cliffs with dynamite, and the powdery pink sand had probably been flown in from another part of the island and raked smooth to create the illusion of unspoiled natural beauty.

Laura walked to the precipice and peered over the edge. It was a straight drop to the water down below, a hundred feet at least, and dizzying. One slip, one wrong step, and she'd fall to her death. The thought of how vulnerable they both were up here, alone on a cliff at the edge of the world, made her shiver.

"Quite the view, huh?"

Laura nodded and took a step back.

"You can even see Abaco from here." Diana pointed at the misty contour of an island on the horizon. "Or maybe that's Bimini. That's where Hemingway lived. Tuna Alley's right around there too. I hear it's a great spot for bluefin."

Laura looked at Diana as she gazed out to sea. Wisps of her hair were flying around her face, and she was smiling.

"Man, it would be great to live here," Diana said.

"Where do you live now?" Laura asked, fishing.

"Oh, you know, here and there. I move around a lot."

Diana's coyness was becoming irritating.

"Almost sounds like you're running from something," Laura said. She meant for this to be a joke, but there was an edge to her voice, and Diana looked at Laura with her piercing gaze.

"I guess we all are, in a way," she said. Then her face softened. "Want me to take a picture of you?"

"Sure." Laura unlocked her phone and handed it to Diana.

Diana took a few steps back, and Laura stood with her hands on her hips and one foot in front of the other, the way she and Chloe had been taught by *Cosmo* to pose. While she waited for Diana to take her picture, she felt a sudden urge to pee. She hadn't gone to the bathroom since breakfast, and the two cocktails she had drunk were creating a mounting pressure in her bladder. She regretted that she hadn't gone at the cabin before they'd left, and she knew she wouldn't be able to hold it for the hike back. She would have to find a spot out here, on this cliff, with some privacy, but there was nothing around but low-lying shrubs.

Diana didn't say *cheese*, so Laura wasn't sure when precisely she took the photo.

"You got it?" Laura asked.

"Yeah, just a sec."

She watched Diana study the photo as if assessing her handiwork. Then Diana walked over and handed the phone back to Laura. It was a decent picture (*Cosmo* was right—one foot in front of the other was always flattering), but for some reason, it had been posted to Laura's Facebook page.

At first, Laura was relieved because if Diana was able to upload the photo, it meant they had reception. But it struck her as odd that Diana had done this.

"Did you just post this to my Facebook page?" she asked. It was obvious that Diana had, but Laura wanted to determine whether it had been intentional or whether Diana was somehow unaware of what she had done.

"Yeah." Diana seemed unconcerned by this bizarre violation of Laura's privacy. "Thought your friend Chloe should see what you're up to."

"But I told you I don't like to post pictures," Laura said and felt the need to add, "I'm a lurker, not a poster."

"Well, she already liked it."

Laura looked at her phone again. Sure enough, the photo had already received three likes: one from Laura's mother, one from Jasmine

Chaudhry, and one from Chloe Shipman. Seeing Chloe's name triggered in Laura a surge of adrenaline. Now that Chloe had liked the picture (Why had she liked it? And so quickly?), Laura felt she couldn't delete it, which only added to her frustration with Diana for blatantly disregarding her wishes. Had she posted the picture on purpose to spite Laura? Or was she just plain rude? Laura's embarrassment, coupled with her urgent need to pee, caused her anger to spike.

"You shouldn't have done that."

"Oh, I think I should have."

Laura stared at Diana, taken aback by her defiance.

"Are you seriously not going to apologize?" Laura's tone was harsh, but she didn't care.

"OK, I'm sorry. But you really need to get out of your own way. Aren't you tired of being lonely?"

"I'm not lonely." Laura felt herself getting defensive.

"Are you sure? All you've talked about this whole time is your friend from high school, but you won't even reach out to her."

"So? She's never reached out to me."

"Yeah, I can see why."

"What is that supposed to mean?" Laura glared at Diana and squeezed her phone like a stress ball. Why was this woman defending Chloe? Chloe was the one who had abandoned her all those years ago.

"Nothing, sorry. Forget it."

She was angry at Diana for probing where she didn't belong, but instead of shutting down the argument, she felt herself leaning in, allowing herself to get even angrier.

"You said it yourself. What happened between us was not my fault."

"Sure, but you obviously miss her," Diana said. "All I'm saying is, sometimes you have to be the bigger person. Pride can make people pretty lonely."

Laura felt her anger bubbling over. It felt juvenile, but she couldn't help it. "I told you, I'm not lonely. You're the one who's lonely. I mean, seriously, what kind of person comes to a romantic couples' resort by herself. That's just sad!"

"Everything OK?"

The man's voice startled Laura. He was young and muscular, and so was his friend. He had a bandanna tied around his head, and his friend had a beard. Both of them were sunburned, but neither of them was wearing a shirt. Laura nodded but said nothing, embarrassed to be caught yelling at a woman she barely knew on a cliff in the middle of nowhere, and it disturbed her how unaware she'd been of the men's approach. Had the men been following them on the trail? How much of their conversation had they overheard? They were tall and strong looking, and it occurred to Laura how easily she and Diana could be overpowered by them. If they screamed, would anybody hear them?

"Everything's fine," Diana said.

The men nodded and headed past them down the trail.

When the men were out of earshot, Diana turned to Laura and said, "I'm not lonely. I'm alone. There's a difference."

The sun was beating down on Laura, and sweat was dripping down her back underneath her bathing suit, and her need to urinate was truly overwhelming now, so she said, "I have to pee," rather abruptly, and walked back into the grove.

Laura made her way between the trees, searching for a private spot. It needed to be out of sight of the trail and any other potential hikers. Deeper in, she found a spot that was surrounded on all sides by trees. She figured that if she couldn't see Diana, Diana couldn't see her. Only then did Laura remember that she was wearing her new romper in addition to her bathing suit, which made peeing doubly inconvenient. Laura had two options: she could either remove the romper and her bathing suit and risk exposing herself to strangers, or she could pull the crotches of both garments to one side and risk peeing on her hand. She opted for the latter and squatted, grimacing at the indignity of the act. But she was so wound up from her argument with Diana and nervous about the possibility of being caught peeing that she was unable to actually pee. To distract herself, she unlocked her phone with her free hand and looked again at the photo that Chloe had liked. With her thumb, she tapped on Chloe's name, pulling up her profile.

Of all the developments in Chloe's adult life, the one that surprised Laura the most was that, at some point in the intervening years, she had started smiling in photographs. Not just smiling but beaming so wildly as to expose her gums. Never in all their years of friendship had Laura ever seen Chloe smile like that. In fact, one of the things Laura had always admired about Chloe was that she only laughed when things were genuinely funny, and she only smiled when something elicited her smile involuntarily. Whenever Laura flicked through Facebook photos of Chloe grinning ecstatically at farmers' markets, she wondered if Chloe actually was that deliriously happy or if she had turned into one of those women who felt the need to telegraph how absolutely amazing her life had turned out. If it was the latter, it saddened Laura, and she wondered what had happened to Chloe to make her feel like this degree of performance was necessary.

Laura scrolled through Chloe's feed and saw that she had posted a picture of her son, taken three days before. Laura pinched the photo with her other hand in order to expand it, but in doing so, she unconsciously released her grip on the layers of fabric she was holding and peed on the romper.

"Fuck," Laura said out loud to no one.

With no toilet paper available, she bounced a little, hoping the air would dry her, but the burning in her thighs finally forced her to stand. The crotch of her ninety-eight-dollar romper was wet.

She knew this compromised image of herself would have elicited Chloe's deep, throaty man laugh, because Chloe would have found it hilarious that, despite Laura's best efforts not to, she had managed to pee all over herself. It was moments like these that made Laura long for the kind of all-consuming friendship they'd had, where they shared the minutiae of their daily lives in one long, unending conversation.

Laura stood up and wiped her wet hand on her romper. She was angry at Diana for posting her picture on Facebook and making judgments about her life while refusing to answer the simple question of why she had come to the resort alone. Laura felt she had earned the right to an answer, so she made her way back through the grove to confront

Diana in the clearing, but Diana was not there. Thinking that she had also taken the opportunity to pee, Laura waited for Diana to return, but she did not. Laura called out Diana's name but was met with silence. She scanned the trail that hugged the edge of the cliff, but there was no sign of her. Laura looked out to sea and shivered despite the heat. All she could hear was the wind in her ears. Diana was gone.

CHAPTER SIX

Laura looked around. Had Diana left after their argument? she wondered. Their fight had been childish and strange, but had it pissed Diana off to such an extent that she walked away? But if so, why hadn't she said anything? People didn't just walk away like that. They didn't just vanish without explanation.

Something on the ground at the cliff's edge caught Laura's eye. She stepped closer and crouched. A blue-and-white evil eye stared up at her. Diana's bracelet. She picked up the silver chain and examined it. The clasp was broken. The sight sent a shiver down her spine. It didn't belong here, this broken bracelet.

Laura rose, concerned. Had Diana slipped and fallen off the cliff? She inched toward the precipice and peered down, bracing herself for evidence of Diana's body sprawled at unnatural angles on the beach below, crushed by the gravity of her fall. But there was nothing, just an empty stretch of sand and an endless expanse of water. She looked out to sea, wondering if Diana's body had perhaps been washed away, but all she could see was the waves foaming on the shore. A stone beneath her shoe dislodged itself and tumbled down the rock face to the beach below. Laura stepped back, shaken. There was no guardrail at the cliff's edge, and only then did she realize how dangerous this trail really was, how wild. She listened, straining to hear something—footsteps, screaming, sounds of struggle—but there was only an eerie silence.

She glanced at the resort in the distance. What had initially appealed to her about the Pink Sands was that everything there—the manicured grounds, the whitewashed cabins, the raked beach—was well taken care of, meticulously managed. But perhaps this sense of control was only an illusion. The resort was, after all, precariously positioned on a narrow strip of land next to the sea, which, while usually beautiful and calm, could also be chaotic and wild. Shore breaks were unpredictable and dangerous. A riptide could pull one under in a flash. Out here in the wilderness, bad things could and did happen.

Laura pocketed the bracelet. She swallowed. Her throat was dry. She glanced at her phone. The battery was down to 5 percent, and the little icon glowed a cautionary red, warning her that only minutes from now her phone would be dead. Not that it mattered, because she no longer had any reception. She held her phone aloft but couldn't get a single bar. It occurred to her how easy it was to disappear. She had no wallet or ID with which to identify herself. No one knew where she was, and if something bad happened to her now, she would not be able to call anyone. Laura thought of Dave and felt a pang of yearning. She wondered what he was doing and if he missed her. She regretted coming on the hike and wished she had gone to the management office with him instead. If she had, none of this would have happened.

She looked back at the way she had come and was gripped with anxiety. She hadn't paid attention to any landmarks as she'd hiked and wasn't sure if she knew the way back. Whenever Laura went anywhere on her own, she always mapped the destination on her phone and calculated the most efficient route, but whenever she found herself in the company of someone who exuded more confidence than she, as Diana had, she tended to cede directional control, even if it led her astray. She hated this quality about herself, how easily she put her faith in other people. Why had she allowed herself to follow Diana so blindly? But then again, wasn't this what vacation was supposed to be for? To drink a few cocktails and loosen the reins a little bit in order to enable relaxation?

Laura glanced at the clock on her phone. Twenty minutes had passed since she'd peed. If Diana had stepped away but planned to return, surely she would have by now. But even as panicky thoughts started to bubble up—Was she OK? Had something bad happened?—Laura tamped them down. It was too soon, she told herself, to assume something bad had happened. Just because Diana was absent didn't mean she was missing. It was very likely that she had walked back to the resort on her own and that Laura would find her drinking a cocktail at the bar.

The sun was lower in the sky now, at an angle that didn't force her to shield her eyes with her hand, and the idea of losing daylight and walking back to the resort in the dark scared her. There were no tiki torches illuminating the path out here the way there were at the Pink Sands. She decided to head back with the hope of spotting Diana along the way.

She made her way through the grove of trees, walking as quickly as she could without tripping on protruding roots. Every rustle in the trees spooked her. She glanced over her shoulder every few feet, but there was no one on the trail, and the longer she walked without seeing a soul, the more alone she felt. It struck her how quickly her perception could change. The remoteness of the island, which had initially appealed to her, now filled her with queasy dread.

When she finally emerged onto the main road, she was overcome with relief to be within view of passing cars. The man and his truck, however, were gone. She didn't know if this was good or bad. Had Diana encountered him again, and had he given her a ride back to the resort? Had he abducted her? Laura told herself that, if anything, it was likely the former, and she kept walking, the afternoon sun bearing down on her.

Up ahead, she spotted two men standing next to a black sedan that was parked on the far side of the road. One wore a bandanna and the other had a beard. Laura recognized them as the hikers she and Diana had crossed paths with earlier. Only then they had both been shirtless, and now the one with the beard was wearing a blue T-shirt that said *Eleuthera* in bold letters and featured an illustration of the island. It was the same T-shirt Diana had bought. Why was he wearing her T-shirt? Laura watched the man slam the trunk of the car and slide into the passenger seat, as his friend started the engine. New panicky thoughts bubbled up: Had Diana bumped into the men on the trail? Had they taken the T-shirt away from her? Why would they do that? Had they hurt her? What was in the trunk of their car?

As she watched the car speed off down the highway, she tried to make out the license plate number, but she was too far away. She told herself to take a breath and calm down. There was probably a logical explanation for all of this. This wasn't the first time she had let her imagination run wild. She knew she tended to move through the world this way, with a constant, heightened awareness of risk. She was never shocked when calamities happened. Whenever she turned on the news and saw a report about a plane crash or other mass-casualty event, instead of shaking her head in consternation, she would just nod, unsurprised. Of course people had died. To Laura, it was a miracle that anyone was alive at all. The human body was so fragile, so vulnerable, so perverse in its design, its vital organs encased not in a tough, protective shell but in soft, pierceable flesh. Human beings walked around with their underbellies exposed, just asking to be hurt.

"You know you're a catastrophizer, right?" Dave asked her this the first night they cooked dinner at her apartment. She'd caught him slicing a raw chicken breast on a wooden cutting board and cried out, "Not that one!" and handed him a plastic cutting board to use instead. But it was too late; the raw chicken juice potentially teeming with E. coli had already seeped into the porous fissures of the wood. She scrubbed the board vigorously with soap and hot water, and when she was finished, she looked up and caught Dave eyeing her strangely. He asked his question in an accusatory way, as if it were a bad thing, but she had always thought her tendency to assume the worst in any given situation was what enabled her to sidestep disaster. Wasn't it a Darwinian survival trait that had kept her alive thus far?

"Bad things happen all the time," she said in her defense.

"Sure, but even when bad things happen, they're never the bad things you expect."

Dave had a point. Things, good or bad, didn't usually unfold the way she anticipated they would, so, technically, she realized, standing there in her kitchen, there was no point in worrying. For a moment, she felt overcome with relief, but then she was struck by a new fear: If Dave was right, if disasters could not be predicted with any degree of accuracy, didn't that mean she should fear them even more? Didn't that mean disasters she couldn't fathom, catastrophes that were so terrifying they were beyond the scope of her imagination, were always lurking in her periphery, crouched on their haunches, poised to strike? It made her wonder then how many disasters she had narrowly avoided in life, how many brushes with death she had unknowingly survived.

And now that Diana had suddenly vanished, even as Laura hoped for the best, she couldn't help but imagine the worst.

When Laura finally spotted the familiar white gate of the Pink Sands, she exhaled with relief. Her phone had died, and she couldn't wait to be swaddled within the resort's walls again, where everything was safe and everyone accounted for.

The security guard opened the gate for her and waved her through. When she arrived at the white gazebo, Priscilla was getting off the phone.

"Can I help you?" she asked.

Laura stared at Priscilla, at her meticulously applied eyeliner, at her crisp white uniform, at her black hair that was swept into an elegant bun. She spoke her next words slowly to sound calm rather than worried, which was how she felt.

"I was hiking with another guest, but we were separated on the Castaway Point Trail. Have you seen a woman walk past here in the past hour or so? Her name is Diana, and she's staying in cabin twelve."

Priscilla's brows furrowed slightly. "No."

"I'm concerned something might have happened to her. Can you please call her cabin?"

Priscilla picked up the phone. As she dialed the number for cabin twelve, Laura walked over to a glass dispenser that was filled with cucumber water. She poured some into a plastic cup, drank it in one go, and then poured herself another. As she finished her second cup, Priscilla hung up the phone.

"No one is answering, but she's probably somewhere on the grounds. I'm sure she'll turn up soon."

It irked Laura that Priscilla didn't seem remotely worried. Wasn't Diana's inexplicable absence, at the very least, cause for a little concern? But the way Priscilla was standing there, politely indifferent, made Laura reconsider. Technically, she had no proof that something bad had happened to Diana, so Priscilla was probably right to be unworried. There was probably no reason to be alarmed.

Laura thanked Priscilla and left the gazebo and made her way down the paved path. Still, as she walked past the Seahorse, she looked for Diana at the bar, but there was no sign of her. She crossed the beach, scanning the lounge chairs and umbrellas, but Diana was not there either. Wanting to satisfy herself that perhaps Diana had returned to her cabin and was simply not answering her phone, Laura headed across the beach, all the way to cabin twelve, climbed the steps of the little porch, and knocked on the sliding glass door. She waited, tapping sand from her shoes, but no one came to the door. She knocked again, louder this time, and peered inside, but the curtains were drawn, obscuring her view. Laura was not typically a nosy person, but she felt compelled, under the circumstances, to see if Diana was inside. And if she was being honest with herself, she was curious to see what her cabin looked like. She tugged gently at the handle and found that the glass door slid open easily on its rollers. She felt anxious suddenly. Technically, she was breaking and entering, which was illegal, but she reminded herself that her primary concern was Diana's safety. If examining her belongings yielded a clue to her whereabouts, it might help Laura figure out what had happened. Still, she couldn't help but also feel a little rush of adrenaline as she stepped over the threshold.

It was strange being inside Diana's cabin in that it was identical to hers and Dave's—it had the same white bed and the same teak furniture—but the layout was reversed, which gave Laura the impression that Diana's cabin was a mirror image of her own. As she crossed the tile floor, she momentarily felt as though she were stepping inside someone else's life and wondered if this was what it felt like to be Diana. It was fascinating to look at the sandals she'd left by the door, the tote bag that was slung on a chair, but then immediately she felt guilty, like a voyeur, studying these details about Diana without her permission.

"Hello?" she said.

There was no answer. She was acutely aware that Diana could appear at any moment and demand to know what she was doing in her cabin. This set Laura on edge because as much as she wanted to find Diana, she was unprepared for their reunion. She didn't know what she would say to her. They had parted ways so abruptly, and their argument on the cliff had been so bizarre. She couldn't remember the last time she'd fought in public, let alone with a stranger, and it embarrassed her to think about it now. But even as she tried to forget their fight, she kept replaying it in her mind. Why had she gotten so angry with Diana for posting that picture of her on Facebook? Why had Chloe liked it? And why had Laura told Diana about Chloe in the first place? She hadn't spoken of their falling-out in years and didn't understand why she had felt the need to divulge all those personal details to a stranger. But that was the thing about Diana. She made Laura want to tell her things.

Laura had never snooped around like this before and didn't know what exactly she was looking for. Everything looked more or less as she'd expected. The only oddity was that several items of clothing had been left crumpled on the floor, making it look as though she'd gone somewhere in a rush. New panicky thoughts bubbled up: Had she been forced to vacate quickly without having a chance to pack? Was this what it looked like when a person fled without warning? But Laura pushed the thoughts out of her mind. Diana was probably just a messy traveler.

She headed into the bathroom. A makeup bag was open on the ledge above the sink. She examined Diana's foundation (Laura Mercier) and her eye shadow palette (MAC) and her various eyeliners and mascaras. Compared to the other women at the resort, Diana always looked casual and undone, so the fact that she had all this expensive makeup was incongruous with the image Laura had been assembling in her mind. The real Diana, whoever she was, seemed even more elusive to her now.

On the ledge next to the makeup bag was a travel-size bottle of perfume. Laura spritzed some onto her wrist and sniffed. It was woodsy and peppery, and it instantly made Laura feel Diana's presence in the room. She realized she'd smelled this fragrance before. That night on the beach with the sleeping pill.

"Hello?"

Laura froze when she heard the voice. She poked her head out of the bathroom as a woman entered the cabin, pushing a cart full of cleaning supplies.

"Housekeeping," the woman said with a Bahamian accent. "Is it OK if I clean?"

Laura could not discern if the housekeeper knew she was trespassing but was too polite to say anything, or if she actually thought Laura was staying in cabin twelve, but she didn't want to find out, so she said, "Yes, that would be great," and quickly left the cabin.

She was halfway down the beach before she realized the travel-size perfume bottle was still in her hand. She paused, her feet sinking in the deep sand, and considered turning back, but returning it now would be too embarrassing, so she pocketed it and headed back to her cabin.

"Where've you been?" Dave was lying on the bed watching TV when she stepped through the sliding glass door. His face flooded with relief when he saw her.

Laura froze. She had been so preoccupied with Diana that she had forgotten about him.

"I texted you, but you never texted me back," he said, turning off the TV.

"My phone died," she said and plugged her phone into the charger next to her side of the bed.

"I went by the gift shop, but you weren't there. Where were you?"

She didn't know what to say. She felt guilty that she'd poked around Diana's cabin and didn't know if she should tell him. She hadn't found anything revelatory. If anything, her little mission had only yielded more questions.

"I went for a hike," she said.

He looked at her, confused. "Alone?"

"No," she ventured carefully. "With Diana."

"Who's that?"

Laura's phone screen came to life, and sure enough she saw several texts appear, all of them from Dave.

> U there?
>
> I'm back at the cabin where r u?
>
> Just called u and got vm
>
> Where r u?
>
> I'm getting worried

"She's the woman who came here alone."

Whatever relief Dave's face exhibited when she walked through the door was quickly replaced with confused concern.

"Why did you go on a hike with her?"

"Because I wanted to go on a hike. And you were busy with Carl."

She watched him clench his jaw. His voice took on a defensive tone. "For the record, I was 'busy with Carl' because Marcus Lowry is in the middle of a messy corporate audit. You need to keep your phone charged."

"Messy why?" she asked, trying to change the subject.

"He moved some personal assets to an offshore account and didn't tell us. But that's not the point. I had no way to reach you."

Dave always kept his phone charged so that he could always be reachable by the partners, and whenever he found himself in an area with spotty service, he became visibly anxious.

"I'm sorry," Laura said. Yes, she sometimes forgot to charge her phone, but it wasn't her fault that she'd lost reception.

"You do this a lot, you know? And then you say you're sorry, but you don't actually change."

It was true that she turned her phone off sometimes, such as when she needed to focus on a difficult contract at work, and he had gotten annoyed on occasion when she hadn't responded to his texts in a timely manner. Still, it was odd to see him reacting so strongly now. When she had been single, the only person who had ever cared about her whereabouts was her mother, so it surprised her to see how much Dave cared about where she'd been. She felt another pang of guilt then, this time about Dave. She had been concerned about Diana's safety, but she hadn't considered that he was worried about hers.

"I guess I'm just not used to people wondering where I am," she said.

"I hope that's it." He didn't seem convinced.

"What does that mean?"

"Sometimes, it feels like you want to be inaccessible."

He had used this word once before to describe what it was about her that he had found so attractive, but he seemed irritated by it now. She studied his face: Was he implying that she had purposefully let her phone die? She hadn't, of course, but it disturbed her that he thought she had, especially here, on their vacation, where they had explicitly come to spend time together.

"I'm sorry I made you worry," she said, hoping to assuage him.

"It's OK," he said. He stood up and hugged her. She felt the warmth of his body and was glad to be safely back in the cabin with him.

"You smell different," he said.

"Bad?"

"No, just different. Is that a new shampoo?"

"It's perfume," she said.

"New?"

She hesitated. The optics of how the perfume had come into her possession were embarrassing, and she didn't know how to explain it without upsetting him even more. Still, Diana was gone, so she decided it was important that he know the truth.

"Sort of. It's not mine." She pulled the little bottle out of her pocket. "I went by Diana's cabin, and I took this by accident."

The way Dave looked at her then made Laura regret her words.

It was the same disturbed look he'd given her when she told him she'd taken the sleeping pill.

"Why did you go back to her cabin? And how do you take someone's perfume by accident?"

"I forgot I had it, but then it was too late to go back."

Dave sat back down on the bed, trying to make sense of her words, so Laura sat next to him and told him everything that had happened.

"What do you mean, she 'disappeared'?" he asked when she was finished. The skeptical tone of his voice suggested that he thought she had exaggerated her story, hyperbolized for some salacious effect.

"I mean she's *gone*."

"Why did you go on a hike with her, anyway? You don't even know her."

Laura shrugged. "We went for drinks earlier."

"When earlier? Earlier today? Why?"

"Why does it matter?" A woman was missing, and all he seemed to care about was that they'd been drinking? She was starting to feel like he was cross-examining her.

"I just don't get why you went hiking, loaded, with a total stranger."

"We weren't loaded. And she invited me," Laura said. "I came back here, but you were still with Carl."

Dave got up off the bed and grabbed a Coke from the minibar fridge.

"But I was really looking forward to going on a hike with you." He said this last part quietly, and Laura realized that he wasn't angry so much as hurt.

"I need you to help me find her. I think something might have happened," she said.

But Dave didn't seem very concerned about Diana's well-being. "I'm sure she'll turn up at dinner."

Diana had mentioned that she was planning to meet someone for dinner, so if Dave was right, she would show her face at the Seahorse later and Laura could sort out what had happened. She glanced at her phone. It was almost 4:00 p.m. Dinner was still a few hours off, and she could wait until then. Everything was fine. Besides, this was a precarious moment in their relationship. She and Dave had just had their first tiff, and she felt the need to move on from it in a positive way.

"Do you want to go snorkeling?" Dave asked, looking out the sliding glass door at the sea.

"Sure," she said.

She stripped down to her bathing suit, wrapped a towel around her waist, and followed him out the sliding glass door and down to the beach.

The beautiful couples were sunbathing on their lounge chairs, but Diana was not among them. As Laura studied the couples dozing peacefully, blissful in their ignorance, it surprised her how palpable Diana's absence felt. Her presence at the resort had lent an air of unpredictability to Laura's vacation, and now her disappearance left a strange void. Laura looked up at the limestone cliffs in the distance, where they had been hiking only a few hours ago. How angry she had gotten during their argument. How stunned she'd felt by Diana's bizarre invasion of her privacy. She still didn't know what to make of it.

A cloud passed in front of the sun then, casting the cliffs in shadow, and a chill ran down her spine. It would be dark soon. As disturbed as she was by their fight, she worried that if Diana was still out there, she would be forced to fend for herself in the night. Unless she had fallen and drowned, and her body would wash up on shore. Spooked, Laura looked out at the water, but the sea was calm, unconcerned with her troubles.

Dave, who had been talking to Javarro at the towel hut, returned with two snorkel masks. He gave one to Laura, and they waded into the water, which was surprisingly warm, even this late in the afternoon. Dave pulled his mask on and dove in. He swam far out, but Laura stayed in the shallows. The events of the day left her feeling uneasy, and she wanted to be close to the shore. She waded to the depth of her shoulders and dipped her face in the water.

Under the surface, everything was calm and green. She couldn't see any fish or coral, just the sand on the seafloor, gently rippled by the waves. She focused on the rhythmic sound of her breathing through the plastic mouthpiece. In and out. In and out. It calmed her, and she swam a little deeper out. Then she felt something graze her left leg, and it gave her a jolt. She pulled her face out of the water and tore off the plastic mouthpiece. She looked around, but there was nothing to see. Still, statistics sprang to mind. Thousands of people got stung by stingrays every year. One hundred fifty million worldwide got stung by jellyfish. And the odds of getting attacked and killed by a shark were one in 3.75 million. She exhaled and told herself that she was safe in the cove. Nothing here could hurt her. She looked for Dave and saw him out beyond the breakers.

She put her face back in the water and swam in his direction. But the farther out she got, the murkier the water became, and then the sandbar dropped off, giving way to deep water. She turned back and swam toward the beach. It was a relief to be closer to shore. Then she saw something under the water. A dark shape on the seafloor. About six feet long. It looked like a body.

Laura ripped off her mask, gasping for air, her heart hammering in her chest.

"Dave?"

But he couldn't hear her, because his face was in the water and he was drifting out to sea. She swam toward him, farther out than felt comfortable, the salt burning her eyes.

"Dave!"

Finally, he heard her.

"What?" he asked.

She treaded water because it was too deep to stand.

"I saw something."

"Where?"

She pointed at the spot where she had been snorkeling. She was too scared to go back and look at it alone, afraid of what she might see. They swam over to it together.

"Where is it?"

She pointed at the shadowy mass under the water. They pulled their masks back over their faces and dipped under the waves. Laura had never seen a dead body before, not in real life anyway, and she braced herself for the sight of Diana's bloated corpse. But as they got closer, the murkiness cleared, and the mass revealed itself to be a rusty metal cage. It was anchored to the seabed and filled with dozens of conchs.

Dave signaled for her to surface.

"What is that?" she asked when she pulled her mask off her face. Her eyes burned in the dazzling sunlight.

Dave raked his fingers through his hair and spat in the water. "I think it's a conch pen. The restaurant probably farms their own instead of diving for them."

"Oh." Laura felt her heart slow. She rubbed her burning eyes and felt stupid for how easily she had let herself get swept up by fear.

"I'm getting hungry. You want to grab dinner?" Dave asked.

It was still early, barely five o'clock, but Laura was shaken up and wanted to get out of the water.

"OK," she said.

They swam back to shore and headed to the cabin to shower and change.

When they were seated at the Seahorse, their waitress told them that the special was Caribbean pepper pot, a seafood stew made with locally caught mahi-mahi, crawfish, and shrimp. They ordered one for the table along with a seafood risotto, and though both dishes were excellent, Laura barely registered the pepper pot's rich coconut-and-tomato broth or the risotto's earthy flavor, because she was still rattled. She downed her glass of sauvignon blanc and asked their waitress for another. As she sipped her second glass, she nodded attentively while Dave described a new political podcast he was listening to, but she kept glancing at the door, waiting for Diana to materialize.

"What are you looking at?" he asked at one point and glanced over his shoulder. He turned back and studied Laura intently. "You're still thinking about her, aren't you?"

Of course Laura was still thinking about her. It was now after six, but Diana had not arrived for her dinner date, and the more time passed, the more concerned Laura became that something bad *had* happened, so pretending that everything was fine when everything was likely not fine fomented an unease inside her that was becoming difficult to ignore.

"I'm just worried. She told me she was meeting someone for dinner."

"Maybe she changed her plans," Dave said, sipping his beer.

Laura considered this. Maybe she had. Maybe it was as simple as that.

"Yeah." She sipped her wine. "I'm sure everything's fine."

But then she felt a pit of dread form in her stomach, telling her that everything was not fine. She had watched enough true-crime TV shows to know that in missing persons cases, every passing hour could mean the difference between life and death.

"I just think we should do something," she said suddenly.

Dave looked at her, confused. "What do you think we should do?"

She hesitated, unsure what his reaction would be to her next words.

"I think we should report her missing."

Laura braced herself for Dave's repudiation, but he reached across the table and took her hand.

"You're really worried about her," he said.

She saw concern in his eyes that hadn't been there before.

"I am," she said.

He stroked her hand with his thumb. "Everything's going to be OK."

Maybe it was her second glass of wine or the warmth of his touch, but she felt closer to him in that moment than she had all day.

"She's going to turn up," he said, still holding her hand. She nodded, willing him to be right.

"I think you need some dessert," he said and smiled.

He looked so confident, so certain, and it reassured her, so she ordered a slice of key lime pie to share and did her best to push Diana from her thoughts. But even as they lingered at the table eating the pie, Laura kept glancing at the door, hoping to see Diana appear. She never did.

When they finally left the restaurant, Laura suggested they check in with the concierge to see if there was any news of Diana.

Priscilla was still on shift, filling out paperwork behind the counter.

"Hi," Laura said.

Priscilla looked up from her work.

"I was wondering if you've heard from my friend Diana?"

"You still haven't seen her?" Priscilla asked.

Laura shook her head. "She said she was planning to meet someone for dinner, but she never showed up at the Seahorse," she said.

"Could you please call her cabin?" Dave asked with a smile, his hands in his pockets.

"Of course," Priscilla said and picked up the phone. Laura noticed Priscilla's voice took on a more professional tone than when she had spoken to Laura earlier in the day.

After an indeterminate number of rings, Priscilla hung up.

"She's not answering."

Priscilla looked at Dave when she said this, and Laura wondered to what degree this shift in her behavior, this sudden urgency, had to do with Dave. She often noticed that his presence granted her a degree of authority she didn't have in his absence. This double standard usually annoyed her, but she was glad Dave was here with her now.

"Can you call security?" Laura asked.

"I'm sorry, but guests of the Pink Sands are free to come and go as they please, and they are entitled to their privacy. Unless a guest has been missing for at least twenty-four hours, there is nothing we can do. That said, I will contact you if I get any news." Priscilla's voice had an edge of finality.

There was nothing more to do, so Laura and Dave headed back to their cabin. As they walked in the darkness, Dave took Laura's hand. "It's going to be OK. And the lady had a point. It hasn't even been twenty-four hours."

Laura nodded. His words comforted her a little. She felt like they were a team, and holding hands in the dark felt romantic.

When they got back to the cabin, Dave turned on CNN, but Laura couldn't focus on whatever Anderson Cooper was talking about, so she pulled open the glass door, stepped out onto the porch, and slid the door shut behind her. She scanned the beach, hoping to spot Diana's silhouette, but the sun had set, and it was so dark she couldn't even see the water.

After a while, the glass door slid open behind her, and she felt Dave's arms wrap around her waist. "Why are you hiding out here?"

"I'm not hiding."

They stood in silence, listening to the waves lapping on the shore. The trade winds were picking up, and the palms were swaying overhead.

"If she's not back tomorrow, we'll go look for her, OK?" Dave said. Laura nodded and turned to face him. He tucked a wisp of hair behind her ear and kissed her.

She kissed him back, and he slipped his hand under her shirt and cupped her breast and smiled. She knew that smile, what it meant, and she let him lead her back into the cabin and into bed. Part of her felt strange having sex when a woman was missing, but another part of her was moved that Dave was being so sweet and attentive, and yet another part of her couldn't help but wonder if Dave was using the renewed connection that had resulted from their mutual concern over Diana's disappearance as foreplay.

As Laura lay on the bed and allowed Dave to remove her clothes, she glanced up at the ceiling fan rotating overhead and wondered if the blades had been carved out of real acacia wood or if they had been molded out of plastic that was made to look like real acacia wood.

She tried to focus on the task at hand, but she couldn't help but wonder if an identical ceiling fan was also rotating in Diana's empty cabin. She hadn't noticed one, but she also hadn't looked up at the ceiling while she was there, and she concluded that since everything else in Diana's cabin was identical to hers, the ceiling fan must be too. Dave kissed her, so she kissed him back, even though she was drained from being out in the sun all day. He moved down her body, but she didn't feel aroused. The combination of the cabin's white walls and white bed and white orchids had initially created a romantic atmosphere, but now that Laura had seen the identical objects in Diana's cabin, the effect no longer felt romantic but rather felt mass produced and commercialized.

Dave looked up from between Laura's legs, his eyes hopeful, his eyebrows arched. "Does that feel good?" he asked, which she had learned was his way of saying, *Why is it taking you so long?*

"I probably drank too much wine at dinner," she replied, which was her way of saying, *It's not your fault I can't come.*

But Laura didn't want to disappoint Dave, who was working so hard, God bless him, that a sheen of sweat was visible on his shoulder blades. After all, wasn't this why they had come here, to this couples' resort, with all its mass-produced romanticism?

"Want me to keep going?" he asked.

She smiled and nodded yes. She lay back and closed her eyes and tried to focus on Dave, on how strong his arms felt, on the little moles on his back that she had discovered the first night they had slept together, on how round and tight his ass was, which always aroused her. But arousal still evaded her. She opened her eyes and looked down at Dave, at his darting tongue, at his hands clenching her thighs, but that distracted her, and she felt all sense of momentum wane, so she looked back up at the ceiling fan rotating overhead, and then she closed her eyes. She finally felt a familiar swell rise inside her, then a rush of release. She moaned and lay still.

When Laura opened her eyes, Dave was looking at her with a smile of proud accomplishment. It was the same smile he had when he won a case or signed a new account. But when she closed her eyes, she could not enjoy the pleasant calm that usually followed an orgasm, because what she saw behind her eyelids caused the little hairs on her arms to stand on end. The image would cause her to toss and turn all night in a state of fraught concern. It was Diana's smiling face. She was still out there somewhere, all alone in the dark.

CHAPTER SEVEN

When Laura awoke on Thursday, she gazed at the hazy blue ocean through the sliding glass door and for one oblivious moment luxuriated in the view. Then the events of the previous day, the disappearance of Diana, came rushing back, and she shivered, alert suddenly, the cobwebs gone.

"Morning," Dave said. "I have an idea. Let's stay in bed all day."

He kissed her, and she inhaled his scent, which had become familiar to her. It still felt surreal to be intimate with the body of someone she had desired so greatly from afar. And yet she felt herself breaking gently away.

"I thought you were going to help me look for Diana," she said, searching his face for the teamsmanship she had felt the night before.

"Oh, right," Dave said, but his tone was noncommittal.

He climbed on top of her, and she felt his hardness against her thigh. He kissed her again, longer this time, his tongue searching inside her mouth.

"I'm not really feeling it," she said, pulling away.

"You were feeling it last night," he said with a knowing smile.

She knew what he wanted, and ordinarily she would give it to him, but right now she felt a need to make sure Diana was safe. She placed her hands on his shoulders and pushed him an inch off her body so that they were face-to-face.

"You're going to help me find her, right?"

It was unlike her to reject him, but Laura had been with Diana when she'd disappeared and felt an obligation to find her.

His smile faded. "I think you're getting a little obsessed."

He headed into the bathroom and shut the door. She heard the faucet turn and the water run.

Fuckable. Unfuckable. Obsessed. Men were always trying to label women.

Why did he think she was obsessed? Diana had disappeared on her watch. Wasn't looking for her the right thing to do? Maybe he was jealous. But jealous of what? Did he think her fixation was sexual? Diana was certainly a beautiful woman, but when Laura searched her feelings, it wasn't attraction she felt but a kind of aspirational envy.

Diana seemed to buck convention wherever she went. That, Laura realized suddenly, was what she found so attractive about her: It wasn't that Diana reminded her of Chloe. It was that Diana was the physical manifestation of the woman she and Chloe had wanted to grow up to become—a confident, unmarried woman who traveled the world, unattached and completely free. Laura wasn't in love with Diana; she wanted to *be* her.

But now she was gone. Laura wondered if Diana had survived the night. She replayed the events of the previous day, hoping new clues would surface, but what came to mind was how spontaneously the day had unfolded, how fun it had been. Fun. That was the word for it. Laura couldn't remember the last time she'd had such simple, aimless fun. Normally, her daily existence was divided into blocks of time in which she accomplished tasks that she assigned for herself. An hour to get out the door in the morning, half an hour for lunch. Even exercise was a chore now. Half an hour on the elliptical or, if time allowed, a swim. But accomplishment was all she felt after a workout. Another task she could check off her list. She made checklists for everything now. She had even made one for this vacation. *Go snorkeling. Go on a hike. Visit the Glass*

Window Bridge. She had actually composed the list on her phone to remind herself, in case she forgot, what it was she wanted.

To wander aimlessly, the way she had with Diana, was something she hadn't done since she was a child. She and Chloe used to while away entire weekends without concrete plans and talk late into the night with profound gravitas about nothing in particular, when spending time together was the point, when spontaneous adventures would unfold because they were up for it and had nothing better to do, when the universe consisted of just the two of them, binary stars, orbiting each other, creating their own gravity.

Back then, Laura thought her friendship with Chloe was the first in a series of close, meaningful relationships she would have with women, but life had not turned out that way. None of her other friendships matched the raw intensity of the one she'd had with Chloe.

Until Diana. Who was gone. And possibly in danger. Laura regretted their fight. Yes, Diana had made some blunt comments that had angered her, but she hadn't been wrong in what she'd said. Laura was ashamed that she'd let things escalate and was worried their argument had provoked her disappearance.

And yet, truth be told, the fight had been a little exciting, and Laura missed the drama. It had been years since she'd raised her voice at another woman; she certainly hadn't in adulthood. She and Jasmine exchanged passive-aggressive comments from time to time, and she disagreed with her other colleagues on occasion, but she hadn't flat-out fought with another woman in years. Even in college, she'd never argued with her suitemates, Charlotte and Melissa. She had shared several dorm rooms with them over the years, yet despite their cramped quarters they'd never had a single screaming match. She was still in touch with them, but since Charlotte was pursuing a PhD in France and Melissa was teaching English in Japan, time zones kept them apart, and whenever they did reunite, their friendship felt more like an intermittent game of catch-up.

The last time she'd had a real blowout fight was with Chloe, back in high school.

Now, in her thirties, friendship was careful and polite. Gatherings were called Lady Hangs and were scheduled weeks in advance, over long mass email threads, with dates and times and RSVPs. Wine was brought. Snacks provided. Arrivals were met with great fanfare and the complimenting of one's hair/shoes/coat. The purpose of these Lady Hangs was not to while away the evening but rather, between the hours of 7:00 and 10:00 p.m., to offer mutual validation. Jasmine was a hostess of such Lady Hangs, and they had specific, unspoken rules: Whenever one of the women described an incident in which she'd been persecuted in some way, it was crucial that all the other women took her side fiercely, with an almost hostile loyalty, echoing their dismay about the injustice that had befallen her, even if privately they thought that she was overreacting or that she was actually to blame. Leaving these Lady Hangs, Laura would feel a twinge of sadness for what now passed as friendship.

That was why the burst of emotion she'd displayed in Diana's presence confounded her. She hadn't realized how starved she was for that kind of passion and intimacy. Perhaps that was also why she felt so drawn to Diana and why she missed her.

Dave finally emerged from the bathroom. He didn't turn on the fan, so when Laura went in, she had to wipe the condensation from the mirror with her hand.

After her shower, as she got dressed, she picked up Diana's bracelet, which she'd left on the little ledge above the sink. She had read somewhere that evil eye amulets were ancient talismans meant to shield the wearer from danger. It worried her to know Diana was without hers now. She rubbed the smooth ceramic bead and slipped the bracelet into the pocket of her shorts. Then she rejoined Dave, who was dressed and waiting, and they headed to the Seahorse for breakfast.

The white umbrellas that had been lowered for the night were open, the row of lounge chairs had been straightened, and the beach had been freshly raked. Once they were seated at a table, Laura scanned the bar for Diana, but she was not pouring herself a glass of mango juice from the dispenser, and she was not sitting at a table eating johnnycakes by herself. The other dining couples were murmuring quietly to each other, discussing their plans for the day. None of them seemed to be aware that Diana was absent. Laura felt agitated by their obliviousness but told herself that Diana was probably still sleeping. She'd probably come home late last night from wherever she'd been and decided to skip breakfast so that she could catch up on her rest.

Satisfied with this theory, she glanced at Dave, who studied his menu in silence. When the waitress came by and asked, "How are you two doing this fine morning?" he just nodded politely and asked for coffee and an omelet. When his meal arrived, he ate it in silence, the kind that usually followed a fight, even though they hadn't actually fought. Laura had, however, rejected his advances, and while there were myriad reasons to refuse sex at home—work stress, life stress, the need for sleep—to refuse it here, at this romantic couples' resort in a tropical paradise, laid bare the fact that something between them was wrong. Laura considered attempting some light conversation but decided against it and ate her fruit plate in silence too.

"I'm going to check the beach," she said when she was finished. "In case anyone's seen Diana."

"I'll call the concierge, see if she made it back to her cabin last night," Dave said.

Laura nodded, grateful that even though there was a palpable tension between them, he was still on her side. They were still a team.

They left the restaurant and parted ways. Dave headed back to their cabin, and Laura walked along the beach, scanning the lounge chairs for any sign of Diana. There had to be a reason she was gone. People didn't just disappear. Not like this, not suddenly and without a trace. And yet it wasn't the first time a woman had vacated Laura's life. One day she and Chloe had been best friends, and the next day they were strangers. Back then, Laura had felt Chloe's absence in a palpable way, like the dull ache of a phantom limb. And now that Diana was gone, Laura saw her face every time she closed her eyes, an eerie afterimage seared into her retinas. Wisps of hair. That piercing gaze. A row of straight white teeth.

Laura walked past Wifey and Hubs on their lounge chairs. Hubs was spraying sunscreen on his arms, and Wifey was strategically adjusting the straps of her bikini to avoid tan lines. They both seemed completely unaware of Diana's absence. She spotted Javarro sitting in the towel hut, rinsing snorkel gear in a large plastic bin.

"Morning," she said as she approached.

"Beautiful morning we're having," he said. "Hard to believe a storm's comin'."

Laura looked up at the cloudless sky. "A storm? Really?"

Javarro nodded. "I can feel it. A big one." He dumped a handful of snorkel masks into the bin and swirled them in the water.

"Have you seen the woman from cabin twelve?" Laura asked. "She has short hair and a black bathing suit."

Javarro squinted as he scanned the beach, then shook his head. "No."

Laura studied Javarro, frustrated by his calm, smiling face, by his lack of concern. She managed a tight smile, then walked past him, past the lounge chairs and umbrellas, all the way to the end of the beach. She gazed out at the horizon. It was impossible to believe a storm was on its way. There was barely any breeze at all. All she could hear was the water lapping gently on the shore, but the serenity only heightened her unease.

As she neared the wall of craggy rock at the resort's property line, she noticed flies buzzing around what appeared to be a mound of carrion. Laura stiffened. If Diana had fallen over the edge of the cliff and drowned, her body could have washed up on shore overnight, and this mound might be her cadaver. But as she drew nearer, she saw that it was not a corpse but a pile of empty conchs, thirty at least, probably pulled from the rusty underwater cage, their innards removed by the kitchen staff, their shells abandoned in the hot sun. Disgusted, Laura walked back to her cabin.

When she pulled open the sliding glass door, Dave was on the phone.

"They haven't been able to connect with her," he said when he hung up. "They don't think she went back to her cabin last night."

The news formed a new pit of dread in Laura's stomach, but it also made her strangely relieved to have some proof that her concern was justified, that Diana was most likely missing.

"I want to go back to the spot where she disappeared," she said.

"Now?" he asked. It was clear he didn't want to join her.

She nodded, resolute. He sighed, studying her. Then he shrugged and put on his shoes.

"This isn't how I imagined us going on our first hike together," he said as he tied his laces. "But I guess it is what it is."

They left the cabin and headed across the grounds, past the white gazebo, and out the front gate. As they walked along Queen's Highway toward the trailhead, there was no sign of the T-shirt man and his blue truck or the hikers and their black sedan. Laura hadn't told Dave about them earlier, and it felt odd to mention them now, so she said nothing, but she kept an eye out for them as they walked.

"That's it," she said when she spotted the faded sign for Castaway Point Trail.

They entered the trail, Laura taking the lead and Dave following behind. As they hiked, she clutched the bracelet in her hand, running her thumb over the smooth ceramic bead. She scanned the ground and the surrounding trees, but she didn't know what she was looking for exactly— footprints, a blood trail, torn fabric hanging from a branch? Things cops found at crime scenes on TV. But there was nothing and no one on the trail.

"Wow," Dave said when they emerged into the clearing. "So this is Castaway Point." He walked to the edge of the limestone cliff and, with his hands on his hips, took in the panoramic view. Laura nodded but said nothing. The view was still breathtaking, but it didn't elicit from her the same awed response it had the day before. The sheer drop-off seemed treacherous now, laced with an edge of terror.

"See anything?" Dave asked.

She surveyed the sandy trail and shook her head. There was no sign of Diana.

"What do you want to do?" he asked.

"I think we should go to the police."

Dave squinted at the hazy blue horizon. "I don't think that's a good idea."

"But it's been twenty-four hours," Laura said and headed back down the trail.

Following her, Dave chose his next words carefully. "I don't think you've thought this through, Laura."

They had only been dating for two months, but she recognized the look on his face. It was the same look he gave clients he was "handling," a term he used to describe the way he managed their emotions, but really it meant the way he could be selectively honest, telling only a partial truth. Dave was a savvy lawyer, but Laura was, too, in that she could spot a liar anywhere. She had a knack for ferreting out the truth. It wasn't an innate skill but one she had honed after what happened to her the summer after she graduated from college. That was when she'd promised herself that she would never again be taken for a fool.

That summer, she moved home and spent her days in the public library studying for the LSATs. One afternoon, she spotted a familiar face roaming the stacks. She recognized Jake Hollinger instantly. He was older, his cheekbones more angular, but his eyes were as green as ever. For years, she had wanted nothing more than for him to notice her, but the idea of being spotted by him at the public library on a weekday in the middle of summer made her feel like a loser, and all she wanted in that moment was to disappear. "Phillips?" Too late. He had spotted her. She looked up and smiled, then noticed he was holding a MCAT study guide, and this instantly made her feel less like a loser.

They went for drinks that night, and it felt good to sit next to Jake Hollinger and feel his shoulder rub against hers. At one point, he placed his hand on her thigh and left it there. By then they were both drunk, and she barely remembered him calling an Uber for them to share. She barely remembered him getting out of the car, and she barely remembered him following her into her childhood home and stumbling up the stairs into her bedroom. But when he kissed her, she sobered quickly and realized that the thing she had wished for so fervently in high school was actually about to happen.

It was an out-of-body experience to have him remove her clothes on the bed where she had spent countless nights staring at his yearbook photo and committing it to memory. She was worried her mother might walk in on them, but that danger only added to the thrill. She didn't tell him that she hadn't slept with anyone in college, that she was still a virgin, and that it was evident, based on his facility with her body, that he was not. She said nothing and let him do whatever he wanted, even though, when he entered her, she felt the same kind of uncomfortable pressure she felt at the gynecologist. But afterward, as they lay there, staring up at the glow-in-the-dark stars she'd stuck to her ceiling years ago, she felt a kind of physical intimacy she had never felt before and wondered if this was the beginning of a relationship that had always been destined to unfold but had been stymied for various stupid reasons, the way couples were always held apart in Jane Austen novels, only to be reunited at the end.

After that night, Laura's summer took on a pleasant routine. She and Jake Hollinger would study at the library every day, and sometimes they would have sex. But it surprised her when, one morning, on her way to the library, she spotted Jake across the street kissing Chloe Shipman.

She hadn't seen Chloe since they'd graduated from high school, and she felt shock but also confusion in that moment. Why was the man she was sleeping with kissing her former best friend? It didn't compute. But there they were, plain as day, holding hands and walking down the street like a couple. Because they were a couple. Sorrow hit her like a crushing wave. Laura had come to believe she was in an exciting but undefined relationship with Jake Hollinger, but apparently, to him, the nature of their relationship had been quite clear. She was the woman he was cheating on his girlfriend with.

Laura turned and walked away quickly. In a small, dark part of herself that she didn't want to acknowledge, she had feared something like this might happen. She didn't know why he had slept with her or why he hadn't wanted to date her back then, but then she realized the reason was simple: she wasn't Chloe Shipman and never would be. The wound of humiliation and betrayal bloomed inside her chest, making it hard to breathe. Then, perhaps because the pain was so great, so molten in its intensity, it seemed to cauterize her wound, and just as quickly as it had opened, it closed, and she felt nothing. She was numb. One thing became clear to Laura, though: she would never allow herself to be lied to again.

The rest of that summer dragged by like a dead limb. She avoided the library, kept close to home, and focused on the LSATs. The Law was made of rules and logic, and this soothed her. It was orderly and rational in a way that life was not. When the time came to take the exam, she scored well enough to gain a spot at Yale Law School, and after her first year, she was offered a summer internship at Reinhart, Mader & Stern. There, she dug out lies like a drug-sniffing dog. When she graduated, she was offered a full-time position. At the firm, Laura learned to trust her instincts about liars, to pull self-doubt like a weed, to nurture the quiet, tentative voice in her head and encourage it to grow into a loud, ringing bell that was impossible to ignore.

That bell was ringing now. Dave was definitely lying to her.

"Why don't you want to go to the police?" she asked, studying his face.

His eyes met hers, then darted away, as though sustaining eye contact were physically painful, like touching a hot stove. "What do you think the police are going to do? Put out an APB? I bet the resort's private security is way more capable. She's a guest. It's in the resort's interest to find her," he said.

"But I feel responsible. I was there when she disappeared."

"Oh, I'm well aware you were," he said, an edge in his voice.

"What's that supposed to mean?"

"Ever since we got here, you haven't stopped talking about that woman."

Laura understood that Dave did not feel as personally invested in Diana's safety as she did because he had never spoken to her directly, but still, going to the police was the right thing to do, wasn't it? Why was he being so resistant? He was a good person, wasn't he? It struck Laura that their ethics as a couple had never really been tested until now, and she felt unmoored by his reaction.

"It's a three-mile walk to Gregory Town, and you know what it's like with the police," he said. "We'll be there all day. I don't want to sound insensitive, but we paid a lot of money to come here, and we've only got one more day left. Do you really want to spend it at a police station?"

"No, but what else are we supposed to do?"

"Let security handle it."

"They're not going to do anything."

"Be smart, Laura."

Be smart about what? He was talking to her like they were analyzing a case at work.

Work. Of course.

They had specifically chosen to vacation at the Pink Sands because they had received a discount on an oceanfront cabin courtesy of Marcus Lowry, who was a client of the firm.

"Is this because of Marcus Lowry?" she asked.

Dave swatted at a fly that was buzzing near his face. Standing for so long in the grove was attracting bugs. Laura felt beads of sweat forming on her upper lip and behind her knees. She knew they should keep moving, but now that she'd put him on the spot, they were stuck here.

"I mean, it doesn't help that he's in the middle of an audit," Dave said. "He's really stressed. And this is not the first time the resort has had issues with a guest."

"What do you mean?" she asked.

He sighed and shifted his weight from one foot to the other. "It came up when I was working on the M&A deal. Two years ago, a woman fell off that cliff and died."

"What cliff?"

"The cliff we were just at. Castaway Point."

This was news to Laura. "What woman?"

Dave shrugged. "Some woman. A tourist. She was hiking with her husband, and she fell, and the story got picked up in the press."

Laura squinted, trying to make sense of this new information. "But the cliff isn't part of the resort."

"No, but it's close by, and Marcus promoted it online."

Laura remembered reading about the hike on the resort's website.

"But they didn't do anything to protect the guests," Dave continued.

"What do you mean?" Laura asked.

"They capitalized on the view, but they never built a fence," Dave said.

Laura recalled that there was no protective barrier along the cliff's edge.

"So the woman's family sued for negligence, the resort was found liable, and Marcus had to pay a huge settlement," Dave said. "After that, the resort's reputation tanked, and Marcus had to hire a crisis PR firm to dig them out."

"Jesus."

Dave nodded. "So now, with this"—he gestured vaguely at her—"the optics aren't great."

No, the optics were not great. If they reported Diana missing to the Eleuthera police and the press got ahold of the story, every lurid human-interest article about her disappearance would also mention the Pink Sands and inevitably call back to the previous incident. Connections would be made. Suspicions cast. And the story wouldn't just devastate the resort. The annual billings of Marcus Lowry's global company, The Sands International, constituted a large portion of the firm's book. So if Marcus Lowry found out that the two individuals who'd reported Diana's disappearance were lawyers at the firm that represented his business, there could also be professional repercussions.

"Fine. Let's call the partners. They should know what's going on."

Dave said nothing, just swatted at the flies that had multiplied around his face.

That was when Laura knew. "You already called them."

He didn't say anything. He didn't have to. She knew she was right.

"When?" she asked.

"When you were walking the beach."

"I thought you called the concierge."

"I did, and when the lady said Diana didn't come back to her cabin, I called the partners. And they're really concerned. I mean, have you met Marcus Lowry? He's batshit crazy. For what it's worth, he's the one who wants the resort security to handle this. Not me."

"So you called the partners without telling me?"

"I had to. They have a right to know."

Gone was the feeling that they were a team.

"Well, I had a right to know that you went behind my back," she said.

"I'm actually trying to protect you, Laura."

She wanted to believe him, but she knew he was handling her the way he handled his clients, only telling her a partial truth. Yes, he was trying to protect her, but mostly he was trying to protect himself.

"So you want to go back to the resort, and then what? Go snorkeling? Pretend like this never happened? Pretend like you didn't just call the partners behind my back?"

She didn't expect him to respond because she already knew his answer. How did that Maya Angelou quote go? *When people show you who they are, believe them.* And hadn't he, long ago, shown her exactly who he was? She felt a familiar feeling growing inside her, the white-hot burn of betrayal. She had been lied to before, and maybe it was years of unprocessed anger from those transgressions, but she felt an acrid bile rising in her throat, and rather than tamping it down, she let it spew out of her mouth.

"'I am always pretending. Why am I always pretending?'" she said.

Dave furrowed his brow, trying to place her words, like lyrics to a forgotten song. "What did you say?" he asked.

"That's what you wrote in your notebook in Intro to Modern American Poetry."

Recognition flashed across his face. "How did you know that?"

"I read it the day you sat next to me in class."

"What the fuck, Laura." He stared at her, processing her words, his face a mix of horror and disgust. "You were in that class?"

She nodded.

"That stuff I wrote was private."

"I know."

"Were you ever going to tell me?"

"I don't know. Probably not."

She knew she was bad at this, at being completely truthful, and that it was a problem, especially in relationships that were supposed to be built on foundations of trust and honesty. But she kept things to herself not because it pleased her but because she didn't always know what to do with the little shreds of truth she found. She was afraid of what people would say or do if she revealed their truths to them, so she stored them away, like the spare buttons that came with new shirts and might, just possibly, be useful one day.

"That's really fucked up. You know that, right?" Dave said.

She felt a twinge of guilt then for keeping the secret all this time. But she had always felt he had the power in their relationship, and keeping this little secret to herself made her feel like it balanced things out a little.

"Are you coming or not?" she asked.

It was his last chance to concede, but he didn't move. He was somewhere else.

"OK then," she said and headed down the trail, back the way they had come.

Laura didn't look over her shoulder until she was out of the grove and back on the road, but Dave was not behind her. She turned right and walked three miles, all the way to the police station in Gregory Town.

CHAPTER EIGHT

Gregory Town was more of a village than a town, and the police station was more of a house than a precinct, painted mint green and situated between a handful of single-story houses that were painted yellow and pink and blue and scattered on either side of the crumbling main road. There were no traffic lights or movie theaters in Gregory Town, just a single-pump gas station and a small general store, outside which two heavyset women sat and stared at Laura as she walked past. The sign above the door of the mint-green house said *Gregory Town Police Station*, which was how Laura knew she was at the right place.

It was dark and cool inside the station. A woman was sitting behind a desk, watching a video on her phone. Her cornrows were piled on top of her head in an intricate knot.

"Can I help you?" she asked.

Laura felt nervous. She had never been inside a police station before, let alone one in a foreign country.

"I'd like to report a missing person." She said this louder than she would have liked, to make herself heard over the air conditioner that was thrumming in the window, and the words sounded overly dramatic as they came out of her mouth.

"I'll be right with you," the woman said and, unfazed by Laura's blunt pronouncement, walked to the back of the station and disappeared inside an office.

Laura waited, looking around for something to drink. There was a vending machine against one wall, but she hadn't brought her wallet because Dave had brought his on their hike, and now, in hindsight, it seemed like a stupid decision to have left it back at the cabin.

The woman emerged and beckoned Laura. "Come on in." Laura followed her into the office.

"This is Officer Solomon." The woman gestured at a tall man who was standing behind a desk. His black hair was cut short and graying around his temples.

"Hello," he said. "Have a seat."

The woman left, and Laura sat in one of the folding chairs across from Officer Solomon, who settled into the chair behind his desk, smoothing his black tie against his white shirt. He looked at her with large, wise eyes.

"I understand you're here to report a missing person."

Laura nodded. "Yes."

With elegant hands, Officer Solomon pulled a notebook out from under a stack of papers and flipped to an empty page.

"What is their name?"

Laura wondered if Officer Solomon's notebook was filled with details of burglaries and murders and if he spent most of his days behind his desk, in this tropical paradise, waiting for bad things to happen to people.

"Diana."

"And her surname?"

"I don't know, actually."

Officer Solomon looked up at Laura, seemingly puzzled by this. "What is your name?"

"Laura Phillips."

She watched him write her name underneath Diana's. It made her nervous for some reason to see her name now officially part of the police record, and she picked at the nail polish on her index finger.

"Is Diana a resident of the island?" he asked.

"No, she's a guest at the Pink Sands resort."

Office Solomon smiled. "That's a very nice place. Where is she visiting from?"

"The US, I think. I don't know for sure. I don't know her very well."

Laura peeled off an entire oval of polish and watched it flutter to the floor of Officer Solomon's office. She looked at the nail that was now exposed. It was unsightly, this single bare nail. She squeezed her hands into fists to prevent herself from picking any more.

"And what is your relation to Miss Diana?"

"I'm a friend. Sort of."

"You were traveling together?"

"No, I met her at the resort."

Officer Solomon made another note in his book. "Did she come here with a spouse or a friend?"

"I don't think so. I think she came here alone."

"Can you describe her appearance? Her height and weight?"

Laura didn't know how tall Diana was or how much she weighed, but then again, she never knew how tall people were or how much they weighed, and it seemed odd that these were the attributes the police considered the most pertinent for identification.

"She's about my height, I think. Five feet seven? I don't know how much she weighs. Maybe a hundred forty pounds? She actually looks a bit like me, only with shorter hair. And she was wearing a black bathing suit and jean shorts and a white shirt."

Laura watched Officer Solomon jot down notes and hoped she hadn't insulted Diana by underestimating her height or overestimating her weight. Maybe she was actually five feet eight and weighed 130 pounds? But it was too late now. Her guess was now a part of the official police record.

"Do you have a recent photograph of her?"

Laura was struck by how much information one needed to report a person missing and how little she actually knew about the woman that she had, according to Dave, become obsessed with.

"No, I don't. Sorry."

Officer Solomon stopped writing. "Would you be willing to describe your friend's appearance to our sketch artist?"

"Sure," she said, even though she felt uncertain, since she'd never had to describe anyone's appearance in any forensic detail before.

He put down his pad and stood up. "I'll be right back."

He stepped out of the office and called to someone in a dialect Laura couldn't understand but assumed was Bahamian Creole. He returned, followed by a short man who had a mustache and carried a sketchbook and a small tin box.

"This is Marcel," Officer Solomon said, gesturing at the man.

"Hello," Laura said.

Marcel nodded and sat in the chair next to Laura, then removed a pencil and a razor blade from the box.

"I've never done this before," she said.

Marcel smiled as he sharpened his pencil with the razor blade using short, quick strokes. "Most people haven't; don't worry. Can you tell me what it was about your friend's face that is most memorable to you?"

Laura watched the pencil shavings fall to the floor. She didn't know what it was about Diana that she found so memorable, but it had little to do with the features of her face. Maybe it was her quiet confidence or her enigmatic nature, but how to articulate those qualities in physiognomic terms?

"I don't know," she said and felt a sudden urge to gather the pencil shavings off the floor and throw them in the garbage.

"Take your time," Marcel said. "Most people remember more than they think. Start with the eyes. Can you describe her eyes?"

Laura thought about Diana's eyes. They were big and blue. Unrealistically blue. Gatorade blue.

"They're blue—I remember that," she said, before she realized this was a detail that could not be captured in a black-and-white sketch. "But I guess that's not really helpful."

"What about their shape? Can you see the white around the top and bottom? Do her eyelids have creases, or are they hooded? Is their shape almond or round?"

"I'm not sure."

"Close your eyes. It might help you remember."

Laura nodded and dutifully closed her eyes. At first, she saw nothing but the red veins on the backs of her eyelids, but gradually an image of Diana came into focus. She was standing on the edge of the limestone cliff. Wisps of hair. That piercing gaze. A row of straight white teeth.

"There's no white around the top or bottom. They're creased, not hooded. And almond shaped."

"Good," Marcel said.

"Why don't you tell me what happened," Officer Solomon said. "That might help you remember more."

"We were hiking the Castaway Point Trail when she disappeared," Laura said.

"Castaway Point?" Officer Solomon and Marcel exchanged a look.

"I heard that another woman died there a few years ago," Laura said.

Officer Solomon nodded and made a note in his book. "Yes, it was a terrible tragedy. Is it possible Diana slipped and fell?" he asked.

"I wondered that, but I didn't hear her scream. And when I looked over the edge of the cliff, I didn't see anything down below."

"Where exactly did she go missing?" Officer Solomon asked.

"We were looking at the view, and I really had to pee, so I went into the grove for privacy, and when I came back, she was gone."

"When was this?"

"Yesterday, around one."

Confusion knitted Officer Solomon's brow. "But you're only reporting her missing now?"

Laura shifted in the chair and recrossed her legs. "I assumed we got separated on the trail and that maybe she walked back to the resort by herself, but she never turned up, and now it's been twenty-four hours."

"It is actually a myth that you need to wait twenty-four hours before reporting someone missing. If you have reason to believe someone is in danger, those first twenty-four hours are very important."

Now Laura regretted that she hadn't come forward sooner.

Marcel held up his sketchbook, where he had drawn a pair of eyes. "Does this look right to you?"

Physically, the eyes were similar to Diana's, but they lacked the intensity of her gaze. "Pretty close," Laura said.

"What about her eyebrows? Were they thin and groomed or thick and natural?"

Laura closed her eyes again. She hadn't really noticed Diana's eyebrows, but now that she was trying to conjure them, she heard herself say, "Thick and natural."

She opened her eyes and looked at Officer Solomon. "I think something bad might have happened. I think she could be in danger."

"What makes you think so?"

Laura pulled Diana's bracelet out of her pocket and handed it to him. "I found this on the trail after she disappeared. It belongs to her, and the clasp is broken."

"Yes, I can see that," he said, examining the bracelet.

"Also, she told me she was planning to meet someone for dinner last night, but she never showed up at the Pink Sands restaurant."

Officer Solomon picked up his pen again. "And you think there might be reason to suspect foul play?"

"You mean like a kidnapping?"

"We don't get a lot of abductions here. Most of the crime is on Nassau. But things do happen from time to time. Was there anyone you met on your hike that made you feel unsafe?"

Laura thought about the man with the creepy smile and yellow teeth staring at her from the entrance of the trail. "When we were hiking to the trailhead, Diana bought a T-shirt from a guy who was selling shirts out of the back of his truck. He followed us to the trailhead."

"Do you remember the color of his truck?"

"It was blue."

Officer Solomon glanced at Marcel. "That was probably Freddie."

Marcel nodded in agreement. Officer Solomon looked at Laura. "He's been selling T-shirts there for years, and we've never had a problem, but I will have a talk with him. Maybe he saw something."

"There were also two guys who passed us on the trail," Laura said.

"Can you describe them?"

Laura squinted, trying to visualize the hikers with her half-closed eyes. "One was wearing a bandanna and the other had a beard. I only bring them up because I saw them later, on the road, and one of them was wearing the T-shirt that Diana had bought. That seemed weird to me."

"Did they speak to you?"

"Not really. When they passed us on the trail, one of them said, 'Is everything OK?'"

"Why did he say that?"

"I don't know. We were sort of arguing, before."

"You and Miss Diana?" Officer Solomon asked.

Laura nodded.

"What were you arguing about?"

"Nothing. It was stupid."

The fight was too embarrassing to explain, and Laura felt foolish for even bringing it up. She wondered where Dave was, if he was still waiting on the trail where she had left him or if he had gone back to the resort. Back to the resort, she assumed. She looked down at her hands and noticed that she had unconsciously peeled off three more ovals of nail polish.

"Are her lips thin or full?" Marcel asked.

Laura focused her attention on the sketch of Diana. "Full," she said and picked absently at another nail. It was too late to salvage her manicure, and it was strangely soothing to peel off the remaining ovals of polish.

Marcel roughed in a pair of lips. He moved on to other aspects of Diana's face, the height and prominence of her cheekbones, the strength of her jaw, and the delicate crow's-feet around her eyes. Was her nose aquiline or roman? Nubian or celestial? Laura didn't know the meaning of these words, so Marcel showed her a laminated book filled with anatomical drawings of various noses and chins and ears. Laura found it disturbing that such a book existed, disassembling the human face into its component parts and lining them up for comparison, but she dutifully pointed out specific noses and chins and ears, and Marcel incorporated them into his sketch, and Diana's face gradually took shape on the page.

As Marcel shaded in the wavy hair around Diana's temples, it surprised Laura how many details she was remembering about Diana that she hadn't consciously registered before. The smattering of tiny brown freckles across the bridge of her nose. The elegant planes of her cheekbones and the tiny silver hoop that pierced the cartilage of her right ear. She recalled Diana's gait, the way she seemed to lope instead of walk, with an athletic stance, her hands on her narrow hips, her stubby fingernails that lacked a manicure. Laura didn't know how she knew these things, but she did. Perhaps Dave was right. Perhaps she really was obsessed.

Marcel held up his finished sketch. "What do you think?"

It felt strange to stare at the face and have the face stare back at her. While it was by no means a faithful portrait, it was vaguely recognizable as Diana. But as she looked at it, she began to doubt herself. The picture looked fake, imaginary. Was she overreacting? She had told Officer Solomon that Diana had disappeared, but she realized she had never actually witnessed Diana disappear. She had not been present for the moment of vanishing. Staring at the sketch, she felt crazy suddenly, like an obsessive fanatic who had conjured a fictional woman's face out of thin air. She had no photo of Diana; she didn't even know her last name, let alone her profession or family history. But Diana had a last name. She must. And a profession and a family history. Or at least people who cared about her. She thought of those people, who probably didn't even know yet that Diana was missing, and just as quickly as she'd felt crazy a moment ago, she now felt duty bound to find her. She decided that for the purpose of a missing person alert, the sketch would suffice, so she nodded and said, "That's her."

Marcel handed the finished sketch to Officer Solomon and left the office.

"What happens now?" Laura asked when she and Officer Solomon were alone.

"I'll call the Pink Sands to see if they have contact information for Diana on file. If we cannot reach her by tomorrow, I will activate a missing person alert. Then I'll submit my report to the police chief in Governor's Harbour. If she is an American citizen, we will contact the consulate and see if we can reach her family and obtain a photo of her. Our island is small, so if she's out there, we will find her," Officer Solomon said.

Laura absorbed his words, comforted by the machine she was setting into motion. He pulled a business card out of his desk drawer and handed it to her.

"If you think of anything else, please give me a call."

"OK." Laura stood up and pocketed the card.

"How long are you staying with us?" he asked.

"I'm leaving tomorrow, actually."

"Where is home?"

"New York."

"Ah, the Big Apple. A great city, but too busy for me. I prefer the tranquility of the island." Officer Solomon stood up and extended his hand. "Have you been enjoying your stay?"

"It's very beautiful here," Laura said and shook his hand, even though it felt odd to discuss the beauty and tranquility of the island under the circumstances.

Outside, Laura was once again enveloped by the hot, humid air. She didn't know what she had expected would happen after reporting Diana missing. A flurry of lights and sirens? A pack of hounds released to search the island? But giving a statement was anticlimactic, and she felt ridiculous for having been so unprepared. She didn't even know Diana's last name and hadn't thought to bring a photograph. Not that she had one to bring. When Diana had offered to take a photo of her on the cliff, it hadn't crossed Laura's mind to take one of her in return.

She made her way down the crumbling road, past the gas station and the general store, where the two heavyset women were still sitting, staring at her as she walked past. As she walked, she started to formulate a plan. She needed to figure out Diana's last name. If Priscilla wouldn't tell her for privacy reasons, Laura would scour the internet. After all, even if Diana had erased all her social media accounts, she couldn't scrub her entire online footprint. Shreds of truth would be left behind, and they could be used to glean insight into Diana and maybe even reveal why she'd disappeared.

Laura reached Queen's Highway and turned right, in the direction of the resort. Officer Solomon's words echoed in her mind: *If you have reason to believe someone is in danger, those first twenty-four hours are very important.* She wondered what the chances were that Diana was still alive. She often thought about this, the statistical probabilities of disaster. This obsessive anxiety often prevented her from taking risks, but there was an advantage: it made her very good at her job. When Reinhart, Mader & Stern had signed as a client the global cruise line Gold Coast International, Laura was tasked with drafting the ticket contracts that the passengers were required to sign before they would be allowed to board any of the ships. She was told to make the fine print bulletproof, to protect Gold Coast from liability that could cost the cruise line millions of dollars in class-action litigation. Laura went to work, imagining savage viral outbreaks, treacherous ocean storms, and other horrific force majeures, and she channeled her fear into her work, writing dense clauses that would force all future passengers to sign away their rights to sue Gold Coast should any of these disasters befall them at sea. Her contract was so airtight, so comprehensive in its scope, she developed a reputation for being thorough and exacting and was even nicknamed the Contract Queen.

Laura hadn't always been this way. Like other naively hopeful people, she used to imagine things working out for the best. She would fantasize about her romantic relationships culminating in marriage and children, but after the summer she graduated from college and slept with Jake Hollinger, she learned that he and Chloe were going to be married, and she began to only imagine the ends of things.

When Laura moved back to New Haven to start law school in the fall, she learned from Facebook that Chloe and Jake Hollinger held their wedding at a rustic vineyard. She concluded that love was unsafe and friendships were dangerous. She grew wary when her new classmates invited her to coffee dates and movies, and even as she accepted their invites, she searched for ulterior motives. She didn't trust women anymore. She didn't even trust herself. After all, she had been made a mistress by Jake Hollinger and hadn't even known it.

Later, from Instagram, Laura learned that Chloe and Jake Hollinger bought a house in Syracuse, and when Chloe got pregnant, she posted it to her stories and shared her progress with photos of her growing baby bump. Chloe gave birth to her son during Laura's final year of law school, and when she posted the baby pictures, Laura clicked through them over and over, even though it made her sick to do so. With his blond curls and dark eyelashes, baby Patrick Hollinger was a perfect blend of his parents' best features.

It was around this time that Chloe started smiling in photographs. Even though the life she was living, in a house in a cul-de-sac in Syracuse, New York, looked domestic and suburban and oppressive, the opposite of the life she had said she wanted, Chloe seemed to radiate an ecstatic happiness. Laura couldn't reconcile how antithetical this outcome was to Chloe's childhood dreams and assumed Jake Hollinger was to blame. She had no proof, but it felt good to blame Jake Hollinger for things.

Laura held all this anger and resentment inside of herself, and because she couldn't unleash it on Jake Hollinger directly, she aimed it at all the other men she met, assuming they must be just like him. A new cynicism encased her heart, and like fibrous scar tissue, it strengthened the muscle while simultaneously limiting its range of motion. As she embarked on promising new relationships with interesting men, she envisioned their future breakups like a science fiction writer, conjuring the smoking wreckage of apocalyptic aftermaths. Even in the first blush of infatuation, she packed emotional go bags and wrote scripts in her head, preparing herself for the inevitable end.

After she graduated from law school and started working at the firm, she stopped dating altogether and focused her energy entirely on her job. The Law became her refuge. Its rules gave her solace in a way that love and friendship could not. Contracts had clear terms of engagement, and if those terms were broken, actions could be taken. Damages sought. She reveled in writing contracts. There was power in the precision of legal language, elegance in articulating protections against potential calamities. The Law was safe. Its precedents were comforting. By studying the Law, she made sense of the world and found her place in it as an attorney at Reinhart, Mader & Stern. With this new understanding of her identity, she opened her heart to her work with a profound sense of devotion. Her relationship to the Law was, it turned out, her one true love. It was the only one that had never ended in betrayal.

But then Dave Mitchell came back into her life. When she first saw him at the firm and was reminded of the note he had written to himself all those years ago, she felt a glimmer of hope that perhaps someone who was capable of that kind of introspection was incapable of betraying her. So she opened her heart to him too.

Laura's phone vibrated in her pocket. She realized that she must have stumbled into an area with cell reception and felt a wave of relief as she pulled it out of her pocket. It was probably Dave calling to apologize, she thought. She decided that she would hear him out. Part of her was still angry, but another part of her wanted to make up and salvage what was left of their vacation. But it wasn't Dave calling. It was a 917 number she didn't recognize.

"Hello?" she said.

"Laura. This is Donald Reinhart."

Donald Reinhart's voice was rich and deep, like the amber-colored bourbon he kept on the bar cart in his office. Laura had only ever been inside Donald Reinhart's office once, five years prior, the day she started working at the firm, when he gave her a personal tour. As she'd stared at the rows of important-looking legal volumes lining his built-in bookshelves and the expensive-looking bottles of liquor in his bar cart, he told her to think of the firm as an extended family, even though it was tacitly understood that Laura was never to enter his office again and that she was certainly not welcome to his bourbon.

"I've been informed of the situation that arose on your trip."

The 917 number meant he was calling from his cell phone. She found it odd that he wasn't calling from his office line, considering it was Thursday, a workday. There was a possibility he didn't want the conversation registered on the firm's official call logs.

"Let me give you my understanding, and tell me if it's accurate, OK?"

"OK."

"Yesterday, you and David reported a woman missing to the concierge at the Pink Sands resort, yes?"

"Yes."

"And the woman disappeared from Castaway Point; is that correct?"

"Yes."

"And today you went into town by yourself and reported her missing to the police?"

"Yes."

"Are you aware that the owner of the Pink Sands is a client of ours?"

"Yes."

With each *yes*, Laura felt the pitch of her voice rise by half an octave, which it did when she was nervous, and she forced herself to lower it so that she would sound more confident and self-assured.

"Are you aware that this is not the first time the Pink Sands has had to deal with an incident at Castaway Point?"

"Yes, I'm aware."

"Good, because it's important you understand why we need to react to this situation swiftly and decisively. When the previous incident occurred, our client took a direct hit in the press, and he's now feeling nervous. Given his past experience, I'm sure you can understand how delicate all of this is."

"I do."

"I'm glad to hear that, Laura. The thing I can't understand is why you didn't come to us first."

It was a good question but one she hadn't prepared an answer for. She had never thought of Donald Reinhart as someone she could approach directly about anything.

"I thought she might be in danger, and I know that time is of the essence in these kinds of situations, so I thought the right thing to do was to go to the police."

This, at least, was the truth.

"It's admirable that you were concerned about this woman's safety, but now we have a very unhappy client, I'm afraid."

The tone of Donald Reinhart's voice was warm, but Laura sensed from the careful, deliberate selection of his words that he was angry. She had seen him get angry in meetings before, and it was quietly terrifying, like watching a volcano organize itself before deciding to erupt.

"We're going to convene a meeting of the partners to discuss this, and I'll get back to you, so please keep your phone on, OK?"

She knew his words meant that this was no longer a discussion between two colleagues and that, moving forward, she would not be consulted on how best to solve the problem at hand. Conversations would now be had between the partners without her involvement. She had worked hard for years to place herself on an upward trajectory, to be perceived as a team player, potentially even partner material down the road, and she had been given signs that her efforts were acknowledged—pay raises and invitations to senior-level meetings made her feel like she was held in high esteem—but now she was being cut out of the loop. She told herself that, at least as of this moment, she was still a valued member of the firm, the Contract Queen, no less, so she should stop worrying. After all, she was a Good Girl. She had done the right thing. And whenever possible, one was supposed to do the right thing.

"OK," she said because there was nothing else to say.

The line went dead. She picked absently at a fingernail, but it was bare. She looked down at her hands, which were trembling slightly. She had peeled off the remaining nail polish during the call, save a few jagged bits of red around the edges of her thumbs that looked garish, like dried blood.

It was late afternoon when she got back to the resort. Dave was right: her trip to Gregory Town had taken up most of the day. The beautiful women were packing up their beach bags and heading back to their cabins to get changed for dinner. They had spent the whole day here, surrounded by unchanging splendor. The sky was still blue, still cloudless; there was no sign of a storm. Javarro had been wrong about that,

Laura thought. Another peaceful day had passed, but she felt outside it. Vacations were happening all around, but not to her, and this frustrated her. But it also disgusted her a little that these beautiful people could enjoy themselves so blissfully when so much turmoil was happening in their periphery.

When she entered the cabin, Dave's suitcase was open on the bed, and he was tossing balled-up socks into it.

"What are you doing?" she asked, even though it was obvious what he was doing.

Dave said nothing. Their argument on the trail had been their first real fight, and since tension rarely brewed between them, his abrupt passive aggression seemed strange now. It was unlike him to force her to pry.

"What did you end up doing all day?" she ventured.

Dave grabbed a stack of T-shirts from the standing wardrobe.

"What do you think?" he said, stuffing them into his suitcase. "Damage control. I've been on the phone with the partners all day. Marcus Lowry is freaking out. Because you went to the police, he thinks there's going to be a leak to the press and this whole situation is going to snowball. He's flying in from Miami tonight. This is the first time all day I've been off the phone. We're heading back into a shitstorm tomorrow."

"Do you want to talk about it?"

"Which part do you want to talk about? The part where you left me on the trail? Or the part where you've been lying to me since we started dating?"

She had never heard this contemptuous tone in his voice before. The scornful look in his eye was also new. She felt a familiar cynicism starting to encase her heart. The fibrous scar tissue she had cut away was creeping back up.

"Did you think for a second how going to the police would impact me?" he asked. "Between the two of us, I'm the senior associate. You know that, right?"

It was true. Laura had been at the firm longer, but Dave had two more years of work experience than she did and was technically senior to her, which meant that, according to professional hierarchy, she had stepped out of line. But she reminded herself that he was the one who had gone behind her back and talked to the partners. He had betrayed her too.

"And that shit you said about what I wrote in college. Why didn't you ever tell me that stuff before?" he asked.

"I don't know," she said. "I didn't mean to keep it from you. It just never came up."

"We've been dating for two months, Laura."

"I'm sorry—there just wasn't really a good time to bring it up. Besides, it was embarrassing that you didn't remember me from college."

"So everyone is supposed to remember you? Do you know how narcissistic that is?"

Laura stalled on his words. Why was it narcissistic to feel forgettable? Pathetic, maybe, but narcissistic?

"If you didn't want to tell me before, why did you tell me now?" he asked.

Laura didn't know why she had quoted to him the words she had read in his notebook all those years ago. To embarrass him, maybe? To point out his phoniness? Maybe she had wanted to hurt him the way he had hurt her. But it was too late to take it back. The truth was out there now, and she had learned long ago that when a secret was released into the world, it took on a life of its own, spreading and mutating and destroying everything in its path.

"That stuff I wrote was private. Do you know how creepy it is that you read it over my shoulder and didn't tell me? I mean, what else are you not telling me?"

"Nothing." She felt the pitch of her voice rising again.

"Are you sure? Because I don't know if I can trust you anymore."

She watched him stuff a pair of pants into his suitcase. She figured she should probably pack, too, but she didn't want their vacation to end like this.

"I'm going to get dinner," Dave said, zipping his suitcase shut.

"OK. Let me go change." She hadn't eaten anything since breakfast and was famished.

"Actually, I want to eat by myself," he said.

She watched him pocket his cabin key and his phone. She felt herself tensing suddenly, as though she were bracing herself for a blow to the gut. She recognized this feeling and realized it was her body instinctively preparing for things to fall apart.

"At the restaurant?" she asked.

"Yeah," he said. "At the restaurant."

She felt a sense of crumbling then, as though their relationship were eroding in real time before her eyes. She felt an urge to lunge forward and physically stop him from leaving, stop everything from happening. She needed everything to slow down, to stop, just for a second, so that she could figure out precisely where she'd gone wrong and then rewind and do everything, this trip, this relationship, over again. But at the same time, she knew that if she could have a do-over, she probably wouldn't do any of it differently, so she stayed where she was and did nothing. Things were moving forward, brushing past her, indifferent to her feelings, and there was nothing she could do to stop any of it.

Dave pulled open the sliding glass door, and Laura watched him head outside and down the paved path that led to the Seahorse. She watched him as the clouds gathered overhead, blocking out the sun, casting everything in shadow.

CHAPTER NINE

Laura didn't know what she was supposed to do. Follow Dave or give him space? Eating alone at a romantic restaurant was something Laura couldn't fathom doing, no matter how angry or hurt she was. Then again, Diana had had no problem dining solo at the Seahorse. Laura wondered where she was now. Was she lying somewhere, injured and in pain? Had she been taken by those hikers, and was she trapped, unable to call for help? It infuriated her that Dave was more concerned about his relationship with the partners than he was about Diana's well-being. Ordinarily, Laura cared deeply about her job, but a woman was missing and possibly in danger, and shouldn't that be more important than the opinion of the partners?

Laura wanted to find out more about Diana, but all she had to go on was her first name. She opened her laptop on the bed and typed *Diana Eleuthera* into Google because she didn't know what else to do, but the only hits that appeared were photos of the late Princess Diana and Charles in Eleuthera, where they had spent part of their honeymoon in 1981. She wondered if they had gotten matching Wifey and Hubs T-shirts for the occasion but concluded that they most likely had not.

She needed to figure out Diana's last name, but she was also starving. Seeing as she'd been uninvited to dine at the Seahorse, she would have to acquire food by other means. She flipped through the binder on the coffee table until she found the in-room dining menu. Maybe it was good that Dave had ditched her. Maybe she would dine alone in the cabin. It would be good to have some space. The entrées listed on the menu were mostly the same as the ones offered at the restaurant: whole grilled grouper, conch salad, pepper pot, sashimi sampler, and something called an island burger. Laura didn't remember the last time she'd eaten a burger. She was always eyeing them on menus at trendy gastropubs in the city but invariably ended up ordering a salad instead, in a habit of self-denial. But now she craved meat.

She picked up the phone and pressed the button for in-room dining. When she was connected, she said, "I'd like to order an island burger and fries, please. And a glass of cabernet."

"I'm sorry, miss," the voice said. "We're not offering in-cabin dining tonight because our entire waitstaff is working at the luau. I encourage you to come down to the Seahorse. You won't want to miss it."

"Oh. Thanks," Laura said and hung up.

No part of her wanted to come down to the Seahorse for a luau. She didn't want to see Dave. More precisely, she didn't want Dave to see her and think she had followed him there after he'd expressly told her that he wanted to eat alone. She didn't know what to do, so she curled up in a ball on the massive bed and closed her eyes. But her stomach growled with the knowledge that hot food was being prepared nearby, and she felt even hungrier than before. She opened her eyes. It irritated her that her need for food was stronger than her pride. It made her feel base and feral, like an animal that couldn't control itself.

She sat up, slid her feet into her flip-flops, and dragged herself out of the cabin without changing her clothes or putting on any makeup.

She had missed the sunset. It was already dark out as she walked to the Seahorse. The tiki torches on either side of the path were lit, and ukulele music drifted through the air, which smelled of woodsmoke. From a distance, she could see paper lanterns had been strung up around the restaurant, giving it an ambient, golden glow. Long buffet tables had been set up, each one fitted with a raffia skirt, and guests were standing in lines holding plates, the beautiful women in flowing dresses and men in pastel Bermuda shorts. As she approached the restaurant, a hostess handed her a lei and said, "Aloha." It struck Laura as odd that the resort was hosting a luau. Luaus weren't even Bahamian; they were Hawaiian. When she had first arrived at the Pink Sands, the place seemed to have a unique, magical quality, but now, as she draped the lei around her neck, everything seemed artificial and inauthentic. Even on their own island, the Bahamians had been forced to adopt the culture of another people just to please some tourists who probably didn't know the difference.

The table with the roast pig had the longest line. The pig was displayed on a large platter, its legs outstretched as if in midleap, its eyes black holes. Its mouth was open, giving the impression that it had squealed while being burned alive. Wifey and Hubs were at the front of the line, and a waiter in a chef's hat was carving flesh from its hindquarters and piling it onto Hubs's plate. Hubs, whose face was newly sunburned, was giving a thumbs-up to Wifey, who was taking a picture of him with her phone. All three of them, Wifey, Hubs, and the waiter, were laughing. Laura felt unsettled and suddenly wanted very much to leave.

She looked around for Dave without making direct eye contact with anyone. She had learned this skill in high school, how to locate a boy in a crowded room without catching his eye and then orient herself in such a way as to keep him in her peripheral vision. It was a skill Chloe had taught her, and she had practiced it on Jake Hollinger countless times.

Dave was sitting alone at a table, the same one Diana had sat at when she'd eaten dinner alone, and Laura wondered where she was now. Was she starving, unable to get any food? Laura felt her anxiety rising, so she willed herself to believe Diana was OK. After all, she had looked so calm and cool eating by herself. Maybe she was more resourceful than Laura gave her credit for. Dave, however, did not look calm and cool. His plate was full of pork and some kind of salad, and he was drinking beer and staring at the ocean. Laura felt pity that he was dining solo in the middle of a festive luau, but then she remembered that he had elected to do so.

She picked up a plate and stood at the back of the line, but it was moving slowly because everyone wanted to have their picture taken with the roast pig. She was anxious that at any moment Dave would turn around and see her, and she could feel the beautiful women staring at her and judging her outfit and lack of makeup, and this compounded her anxiety to such a degree that standing in the slow-moving line suddenly felt intolerable.

She eyed another food station, where a waiter was flipping beef patties on a grill. A dozen burgers were arranged in a row on a table in front of him, next to several bottles of wine. They looked tantalizing, and she felt an urgent desire to eat one. She glanced at the beautiful women, knowing that she would draw attention to herself if she abruptly left the line, but her appetite was overwhelming, so without making eye contact with anyone, she walked quickly over to the grill and grabbed a burger and an open bottle of wine and ducked out of the restaurant. She smiled to herself as she walked away from the smoke and lights and music. She kept walking until she reached the far end of the beach, where all she could hear was the sound of the waves lapping gently on the shore.

By the water, the breeze was calm and pleasantly cool. The white umbrellas were closed, and the lounge chairs had been flattened for the night. No one was on the beach because everyone was at the luau. She looked over her shoulder at the way she had come, but it was so dark she couldn't see anything except for the Seahorse glowing in the distance.

She kicked off her flip-flops and sat down on the cold sand. She took a swig of wine and wiped her mouth with the back of her hand. She wedged the bottle in the sand and picked up the burger with both hands and took a bite. The patty had a thick bark, and its warm juice dripped down her chin and over her unsightly fingernails. She took another bite, and maybe it was because she was eating alone on a beach in the dark, or maybe it was because she was eating a burger for the first time in years, but something primal inside her snapped, and she took another bite and then another, not stopping to chew or swallow or wipe the juice that dribbled down her neck and hands and wrists, and she kept eating like that, like a wild thing that didn't know its own name.

When she was finished, she drank half the bottle of wine and then lay down. She was full and buzzed, and the cold sand felt good against her back. She didn't know if Dave was still at the luau or not, and she didn't care. Her phone vibrated in her pocket. She pulled it out. The 917 number was calling again.

"Mr. Reinhart," she said, sitting up.

"Hello again, Laura. Do you have a few minutes to talk?"

She nodded, but when she realized that he couldn't see her, she said, "Yes, of course."

"Good. The other partners and I just met to discuss the situation. We think you've been an exemplary employee, and we've appreciated all the hard work you've put in at the firm. I didn't realize you've been with us for five years. I still remember when you joined us."

Laura exhaled. She *was* an exemplary employee, and it felt good to have her hard work acknowledged by her boss. Dave had made her worry for no reason.

"Five whole years. It feels like a lifetime ago," she said.

"That's why we were all so surprised that you didn't come to us directly to discuss the delicate situation involving your friend."

"I know, and I apologize. I should have come to you first," she said.

"Unfortunately, by not coming to us first, it's the opinion of the partners that you committed an egregious error in judgment."

Laura felt her stomach drop. The only other time she had been accused of having bad judgment was when things had ended badly with Chloe and her mother told her she was terrible at picking friends. Laura had ignored her mother then, but maybe she had been right all along. Maybe she picked the wrong friends and fell for the wrong men and made bad decisions. Maybe she did have bad judgment.

"The partners have taken a vote, and I'm sorry to say that we can no longer offer you employment at the firm."

Laura dug her fingers in the sand. She wasn't sure if she had heard Mr. Reinhart correctly. "I'm sorry?"

"We fully intend to pay out your contract, as well as an additional ten weeks to show our goodwill. What we'll need from you in return is to sign an NDA, which you can do when you return to New York. I'm sorry it has come to this, but we all feel it's the best thing."

Maybe it was because she had just drunk half a bottle of wine, but she truly did not understand what was happening.

"Are you firing me?"

"Yes. Best of luck to you."

The line went dead.

Laura stared at her phone. If they were willing to fire her to appease Marcus Lowry, the situation with Diana was more serious than she'd thought.

She set her phone down on the sand. She was no longer an attorney at Reinhart, Mader & Stern. She was unemployed, something she hadn't been since she'd graduated from law school. Her job at the firm was the only real job she'd ever had, the only adult one anyway. What would happen to her little office, she wondered, and her black cardigan with the tortoiseshell buttons that she draped over the back of her ergonomic chair and wore whenever the air-conditioning got too cold? What would happen to her business cards? She had felt so proud when all five hundred of them had been delivered to her in a long narrow box on her first day. She remembered opening the box and pulling out a card and running her finger over her name embossed in shiny black ink. And what would happen to the email signature that punctuated every email she sent, to remind everyone, including herself, who she was? Who was she if not Laura Phillips | Associate | Reinhart, Mader & Stern? It was the only version of her adult self she had ever known.

It didn't feel real. Maybe it wasn't real. Maybe she had imagined the whole thing. She lay back down on the sand. If she went to sleep right now, maybe she would wake up and discover that the whole thing had been a bad dream. She closed her eyes.

But it was real. It had happened. She opened her eyes and stared up at the sky. It was so black and there were so many stars, which were so densely packed together she couldn't make out any individual constellations. She had read somewhere that because the light from stars traveled trillions of miles to reach her eye, looking up at them was like looking back in time. She felt this way now, like all her bad relationships and bad decisions were tiny pinpricks of light blinking back at her from the past.

As she lay on the beach, a strange thought started to form in her mind. Maybe it was the wine coursing through her veins, but the idea of having a job and going to an office every day seemed stupid and abstract suddenly, like a child's game of dress-up. She didn't understand what was happening to her. For years, her primary objective had been to work hard and make money and enjoy its accompanying status. She had billed so many hours every week to earn her salary, which she had used to buy clothes and shoes and expensive wineglasses. The harder she worked, the more money she made, the nicer things she bought, from more expensive stores, so that she could outwardly signal her increasing level of success. But now that her livelihood had been yanked away, all the success she had achieved and all the nice things she had bought seemed useless, especially here on the island. She had expected to feel panic at the gaping existential void that had just opened up in front of her, but instead she felt relief, as though she had been holding on to a large, unwieldy object for a very long time and could finally let go of it and not care about it anymore.

Besides, it was hard to take her joblessness seriously when the sky was so massive and full of stars that were so ancient they would outlast her and every other living thing on the planet. She thought of Diana then. Was she stranded under these same stars? What if her life was at stake? Under the massive firmament, Laura felt incredibly small then and helpless to find her. The stars were so dizzying that she couldn't tell if they were getting closer or if she was drifting upward toward them, so she closed her eyes and dug her hands into the cold, grainy sand to make sure she wasn't actually floating away.

She didn't know how long she lay like that, but at some point she heard splashing in the water and opened her eyes. She propped herself up on her elbows and squinted at the black water. A dark shape was thrashing in the waves.

Laura jumped up and waded into the water, which was warm like bathwater, and when she was deep enough, she dove in and swam toward the thrashing figure. It wasn't until she was far out, where it was too deep to touch bottom, that she realized the thrashing figure was Diana. Laura was flooded with shock and relief, but when Diana surfaced, gasping for air, the whites of her eyes gleamed with terror. Laura reached out to her, but Diana grabbed her arms and pulled her under. Laura pried at Diana's fingers, trying to free herself, but Diana's grip was strong, and she pulled her deeper down, where it was too dark to see anything. It occurred to Laura that she was drowning, but she was sinking too fast to do anything about it. It was just happening. In a moment, her lungs would fill with water and she would die. Laura tried to scream, but all that came out of her mouth was a furious stream of bubbles.

Laura awoke with a start. She sat up too quickly, and her forehead throbbed. The wine bottle was still wedged in the sand next to her, and a small bird that had been pecking at burger crumbs flew away. She didn't know what time it was, but she knew it must be early morning, because Javarro was down the beach opening the white umbrellas.

The tide had come in, and the water was lapping at her ankles, making her body look like a piece of driftwood that had washed ashore in the night. But her clothes were dry, so she knew she hadn't actually been in the water. There was no sign of Diana, so Laura knew she must have only dreamed that she was drowning, but her heart was hammering inside her chest, and the panic she felt was real.

The sky was overcast, but there was a strange glare to the light that forced Laura to squint. A storm was gathering on the horizon. Javarro was right. It was coming, after all.

This was something Laura could never do in New York, watch a storm gathering in the distance, since the tall buildings always obscured the horizon. As a result, storms in the city were unpredictable, always breaking overhead without warning and forcing her to seek shelter under awnings because she never thought to carry an umbrella. But here, the storm took on a physical shape and moved diagonally across the horizon from left to right, like an actor on a stage. The storm looked like it was still a way off, but Laura guessed it would probably make landfall by evening. She wondered if Diana had survived the night, wherever she was, and if she was in the storm's path.

She stood up and brushed the sand from the backs of her legs. She picked up the empty plate and the wine bottle and headed back to her cabin. Wifey and some of the other beautiful women were doing a sunrise yoga class on the beach. Their bodies were arched in identical poses, and they were being told by their instructor to connect with their breath. They looked serene and judgy at the same time. Laura felt embarrassed and vaguely slutty as she walked past them in yesterday's clothes, the wine bottle evidence of her drunken behavior from the night before.

Dave was standing on the little porch outside the cabin. He was wearing his travel clothes, jeans and a black T-shirt, the same outfit he'd worn on the flight from New York, and he was talking to Officer Solomon, who was wearing a beige uniform jacket over his shirt and tie and had a cap tucked under his arm that was black and white with a red band. It was jarring to see them talking together, two strangers who had entered each other's lives because of her but without her direct involvement. Seeing them together made her feel excluded but also anxious because Officer Solomon's presence probably meant there was news about Diana. Good or bad news, it was unclear, but the range of possibility was so extreme it caused Laura's pulse to quicken as she approached them.

"Did you find her?" Laura asked when she was close enough.

"Good morning, Laura," Officer Solomon said. "No, we haven't located Diana Casey."

Laura absorbed this, surprised. Diana's last name was Casey? This, finally, was a lead.

"We have been in touch with her family in the US, though," Officer Solomon said.

Laura stopped at the base of the porch steps and squinted up at Dave and Officer Solomon.

"So she's American."

"Yes. You were right about that. Diana's parents informed me that she has not been returning their calls. That, along with what you told me, gives me reason to be concerned. So Diana is now formally being considered a missing person. The resort had her passport photo on file, so I will be issuing a missing person alert."

It was chilling to hear Officer Solomon talk about Diana in this way, as though she were a case number, not a person. Laura imagined paperwork being generated and files exchanging hands. It was all so bureaucratic.

"Where've you been?" Dave asked. He didn't step down from the porch but stayed where he was, with a distant, slightly stiff air about him. Laura didn't know if he was acting formal because he was in the presence of a cop or because he was still smarting from their fight.

"I fell asleep on the beach last night." She held up her plate and wine bottle as evidence. She was embarrassed saying this in front of Officer Solomon, but she felt it wasn't right to lie in front of a cop.

"All night?" Dave seemed skeptical.

"I think so. I just woke up a little while ago."

Dave looked at Officer Solomon. "Can you give us a few minutes?"

"Of course." Officer Solomon stepped down from the porch. "I'm going to check in with security. Thank you, David, for telling me the details of your conversation with Diana."

Laura looked at Dave, confused. Conversation? When had he spoken to Diana? But Dave avoided her eye.

Officer Solomon touched Laura's arm as he passed. "I would like to ask you a few more questions later, when you have a moment."

"Sure," Laura said, but her stare remained focused on Dave. When Officer Solomon was out of earshot, she said, "You never told me you had a conversation with Diana."

Dave shrugged. "There's a lot you didn't tell me either."

He pulled open the sliding glass door and went inside. Laura could tell by his body language that he was still angry and probably wanted to fight some more, but there was sand in her hair and her skin itched, and she wanted a shower and a cup of coffee and to forget that last night had even happened. She arranged her face into its most neutral expression and followed him inside.

"Where were you, really?" Dave asked after she pulled the glass door shut. "Because you never texted me." He glared at her with his arms crossed, not even trying to be passive aggressive.

"I told you, I fell asleep on the beach. Sorry I didn't text you," she said and set the empty plate and wine bottle down on the coffee table. "But you didn't text me either."

"So, what, you just wandered the beach all night?" he asked, as if that were the most ridiculous thing in the world.

"I wasn't having a great night, OK? After you left, Reinhart called and fired me."

What surprised Laura was the lack of embarrassment she felt when she said the words out loud. She felt brazen, like a reckless teenager who had just been kicked out of school. Having nothing to lose made her feel a strange kind of power. Everything seemed possible, and yet nothing seemed to matter. She watched Dave absorb the information. He was still angry, but she could sense him softening.

"I didn't think they'd actually go through with it," he said as he slid his laptop into his messenger bag.

"Wait. Did you know the partners were going to fire me?" she asked.

Dave said nothing as he unplugged his laptop power cord from the wall.

"Why didn't you say anything? You could have warned me."

She watched him wrap the cord into a tight coil.

"Is that why you didn't want to have dinner with me last night? Because you knew they were going to fire me?"

"They told me not to say anything. It was awkward."

Laura stared at Dave. Because he was so good looking, and because good-looking people seemed to move through life on their own terms, she didn't think of him as a particularly obedient person, but he seemed pathetic now for doing whatever the partners told him to do.

"A heads-up would have been nice," she said.

He shrugged as he stuffed his coiled power cord into his messenger bag.

"And why didn't you tell me you had a conversation with Diana? When did you talk to her?"

"I don't think you're in a position to ask questions here. You haven't exactly been honest with me," he said and slung his messenger bag across his chest.

"What is that supposed to mean?"

"Why didn't you tell me about the guy in the truck?" he asked.

"What guy?"

"The cop said you saw a guy in a blue truck on the road. Why didn't you tell me?"

He meant Freddie.

"I don't know."

"Or the hikers. Why didn't you tell me about them?"

"I don't know. What did you talk about with Diana?" she asked.

"The cop didn't even know who I was. It was embarrassing. Why didn't you tell him we were here together?"

"I don't know, Dave."

She didn't like how he was steering the conversation and pelting her with questions she couldn't answer. She didn't know why she hadn't mentioned him to Officer Solomon, but at the time, it hadn't seemed pertinent to the topic of Diana's disappearance. She felt Dave studying her face, waiting for it to reveal some ugly truth she was trying to conceal. But he was lying to her too, telling her only partial truths.

"What were you and Carl Reyes doing at the management office that took so long?"

Dave grabbed his suitcase and extended its telescoping handle. "You know, the whole time we've been here, I think you spent more time with her than with me. You let her hijack our entire vacation."

He was deflecting. Why was he deflecting?

"You didn't answer my question," she said.

"I told you. Marcus Lowry has complicated tax implications," he said and rolled his suitcase to the door.

"What did you talk about with Diana?"

"Nothing. Look, last night, I thought a lot about our situation, and I think you actually wanted to go on vacation by yourself, but for whatever reason you were too scared, so you used me."

"*Used* you? That's fucked up, Dave."

Where was this coming from? He seemed unfamiliar to her suddenly, a stranger.

"I'm sorry your friend is missing, and I'm sorry you got fired, but I think when we get back, we should take a break."

It occurred to Laura then how fragile relationships were, how easily they could be snuffed out. Was this what Dave had been thinking about at the luau? she wondered. Had he plotted their breakup while staring out to sea, eating his plate of pork? Had this decision come to him suddenly, or had he been feeling this way for a while? After all, he knew she was going to be fired, so did he figure he would cut his losses and move on? She couldn't believe he hadn't warned her about her impending joblessness and then proceeded to blame her for avoiding him all night.

"Are you going to call Tafari?" she asked.

"Who's Tafari?"

She searched his face, but he just stared at her blankly.

"The taxi driver," she said. "Who brought us here from the airport? Who told you his whole life story?"

Dave shook his head, genuinely confused. "I don't remember any of that."

"He gave you his card."

"I guess I threw it out."

Laura stared at Dave. He was so blasé, but only three days ago, he'd been so animated in the taxi, so engaged in conversation, so curious about Tafari's life. Or at least he had seemed that way. In that moment, she realized how perfectly suited he was to his job. He wasn't a great contract writer like she was or a strategic thinker like Donald Reinhart, but he was handsome and charming and well liked by everyone at the firm, especially the partners, who always seemed to assign him to accounts that were way above his pay grade, like The Sands International. The partners didn't like dealing with Marcus Lowry because he was a hostile and relentless client, but his billings accounted for a large portion of the firm's revenue, so they had to make him feel respected and well taken care of. Dave didn't like Marcus Lowry either, but he knew how to make him feel special and important.

Dave had always been this way, even back in college. Laura's first impression of him had been that he could make anyone like him. But that wasn't why she'd fallen for him all those years ago. It was the note he wrote in their poetry seminar. That shimmer of vulnerability, that glimpse of his inner child. These past two months, she had been waiting for that shimmer to reappear, but it hadn't, and now she wondered if it ever would. She didn't know why people couldn't just stay their childhood selves forever, why they had to bury the best parts of themselves when they grew up, or else jettison them completely, but that was what people did.

"That thing you wrote in your notebook," she asked, "about being a pretender. What did it mean?"

Dave rubbed his face with his hands, exasperated.

"Jesus, Laura, I don't know. It was a long time ago. It didn't mean anything."

She had always assumed the words he wrote back then had been significant, but maybe she had misread him completely. Were those introspective qualities she had endowed him with just her own projections? Was he, in fact, exactly what he looked like—a handsome, charming, savvy pretender? A beautiful shell? Were people disposable to him? Was she?

Laura felt sick suddenly, nauseous. Dave seemed ugly to her now. In fact, she hated him. She never wanted to see him again.

"I think you're right," she said. "This isn't working anymore."

Dave checked the time on his phone.

"We should go. Our flight leaves at eleven."

"You go ahead. I'll catch a later flight." The words flew out of her mouth, surprising them both.

Dave studied her face, waiting to see if she was serious or if she would take back her words, but when she said nothing, he said, "If that's what you want."

"That's what I want." She couldn't fathom sitting next to him on a plane now.

"OK, then. I'd better get to the airport," he said.

She watched him pull open the sliding glass door and carry his suitcase out of the cabin and down the porch steps, then set his suitcase down on the path and roll it away.

Laura shut the sliding glass door, headed into the bathroom, and turned on the shower. She peeled off her clothes and let the hot water drum on her back until the steam grew so thick she couldn't see anything. When she was finished, she turned off the water, wrapped a towel around her body, and twisted another one into a turban on her head. She opened her laptop on the bed and scanned Kayak for cheap flights back to New York. There was one leaving at 1:00 p.m., which would give her enough time to get to the airport but probably not enough time to fit in one last swim in the sea. Not that it mattered anyway, since checkout was at 11:00 a.m. and she still had to pack. She paid the change fee with her credit card and called the front desk and asked them to arrange a taxi to the airport and to send a porter to come pick her up.

She pulled the towel off her head and combed her fingers through her damp hair. She headed back into the bathroom and pulled the blow-dryer out of the wicker basket even though she had no desire to blow-dry her hair. Then she realized: Dave was gone. There was no one she had to please anymore. This realization rattled her, but it was also a little freeing. She tossed the blow-dryer back in the wicker basket, pulled her damp hair into a bun, and strode out of the bathroom.

She pulled on her jeans, which, after a few days of wearing dresses, felt stiff and unnatural, as though they belonged to someone else, which, in a way, they did. She took her T-shirts and maxi dresses out of the standing wardrobe and rolled them up, making them as compact as possible, and stuffed them into her carry-on bag. She wasn't worried about wrinkling them because all her clothes would need to be washed when she got home anyway. She pulled her pee-stained romper off its hanger. As she'd predicted, it had lost its newness and, with it, its potential, so she rolled it up and tucked it into her bag along with the rest of her clothes. She went back into the bathroom and gathered her toiletries and all the little complimentary bottles of shower gel and body lotion and crammed them into her makeup bag. She spotted the evil eye bracelet on the ledge above the sink. She felt guilty leaving the island with Diana still missing, but she told herself that the police had everything in hand. She had set a machine into motion, and that was all she could do. She slipped the bracelet into her pocket. She spotted Diana's travel-size bottle of perfume on the edge of the sink and spritzed some onto her wrist. She felt guilty doing this, too, assuming Diana's belongings as her own. But they were all Laura had left of her.

Then she remembered: *Casey*. She returned to her laptop on the bed and typed *Diana Casey* into Google. Several hits appeared. She clicked the first link, and it led her to a professional website that featured a photo of Diana and described her as an award-winning documentary filmmaker. She stared at Diana's photo, processing this. It was strange to know so much about Diana so suddenly. She had never met a documentary filmmaker before but assumed that since Diana's profession depended on her extracting personal information from strangers, it made sense that she had managed to elicit stories from Laura's past. She clicked on the *About* page, hoping to find an email address or a phone number, but there was only a standard contact form. According to the website, Diana's most recent film, *What They Don't Want You to Know*, uncovered financial crimes on Wall Street and had won some awards at film festivals. Diana's words echoed in Laura's mind: *I just hated the feeling of being watched.* New panicky thoughts bubbled to the surface: Had her film exposed some unsavory characters? Had someone threatened her? *I really needed to get away.* Was her vacation actually an escape? Why else would she delete her social media a week before leaving the country? Was she on the run? What if the police never found her? What would happen then? And how long was a woman considered missing if she was never found?

Laura googled this. Seven years. Seven seemed to Laura an arbitrary number, but somewhere along the way, society had deemed it a reasonable amount of time. She kept her tax returns for seven years. It took seven years to establish good credit. Felony arrests were reported on background checks for up to seven years after criminals were released from prison. And apparently, seven was the number of years that society allotted for a woman who was missing to be found. If not, she would be declared legally dead. Laura knew that the probability of finding a missing person was highest in the first twenty-four hours after they disappeared and plummeted after forty-eight. Diana had been missing for forty-five.

She headed back into the bathroom. She dropped the little perfume bottle into her makeup bag and stuffed her makeup bag into her carry-on. She tried to wedge her flip-flops into her bag as well, but it was a struggle to make them fit. Then she remembered that she had originally packed them in Dave's suitcase, but he was gone now. She felt a pang then. There was no one to talk to, no one to wait with her bag at the airport while she went to the bathroom. She was all alone. Just like Diana. It was a familiar feeling but a sad one.

She carried her bag out to the little porch and sat down on the steps to wait for the porter. She had gotten used to the blue skies and the placid water and assumed every day here would be the same, but the sky was gray now, and the palm trees were swaying in the wind. The air smelled earthy and anticipatory of rain. It was strange to see the island experiencing real weather. Then the sky opened, and the storm that had been traveling across the horizon earlier that morning suddenly arrived. At first, the rain fell in fat, wet drops, like tiny exploding water balloons, and then it fell in hard, fast sheets, like a wall of sound. The beautiful women on the beach shrieked and hid under the white umbrellas as the downpour turned the pink sand brown. Only Hubs stood in the downpour, with his arms outstretched, genuinely unbothered, and coaxed Wifey to join him, and she did. It was pouring rain on their honeymoon, but they seemed to be embracing it.

A golf cart pulled up in front of the cabin, and the porter yelled out, "Good morning, miss," over the din of the rain. Laura stood up as he opened a giant golf umbrella and jogged over to her. He held the umbrella over her head with one hand and picked up her bag with the other and escorted her down the porch steps. He hoisted her bag into the back of the cart, closed his umbrella, and slid into the driver's seat. Laura climbed into the back. He tossed her a smile over his shoulder and, putting the cart into gear, drove them down the path.

Laura looked out at the sea, trying to memorize it, but the torrential rain obscured her view. She wondered if Diana was out there somewhere, alone in the storm.

When the golf cart arrived at the white gazebo, the porter yelled, "Here we are." He opened his umbrella again, grabbed Laura's bag, and escorted her up the steps. The rain was drumming so loudly on the gazebo's wooden roof that Laura had to yell, "Thank you," when the porter set her bag down on the floor. He smiled and nodded, then headed back to his golf cart and drove away.

It wasn't until the porter was gone that Laura noticed Priscilla was not alone in the gazebo. Officer Solomon was standing next to her, and both of them were hunched over her computer.

"Hi, I'm checking out," Laura said, gesturing at her carry-on bag. They both straightened when they saw her.

"Hello again," Officer Solomon said.

"I'm afraid the current is off across the island," Priscilla said to Laura stiffly, as though Laura's presence made her uncomfortable.

"The current?" Laura asked.

"The power is out and the internet is down," Officer Solomon clarified. "Because of the tropical storm."

"I thought it wouldn't make landfall until tonight," Laura said.

"Mother Nature can be a little unpredictable around here," Officer Solomon said.

She had never been in a tropical storm before. She had only ever watched footage on the news, of fallen trees and cars floating in floodwaters and homes destroyed by the wind. She had a sudden urge to get off the island.

"Is my taxi here?" she asked.

"I had to cancel it," Priscilla said, staring at her computer. It was unnerving the way she was avoiding Laura's eye.

"Why did you do that?" Laura asked.

"I asked her to," Officer Solomon said. "I have a few more questions I'd like to ask you."

Laura thought it was presumptuous of Officer Solomon to cancel the taxi without her permission, but as irritated as she was, it didn't feel appropriate to get angry at a cop.

"I'd like to help you with the investigation, but my flight's at one," she said.

"I imagine your flight will be canceled, so I suggest you wait out the storm. And the safest place to do that is right here," he said.

He made a good point, but it was odd the way he was standing there with his notebook. He was being friendly and polite, and yet there was a firmness to his voice and posture, like his request was actually a command.

"Besides, once you return to New York, things will become complicated."

Over the course of their conversation, he had moved and was now standing between her and the door, and this made her feel trapped suddenly. She was not a citizen of the island and didn't actually know what her rights were, and this made her uneasy. Would she need to call the consulate? Would she need a lawyer? She didn't know any Bahamian lawyers. But she did want to help find Diana. And since a tropical storm was raging outside, it made sense to stay, at least until it was over.

"OK," she said and swallowed. Her throat was dry. "Whatever you need."

Officer Solomon closed his notebook and smiled. "Good. How about we find a quiet place to talk."

CHAPTER TEN

The quiet place Officer Solomon had in mind to talk was a cabin situated behind the gazebo. They walked over to it, sharing Officer Solomon's umbrella. It was the only building on the resort grounds that wasn't painted white, and it was raining so heavily Laura didn't even see it until she was standing right in front of the door and noticed a sign that said *Admin*.

Inside the cabin, there were no orchids or glass dispensers filled with cucumber water, just an old wooden desk, a few mismatched chairs, and a fan in the corner.

"Please," said Officer Solomon, gesturing at one of the chairs. "Have a seat."

Laura sat down and pushed a wet strand of hair off her face.

"I would like to go over your statement again," he said, sitting at the desk and pulling out his notebook. "I think there are a few details you left out."

"I'm pretty sure I told you everything I know."

"I spoke with David this morning, and I don't think that's true."

Laura stared at Officer Solomon, her mind racing, trying to think of what Dave could have possibly told him, but she could think of nothing.

"OK," she said. "I'm happy to help."

Truthfully, though, Laura was not happy to help. Yes, she had reported Diana missing and wanted desperately for her to be found, but her T-shirt was damp, and her jeans had gotten wet and now clung uncomfortably to her thighs, and all she wanted was to go home. But Officer Solomon was looking at her with suspicion, so she had to play the part of the Good Girl, which was something she knew how to do because she had been one all her life. Good Girls were taught to be mindful and accommodating. They listened more than they spoke. They perched on the edge of chairs, careful not to take up too much space. They didn't interrupt, didn't inconvenience anyone, and were careful not to draw too much attention to themselves. They answered questions thoughtfully and thoroughly because they were, above all, Happy To Help.

"David mentioned that the morning of Diana's disappearance, you and she had been drinking alcohol. Is that true?"

Seriously, Dave?

He had betrayed her with the partners, and now he was casting doubt on her with the cop? *Why?*

"Yes," she said, keeping her voice light. "We had a couple drinks at the bar, but that's pretty standard at an all-inclusive resort, right?"

"Of course. But it struck me as odd that you didn't mention the alcohol when you reported her missing."

Laura shrugged, casual. "Honestly, it didn't seem relevant."

"How many drinks would you say you had?"

"Two." She watched him make a note of this in his book. "Why does it matter?"

Officer Solomon shrugged, matching her casual tone. "It doesn't, necessarily. But sometimes alcohol can affect the way we remember things. Especially when it's mixed with drugs."

"I didn't do any drugs."

"Are you sure?" Officer Solomon consulted his notes. "According to David, you took a sleeping pill the night before. Is that not true?"

Fucking Dave.

Laura uncrossed and recrossed her legs. What was he trying to do, paint her as some kind of addict? She was stung but kept her voice even. She had nothing to hide.

"OK, yes, that's true. I couldn't sleep my first night here, so I went for a walk on the beach and met Diana, and she gave me a sleeping pill. And I'm glad she did, because it was the only reason I was able to fall asleep."

"Can you tell me more about your relationship with Diana?" Officer Solomon asked.

"We didn't really have a relationship. I only met her three days ago."

"You make it sound as if it was a casual friendship."

"It was."

Officer Solomon referred to his notes.

"The word David used was 'obsessive.'"

Obsessive? What the hell, Dave?

She felt a flash of fear then. Why had he thrown her under the bus? Was it to cast suspicion onto her so that he could throw it off himself? But why did he feel the need for self-preservation? He didn't even know Diana. She watched Officer Solomon make a note in his book. Then she recalled that Dave had, unbeknownst to her, spoken to Diana.

"What did Dave and Diana talk about?" she asked.

"I would prefer to focus on you and Diana," Officer Solomon said. "David told me that you were fixated on the fact that she came to the island alone."

Laura studied Officer Solomon for clues, but his inscrutable face betrayed nothing. Still, his coyness made her think he knew more than he was letting on.

"I mean, it definitely seemed weird to me that a woman would choose to come to a romantic couples' resort by herself," she said. "I probably talked about it more than I should have, but I wouldn't say I was obsessed with her."

"But you did enter her cabin when she wasn't present; is that correct?" he asked.

Laura felt the little hairs on her arms stand up. Dave must have told him this too.

"Yes. Because I was looking for her," she said.

"Are you aware that it is illegal to enter another guest's cabin without their permission?" he asked.

She felt her entire body tensing. His line of questioning made her think he was digging for a suspect. If that was true, it meant something bad *had* happened to Diana. Was she dead? The thought sent a chill down Laura's spine.

"I was worried about Diana. No one knew where she was."

"Did anything happen when you were inside her cabin? Anything unusual?"

"No. She wasn't there, so I left."

"Did you take anything that belonged to her?"

"No."

"No?" Officer Solomon studied Laura. "You didn't steal a bottle of her perfume?"

What was Dave's game here?

"OK, yeah. But I didn't steal it. I took it by accident," she said.

"So you did take something from her cabin."

"Yes."

"Why did you lie to me just now?" he asked.

Fuck. Laura was no longer an attorney at Reinhart, Mader & Stern, but her lawyerly instincts were still intact, and they told her she knew better than to lie to a cop. The problem was she was nervous. She wasn't used to being interrogated. Legally, she was within her rights to stop the interview or request a lawyer, but she knew that would make her look like she had something to hide. And she had nothing to hide. Still, she couldn't believe how events had conspired to land her in this situation. How had a few innocent cocktails and a hike turned into this?

"I didn't lie. I just forgot. I'm sorry."

"Why did you take it?" Officer Solomon asked.

She had taken the perfume by accident. She wasn't a creepy stalker. But she knew how details like this could be taken out of context and blown out of proportion. She had to be smart. She had to protect herself because no one else would.

"I don't know. I was just trying it on to see what it smelled like. And then I left her cabin and forgot I still had it in my hand." It embarrassed Laura to say this out loud.

"Where is it now, the perfume?"

"I still have it."

"You are also in possession of her bracelet; is that correct?"

She nodded reluctantly.

"You stole her perfume and took her bracelet. Do you think that might be why David was concerned about you?"

She shifted in her seat, uncomfortable in her damp clothes. The rain was drumming so loudly on the roof that it was giving her a headache.

"I get how it looks, but I really think he was overreacting."

Officer Solomon nodded but seemed unconvinced. He rotated his pen between his fingers. "I spoke to Freddie, by the way, and he confirmed that he saw you and Diana enter the Castaway Point Trail together."

"What about the hikers? Did you find them?" she asked.

"No, we canvassed other hotels in the area, but we couldn't identify any travelers matching their description."

Laura processed this. That meant the two hikers were still out there somewhere. If Diana had been hurt or kidnapped, it made sense that her attackers could have been the two strong men who happened to be on the cliff right before she disappeared.

"David told me about an obsessive friendship you had some years ago that ended in violence," Officer Solomon said, looking at his notes. "With someone named Chloe?"

Laura felt a rivulet of sweat trickle down her back. She'd forgotten that she had told Dave about Chloe and her broken wrist.

"My friendship with Chloe wasn't obsessive." She tried to make her voice sound neutral, but it came out sounding shrill.

"According to Dave, you have a history of obsessive relationships with women."

She hadn't told Dave much about Chloe because intense, complicated friendships didn't happen for men in the same way they did for women, so it was hard to explain. But one night over Mexican food, three weeks into their relationship, they had gotten drunk on margaritas, and she had told him how, back in high school, she and Chloe had been inseparable until they weren't. At the time, Dave hadn't seemed very interested in the story, and Laura thought he wasn't even really paying attention, but apparently, he had been listening after all. She had trusted him with one of her most intimate secrets, and he had quietly filed it away, her little shred of truth, waiting to deploy it if it ever became useful.

Her simmering anger started to boil.

"It was a long time ago," she said.

"Whatever you can remember."

"We got into a stupid fight. Chloe pushed me, and I pushed her back, and she fell and broke her wrist. It was an accident."

"In your earlier statement, you mentioned that you and Diana had an argument before she disappeared," Officer Solomon said.

"Yeah. Why does that matter?"

"It might not, but I am trying to get an accurate picture of what happened. What was the argument about?"

"I told you. It was stupid. Diana took a picture of me and posted it to my Facebook page without asking. I was annoyed, so I snapped at her. It wasn't a big deal."

"Most arguments start over stupid things, but sometimes they escalate. Like it did with Chloe."

"I feel like you're accusing me of something."

"I am simply trying to figure out what happened."

But he was focusing on the wrong thing. Diana was missing, alone in a tropical storm, and as each hour passed, the odds of finding her were diminishing rapidly. There was a very real chance it was already too late, that she was dead, maybe even murdered.

"You really think I had something to do with this?" Laura could barely hide her frustration. "You think I pushed her off the cliff or something?"

"That's not what I am saying."

But it was. With three words—*obsessive*, *friendship*, and *violence*—he was trying to establish a pattern of behavior. She knew this strategy, had seen it used in court. She had been a witness of Chloe's accident and was the last person to see Diana before she disappeared, and Officer Solomon was trying to build an analogous relationship between the two events. If there was violence in one event, it was logical to assume there might have been violence in the other. He was looking at her differently now, like she was a bad person, a criminal. The only other time she had been looked at in this way was after Chloe's wrist had been broken and everyone at school stared at her like she was a dangerous person, someone capable of violence.

"Even if I did do something bad, which I didn't, why would I come to the police station and report her missing?" Laura asked. "This doesn't make sense."

"People insert themselves in investigations for many different reasons," Officer Solomon said calmly. "Sometimes, they feel guilty about a crime they committed, and their way of managing their guilt is to become involved with the police. To appear helpful. Other people are attracted to the attention." His tone was matter of fact, as if he had come to this conclusion about her before they had even started the interview.

"And you think I'm one of those people."

"I didn't say that."

But she knew it was what he meant. It was startling how quickly perception could change, how abruptly one's reputation could be destroyed. And reputations mattered, even outside the context of high school social hierarchies. Laura had thought that by reporting Diana's disappearance to the police, she had done her civic duty, but all she had really accomplished was to put a target on her back. And Dave was using it to his advantage.

His words echoed in her mind then: *I think she's a spy*. He had said this as a joke during their silly game on their first morning at the resort, but what if it wasn't a joke? What if Diana wasn't at the Pink Sands on vacation? What if she had come on assignment? What if she *was* a spy? New panicky thoughts bubbled up: Diana's previous documentary had exposed financial crimes on Wall Street, and hadn't Dave said that

Marcus Lowry was hiding money in an offshore account? What if the Pink Sands was involved in some shady business dealings, and what if Diana was intending to make the resort the subject of her next exposé? Maybe Dave knew all this, and maybe his conversation with Diana was not nothing. Maybe it was something.

The way Dave had been so unnecessarily cruel made her think he had an ulterior motive. More panicky thoughts bubbled up, too ludicrous to believe, but she couldn't stop them now as they flooded her brain—Dave had seemed so romantic and spontaneous when he'd suggested they take a trip to Eleuthera, but was it possible their short vacation had been purposefully scheduled to overlap with Diana's stay? Was she a threat that needed to be neutralized? Was that why he hadn't been motivated to search for her? Why had he stayed at the management office for so long the day she went missing? Was it so that he would be accounted for if she disappeared? Was Carl Reyes his alibi? If some version of this was even remotely true, the one thing Dave couldn't have anticipated was Laura's burgeoning friendship with Diana. It was an unexpected complication. Was that why Dave had offered her up to Officer Solomon? After all, what better way to throw a cop off the scent than with a suspect who had a history of obsession and violence? Was that fucker trying to make her his patsy?

Her anger was roiling now. It was all she could do to contain it. Officer Solomon turned a page of his notebook, and she glimpsed a small black-and-white photo of herself. It was disturbing to see her own eyes staring back at her.

"Why do you have a copy of my passport?" she asked.

"I requested it from the concierge."

Water was starting to drip from the ceiling. The muggy air made it hard to breathe. She felt her chest constrict. Officer Solomon and Priscilla had obviously had a conversation about her behind her back. Confidential information about her had exchanged hands without her consent. It wasn't right.

"Why do you need it?" she asked.

"My job is to gather all relevant information, and since you are the last person who saw Diana before she disappeared, you are very relevant to this case. That is why I would appreciate if you would cooperate with the investigation and extend your stay for another forty-eight hours."

Laura had been a lawyer long enough to know what it meant when cops used words like *appreciate* and *cooperate*. He wasn't arresting her, but she was now a suspect in Diana's case, or at the very least a person of interest. Even though she had done nothing wrong, she knew that anything she said could be used against her. Refusing to cooperate would not help her either. If she tried to leave the island now, it would make her look like she was trying to flee because she had something to hide. Officer Solomon was acting casual, but he had probably already sent a photocopy of her passport to the airport's customs officers, to alert them in case she tried to vacate the island. He had no grounds to forcibly detain her, not without incriminating evidence, but resisting him now would only motivate him to find grounds and bring criminal charges against her. The optics were not on her side. Dave had made sure of that.

She had to be smart. She needed to play the game. Not only because she wanted to find Diana but because she now had to clear her own name. Not to mention the fact that she was stuck here, in a tropical storm. Oddly, though, for the first time in five years, she had no job to go back to. Technically, there was nowhere she needed to be on Monday morning.

"Sure." She kept her voice calm even though she was terrified. "I'm happy to help."

Outside, it was still raining heavily, and the palm trees were thrashing in the wind. Laura and Officer Solomon stood under the cabin's little awning and surveyed a stream of muddy water that had formed along the paved path and was gushing at their feet.

"For now, you should hunker down and stay dry, and this is probably the safest place on the island," Officer Solomon yelled over the wind, as he opened his umbrella. "I will be in touch." He nodded goodbye, then jumped over the stream and ran through the rain to the jeep that was parked on the far side of the path.

Laura watched him go. She couldn't afford another two nights at the Pink Sands at full price, especially now that she was unemployed. She pulled out her phone to search for alternate accommodation, but the internet was still down. She pocketed her phone. Maybe Priscilla would agree to give her a discount. She studied the rushing stream, trying to gauge if she could cross it without getting her shoes soaked. But there was no way. It was too deep and the rain was torrential, so she would be drenched no matter what.

"Fuck it," she said and, bracing herself, jumped across the stream, splashing mud onto her jeans in the process, and ran back to the white gazebo.

She climbed the slippery steps and walked straight into a group of guests huddled around the counter. They were shaking rain from their jackets and fumbling with their suitcases as Priscilla attended to their needs. They had just arrived at the resort, but because the power was out, she was checking them in manually on a clipboard. Another employee handed out complimentary glasses of rum punch to quell the wet, unhappy guests.

Laura pushed her way to the counter and caught Priscilla's eye. "I'm going to need to extend my stay," she said.

Priscilla's pristine bun had come undone, and sweat beaded her forehead. "I'm sorry, Miss Laura, but the Pineapple Festival starts tomorrow, and we've had an influx of guests, as you can see. Several departing guests have also been grounded by the storm, so unfortunately, we are completely booked up at the moment."

Laura pushed the wet hair off her face and stared at Priscilla intently, as though looking at her would change the fact that she no longer had a place to stay. "Where am I supposed to go?" she asked, panic rising in her chest.

Without looking up from her clipboard, Priscilla said, "I'm sorry, but we cannot accommodate you at this time."

This wasn't happening. She couldn't be kicked out of the hotel in the middle of a tropical storm.

"Can you call someone for me?" Laura asked.

"I would be happy to help you, but our phones are down. I'm very sorry about that."

Laura kept staring at Priscilla, waiting for her to offer some kind of solution, while the new guests jostled her to get access to the complimentary rum punch, but Priscilla said nothing more and instead handed a credit card back to a guest and asked to see his passport.

Laura had done everything they asked her to do. She had answered their questions and tolerated their judgment and even agreed to extend her stay at her own expense on this godforsaken island, and they had no room for her now? She had followed the rules, all of the rules, all of her life, and for what? What had been the point of it all? She had gotten straight A's and had gone to a good college and had gotten a good job and worked hard and paid her taxes and was nice to strangers and had never been arrested, had never even been pulled over for a speeding ticket. She was a Good Girl who followed the rules, and when someone was in danger, she had been taught that the right thing to do was to go to the police, so that was what she did. And for what? What was the point of following the rules if the result was to be treated like a criminal? She felt like she was in free fall but also like she was trapped. She couldn't leave the island, but she had nowhere to go and no one to help her. This realization caused something deep inside of her to snap, and the rage that had been simmering politely burst forth and flowed out of her like lava. Maybe everyone was right about her. Maybe Officer Solomon and Priscilla and Donald Reinhart and Dave and Chloe were right. Maybe she had spent her entire life in denial, hiding behind skirt suits and business cards and the Law, and it was all a sham. Maybe she had never been Laura Phillips | Associate | Reinhart, Mader & Stern. Maybe she had never been a Good Girl, not really. Maybe she actually was the person that everyone in her life clearly wanted her to be. Maybe everyone could see the truth as plain as day, and maybe she was the one who should stop fucking pretending. If everyone was so determined to believe the worst about her, why not give them exactly what they wanted: proof, once and for all, that she was, indeed, a criminal?

She pulled her carry-on bag out of the pile of suitcases, slung it over her shoulder, and left the white gazebo. Ignoring the relentless rain that drenched her yet again, she sloshed through the deep puddles that had formed on the path, and in one last act as an accommodating Good Girl, she pulled a complimentary white bicycle off the complimentary white bike rack, stuffed her carry-on bag into the front basket, and pedaled out the front gate and onto the road.

She turned left and headed north up Queen's Highway. She pedaled slowly at first, the wide-set handlebars wobbling in her hands, her feet slipping on the pedals. But once she gained momentum, she pedaled harder. She heard a security guard chasing her, yelling at her to stop, but she only pedaled faster without looking back.

CHAPTER ELEVEN

Laura pedaled as fast as she could up Queen's Highway, but the wind was strong, the road was slick, and she had to veer often to avoid potholes full of muddy water. She looked over her shoulder at one point and could no longer see the security guard chasing her, but she kept pedaling hard anyway, even as the rain pounded against her back and streamed down her face. Her wet hair clung to her neck, her clothes were soaked through, and she didn't know where she was going, but she was a thief now, which meant she couldn't stop.

Officer Solomon had told her to hunker down, but what he really meant was that she wasn't allowed to leave. She was trapped here, and any minute he could track her down and arrest her.

She had no way to know if Diana was dead or even murdered, but she had been missing for more than forty-eight hours, and time was ticking away.

It struck Laura then how fragile life was and how easily things could have gone a different way. Had she not gone on the hike with Diana, both of them would be fine now. Diana would be enjoying her vacation and planning her next documentary. Laura would still have her job, and her relationship would presumably still be intact, and she would be on a plane right now headed back to New York, reminiscing about her pleasant holiday. Her mother assumed she was on the flight with Dave, and Dave assumed she would be on a later flight, but neither of those things was true. It was not unlike those first few hours after Diana had disappeared, when she was unaccounted for but not yet officially missing. No one knew Laura was alone, marooned on an island in the middle of nowhere in a storm, and no one had any reason to be concerned. She had been afraid that this, or something like this, might happen to her one day, and now it had.

She kept pedaling. There was no one on the road. She felt homesick suddenly and wanted to call her mom. It had been ingrained in her that making an outgoing call in a foreign country was forbidden unless it was an emergency. This, however, felt like an emergency. But when she slowed the bike and pulled her phone out of her pocket, it had no reception. She tucked it away and kept pedaling.

Occasionally, she passed tall wrought iron gates with signs that advertised private beach resorts. The Ocean Club. Pineapple Grove. Breezes Resort & Spa. She considered stopping and inquiring about a room, but all the gates were locked due to the storm. She couldn't afford the exorbitant nightly rate, anyway, seeing as she was newly unemployed. She wondered if this was how the locals felt when they drove past these gates every day, barred entry from some of the most beautiful spots on their own island. She felt disgusted with herself, too, because what had initially appealed to her about Eleuthera was the exclusivity of the Pink Sands resort, its manicured grounds and immaculate white cabins, not the island's natural beauty.

The wind picked up, and a giant palm frond broke off a tree and fell directly in her path, forcing her to swerve. It wasn't safe out here. She needed to get out of the storm. For the first time, she felt truly scared. She was all alone and didn't know what to do. She didn't belong here. She was an outcast, with nowhere to go and no way to leave. She felt a surge of fear then and stood up in the saddle as she pedaled.

She took a deep breath and exhaled through her mouth. The rhythmic pedaling calmed her a little. She hadn't been on a bike in years and had forgotten what this felt like, pumping, then coasting, the wind in her hair. As scared as she was, there was a certain satisfaction in moving at a velocity created entirely by her own power. The last time she'd been on a bike was the summer before she started high school. She had forgotten about that summer, but as she pedaled, the memory of it came back to her in crisp detail.

That summer, it seemed like everyone she knew was traveling to Europe or overnight camp or other places where exciting, life-changing things happened, but she had nothing to do all day except bike aimlessly around town. The only consolation was that Chloe was stuck at home too. They spent every day together that summer. It was the summer before they met Jake Hollinger, the summer before the contract came between them. They didn't know it then, but that was the last summer they would spend as best friends.

One day in July, they biked down to the river. As they pushed their bikes through the underbrush that separated the bike path from the river's edge, they came upon a stony little beach. It was surrounded on all sides by trees, which made it completely hidden from view of the bike path, and the dappled sunlight that came through the leaf canopy overhead gave it a private, enchanted quality. They waded into the river up to their knees and spent the whole day casting stones into the water. In the late afternoon, when the air cooled off and the sun dipped below the trees, Laura felt a profound sadness as they pushed their bikes back onto the path. As they rode home, everything around them seemed drab and unmagical.

They returned to the spot the following day, and Chloe, who always made things more beautiful than they needed to be, brought her art supplies, and they spent the afternoon painting hearts and flowers on a large, flat boulder and stripes around the trunks of the surrounding trees. The day after that, they brought sandwiches and beads and fishing line and made necklaces, but mostly they just sunbathed and cast stones into the water. They never told anyone about the spot, partly to keep its location hidden but also because they knew that what they did there all day long was childish and they didn't want to be embarrassed. They were, after all, about to enter ninth grade at a high school that was twice as big as their middle school and too far away to bike to. So they kept the spot a secret but continued to return to it every day.

One day in August, when they pushed their bikes through the underbrush, they found the spot littered with broken beer bottles and cigarette butts and a Swiss Army knife. They wandered the site in silent shock. Laura kicked at the broken glass. The spot no longer felt enchanted. She didn't know if it had lost its magic in the act of desecration or if its discovery by others enabled her to see that there had been no magic there at all, just two foolish girls who had painted some rocks and trees. Neither of them said a word; they just pushed their bikes back onto the path and rode home in silence.

They never returned to the spot after that. They spent the remaining days of that summer at the mall instead, where they bought bus passes and shopped for back-to-school clothes. By then, their friends had come home from Europe and overnight camp with stories and nose rings and photos of long-distance boyfriends. They never told anyone about the spot. Only once, when Jake Hollinger asked what they had done all summer, Laura blurted that they used to go to a spot by the river, but Chloe dismissed it as a stupid thing they'd done and changed the subject. Laura said nothing then, but the air around her face seemed to vibrate, as if she'd just been slapped.

To Laura, her friendship with Chloe became a cautionary tale of the frightening fate that could befall a pair of binary stars, who, by orbiting each other too closely, collapsed into each other. In time, she learned to keep everyone she met safely at arm's length, never allowing herself to fall into anyone's orbit and never letting anyone get close enough to enter hers.

But with Diana, she had felt the electric hope of meeting someone with whom she could share a profound connection. Only now, Diana was most likely gone forever, murdered or lost at the bottom of the sea, her body entangled in the undulating tentacles of a coral reef.

Laura had read somewhere that Charles Darwin had been fascinated by coral reefs because of their seemingly impossible randomness, how they would appear on the ocean floor suddenly and without explanation, tiny oases teeming with life in what was otherwise a watery desert. He was mystified by how these little pockets of life could flourish in such a vast abyss of nothingness, as though fed by some unseen magic. This phenomenon so perplexed him it became known as Darwin's Paradox. More and more, it seemed to Laura that life was like this: brief moments of intense yet inexplicable connection, followed by long stretches of aching loneliness.

Laura sat back down in the saddle and coasted, wiping the wetness from her face. The wind was getting stronger, and there was no shelter anywhere. But at the same time, there were no demands on her, no expectations to be met, and this evoked in her a strange sense of freedom.

After a while, the flat road rose up, and she had to stand in the saddle and pedal hard to scale the hill. Her carry-on bag in the front basket was heavy and lopsided, though, and it caused the bike to tilt to one side, which made steering difficult. She finally crested the hill and coasted down the other side, but the steep descent made her handlebars rattle violently. She squeezed the hand brakes until her knuckles turned white, but the bike barely slowed, and she felt the paralyzing fear that accompanied a sudden loss of control. She jammed her heel on the ground, but that just caused the bike to skid off the slick road, and suddenly she was flying over the handlebars and into a ditch.

She lay on her back for an indeterminate amount of time, staring up at the gray sky, blinking back the rain that was falling in her eyes. When she finally got her bearings, she sat up and took stock of her injuries. Her wet jeans were ripped at the knees and stained with blood, and her right hand was scraped and encrusted with dirt.

She wondered if she could sue the Pink Sands for damages, since she had been injured while using one of their complimentary bicycles, but then she remembered that she had signed a liability waiver when she and Dave had checked in, and she had drafted enough contracts of adhesion to know that she had signed away her right to pursue compensation for any injuries sustained at the resort. Besides, she wasn't even on the resort's grounds, and she had stolen the bike. The fault lay entirely with her. She remembered Diana's words then: *Were you always like this? A lawyer?* But she knew what Diana actually meant was, *Were you always this fearful a person?* Laura hadn't always been this way. She remembered being young and carefree and not feeling so much fear. What had happened to her? How had she let herself become like this?

Diana wasn't fearful. She was a filmmaker who was brave enough to stand up to corruption and expose the truth. Laura admired this about her but was scared for her now. What if her courage had made her a target? What if it had gotten her killed?

Laura stood up slowly and walked over to the bike, which was lying on the ground at an odd angle. The chain had fallen off and dangled loosely. She pulled the bike upright and tried to realign the chain, but her hand kept shaking, and all she succeeded in doing was getting grease all over herself. She needed help, but there was no one. Eventually, a truck approached, but it just roared past, spraying mud, indifferent to her bloody knees and throbbing hand.

She felt hot tears streak her face and wiped them away with her arm. She didn't know why she was crying exactly. Maybe it was because she was drenched and shivering. Maybe it was because Diana was missing and likely dead. Or maybe it was because after all these years she still missed Chloe. Maybe it wasn't even Chloe she missed. Maybe it was just the magic of their friendship, which probably wasn't even magic at all but a sense of youth, her youth, which was gone now. Maybe she was grieving its loss.

Laura pulled her phone out of her pocket. The screen was a spiderweb of cracked glass, but inexplicably, she had one bar of service.

Her mother answered after the second ring.

"Laura?"

The reception was bad, and her mother's voice sounded far away and was interspersed with static, but hearing it filled Laura with relief.

"Mom?"

"Where are you?"

Laura looked around, but there were no signs or landmarks indicating her exact location. All she could see in either direction was the road disappearing into the horizon.

"I don't know."

"What do you mean? You're not back yet?"

It occurred to Laura that her mother didn't know she was stranded in a tropical storm, or that she had lost her job, or that Dave had broken up with her, or that she was involved in a missing persons investigation. She suddenly wanted to tell her mother everything, the way she used to when she was a child, when she would recount every little thing that happened between her and Chloe that day, and her mother would listen quietly and then say something like, *I never liked that girl*, and give Laura a hug and make her a snack.

"I'm still on the island." Laura tried to keep her voice even, but her words came out wobbly.

"I heard on the news there's a storm where you are. Why haven't you left yet?"

She could hear concern in her mother's voice.

"My flight was canceled."

"Is Dave OK?"

"He left earlier. We broke up."

"Why? What happened?"

Laura suddenly felt exhausted at the prospect of recounting the entire story to her mother. And she didn't know what to tell her about Dave. She didn't know what to believe. All she knew was that she was exhausted and wanted to sit down, but the ground was wet, so she paced back and forth across the highway, daring someone to drive by, but no one did.

"It's a long story."

"You're scaring me, Laura. Are you hurt?"

She studied the specks of gravel that were embedded in the flesh of her palm. It was, incidentally, the same hand that she had, three months before, sliced open with her broken wineglass while on the phone with her mother. The only evidence of that injury now was a thin white scar.

"No."

"What's going on? Are you OK?"

She felt the emotion welling in her voice. "No."

"What happened?"

She stared at the stormy sea in the distance. "Mom, why didn't you like Chloe?"

"What?"

"She was my best friend, but you never liked her."

In between the crackles of static, she heard her mother sigh. She was quiet for a long time. Finally, she said, "What I didn't like was how much you opened your heart to her and how easily you got hurt. You always let yourself get so hurt by people."

Laura wiped her nose with her arm.

"Where are you right now?" her mother asked.

"I'm outside."

"Are you crazy? You need to get out of the storm. Have you eaten today?"

"No."

"Go inside and get something to eat. You'll feel better after you eat."

No matter what Laura's problem was, food was always her mother's solution. She wondered if her mother had always been this way, or if this was something that happened when one became a parent.

"I have to stay here for another night, at least," she said. "But the resort is booked up, and I don't know what to do."

"After you eat, go find another hotel. I'm sure there are a lot of hotels there. It's a touristy island, isn't it?"

It seemed easy enough when her mother framed it this way. All she had to do was eat something and find a new place to stay. The clarity and simplicity of this objective calmed her, and she felt herself nodding and exhaling slowly through her mouth.

"OK," she said.

"Laura—"

"Mom?"

She heard a loud crackle of static and then three quick tones indicating the call had been dropped. She stared at her cracked phone, but the single bar was gone. She stuffed it back in her pocket. She flipped the bike upside down and fed the chain slowly, link by link, back onto the cogset. She turned the bike upright again and wheeled it onto the road. She wedged her carry-on bag back into the basket, climbed into the saddle, and started pedaling. Her bloody knees throbbed, but she ignored the pain and kept biking north.

The highway gradually veered inland, away from the sea. Occasionally, a truck drove past, but mostly she was alone on the road. She pedaled past fallen trees and downed power lines and giant palm fronds that were splayed like dead bodies in the road.

Eventually, a small building came into view. It was painted lime green and had a white wraparound porch and a billboard that said *Conchy Joe's Motel & Restaurant*. A sign in the window said *Open*, so Laura leaned her bike against the railing, grabbed her carry-on, and headed inside.

It was a relief to be out of the rain, but it took a minute for Laura's eyes to adjust to the relative darkness of the restaurant. Ten tables were arranged in two rows, and several of them were occupied by families, both tourists and locals, eating platters of fried food. Laura made her way to an empty table at the back and sat down.

The laminated menu on the table said *Conchy Joe's—Come as a guest, leave as family*, and the offerings consisted exclusively of conch-themed dishes: fried conch, conch salad, conch fritters, and something called conch bites, which Laura assumed were like conch fritters but smaller. Fittingly, every windowsill and available surface was decorated with a conch shell. A waitress approached and wiped down Laura's table with a damp rag even though it was already clean.

"I see you got caught in the storm," she said.

Laura nodded and dried her face with a napkin. "I'm so glad you're open."

"The current is down most every place on the island, but we've got a generator." She nodded at the other diners. "People been comin' from all around for a hot meal." She tucked the rag into the sash of her apron and pulled a pad and pencil out of her pocket. "What can I get you?"

Laura had resisted trying conch out of fear and revulsion, but faced with hunger and no other options, she ordered conch fritters and a Diet Coke. The waitress nodded, then disappeared behind a door that Laura assumed led to the kitchen. As she waited for her meal to arrive, she glanced at the other diners and became acutely aware that she was the only person in the restaurant who was sitting alone. There was nowhere to hide and no dark beach to skulk off to, so to avoid making eye contact with anyone, she picked up the menu and read it in its entirety three times, even though she had already placed her order. She learned from the menu that the motel was located behind the restaurant, and it offered room service, which Laura found surprising.

When she grew bored of reading, she studied the other diners. The mother at the table across from her was cutting up pieces of conch for her young son and listening to whatever her husband was saying, but she didn't meet Laura's eye. In fact, no one was looking at Laura. No one seemed to care that she was a woman dining alone. Only when she glanced out the window did she see a woman staring at her on the other side of the glass, but when she looked closer, she realized it was only her reflection.

The conch fritters arrived with a side of fries. Laura drank half of her Diet Coke in one long gulp, then bit into a fritter and felt the oil release in her mouth. She expected the conch to have a strong, fishy taste, but its flavor was surprisingly delicate, like crab. Since she was eating alone, there was no one she needed to accommodate or make conversation with, and this allowed her to focus entirely on the flavor of the food, which made for a more sensory experience. Laura felt stupid suddenly, thinking of all the tuna tataki she had missed out on in life because she had been too afraid to eat by herself.

Perhaps this was what had appealed to Diana about dining alone at the Seahorse.

She wondered if Diana was alive and if she'd found food and shelter from the storm, or if she was dead and Officer Solomon would track Laura down and interrogate her again, this time as a suspect in her murder. Laura suppressed the panicky thought and cut into another fritter. Under the crispy batter coating, the conch's flesh was gummy and white, which she supposed was to be expected, considering it was a snail from the sea. It was impressive to Laura that a creature as simple and limbless as a sea snail could build such a beautiful, ornate shell with which to protect itself from the brutality of ocean life. She had read somewhere that the longer a conch lived, the stronger and more intricate its shell became, taking on the shape and story of its life. In a way, people were no different. They all built such beautiful, ornate shells to encase their soft, fragile selves. Still, having a shell didn't seem to be enough to survive life's cruel savagery. After all, it was so easy to be destroyed. Millions of conch shells were crushed every day, pulverized by ocean waves into a fine pink powder, which gave the beaches their color. When she arrived at the resort, Laura had been awed by the pink-sand beach because of its exotic, almost surreal splendor, but its beauty, like so much of the world's beauty, was born of violent destruction.

When Laura finished her meal, she felt better, just as her mother had said she would. She signaled the waitress for the check, and when she paid it with her credit card, she asked if there was any vacancy at the motel. The waitress said yes and ushered her into an adjoining room, where she booked Laura into room number 8. Laura took the key and headed outside, where it was still raining. She walked her bike around the back of the restaurant to the strip of motel rooms, unlocked the door marked *#8*, and wheeled the bike inside.

It was a relief to close the door and lock it. She closed her eyes and exhaled, feeling the tension drain from her neck and shoulders. She was inside. She was safe. She opened her eyes. The room was small and spare but clean. There were no orchids or teak armchairs, just a queen-size bed and a small TV. The walls were painted the same lime-green color as the exterior of the restaurant, with curtains and bedspread and pillows to match. Laura set her phone down on the nightstand, pulled off her wet clothes, and headed into the bathroom. There was no double vanity or rainforest showerhead, just a narrow tub with an old shower curtain, but the water was hot and the pressure was strong, and Laura stood under the stream until her skin turned red and raw.

Afterward, she dried herself off and dug some Band-Aids out of her makeup bag and applied them to her wounds. She pulled on a fresh T-shirt and boxer shorts and slid into bed. It felt good to be warm and dry. It felt good to be lying down. There was serenity in her basic needs being met. She was weary from biking and felt as though all her emotions had been wrung from her body and all that was left of her was skin and bones. She couldn't go home, and if Diana was dead, the authorities would come for her, and there was nothing she could do. So she closed her eyes. There was a sweet release in the act of surrender. Before she knew it, she felt her limbs grow leaden and she fell asleep.

When she awoke, the room was dark, so she assumed it was the middle of the night. She groped blindly for her phone, and when she felt its familiar shape on the nightstand, she held it up to her face. The bright light from the screen made her squint: it was 9:47 a.m. She had slept through the entire night. It only seemed dark out because the drapes on the windows were blocking the daylight. She rubbed her eyes. She couldn't remember the last time she had slept through an entire night in a bed that wasn't her own.

She tried to check her email on her phone, but the internet was still down. She climbed out of bed and pulled back the curtain. The sky was blue and cloudless. A man was picking up fallen palm fronds that were scattered across the parking lot. Laura headed into the bathroom and took a shower. Afterward, she pulled on a tank top and her shorts, which had dried overnight, and headed to the restaurant for breakfast.

Inside the restaurant, two older men were drinking coffee at the bar, and the waitress who had served Laura the night before was wiping the laminated menus with a rag. Laura sat at the same table where she had eaten dinner the day before, and when the waitress came to take her order, she requested eggs, toast, and coffee. While she waited, she noticed on the table next to hers a slim, folded newspaper called the *Eleutheran*. On the front page, next to a story about the storm, there was a photo of Diana and a headline that read, *American Tourist Goes Missing at Castaway Point*. Laura picked up the newspaper.

Police are seeking the public's assistance in locating Diana Casey, a 35-year-old American woman who went missing on June 5. Casey, who is described as a Caucasian female about five feet seven in height, was last seen around 1:00 p.m. on the Castaway Point Trail wearing blue jean shorts and a white top. She was a guest of the Pink Sands resort. Police are appealing to anyone with information regarding her whereabouts.

Laura studied Diana's smiling face, which had been cropped, it seemed, from a larger group photo. She wondered how many other people were reading the article right now and if this new public awareness would result in a fresh lead. It was reassuring to know the story was out there, but it was also chilling because Laura, having read countless stories like this one over the course of her life, knew how most of them ended.

The waitress returned with her breakfast.

"You going to the Pineapple Festival?" she asked, topping up Laura's coffee.

"I don't think so," Laura said. She wanted to go home, but she wasn't allowed to. She was mad at Dave and mad at the world, and she had no desire to go anywhere else, least of all to a festival full of happy people. She wanted to go back to bed.

"The storm ended just in time. The festival's going to be a jam-up," the waitress said and walked away.

Laura ate her breakfast and sipped her coffee slowly, rereading the article several times. When she finished her meal, she paid her bill, rolled up the newspaper, and stuffed it in her back pocket. On her way out, she caught a woman staring at her from a table by the door.

"I know you." It was Wifey. She was smiling brightly at Laura. "You were staying at the Pink Sands."

"I was," Laura said, momentarily blindsided. It was jarring to see Wifey in a context outside the resort.

"I knew it. See, hon? I was right." Wifey looked over at Hubs, who was sitting across the table, perusing the menu. Hubs looked up and smiled vacantly at Laura.

"That was quite the storm yesterday, huh?" Wifey said.

Laura nodded. "It was pretty bad."

"At the resort, they told us we had to come here because this place has the best conch on the island," Wifey said.

"The food here is great," Laura confirmed, as if she were suddenly an expert in conch.

"Where's that beautiful man you were with?" Wifey asked, looking behind Laura for evidence of Dave.

"Oh, he's still sleeping," Laura said reflexively, then grew embarrassed. She didn't know why she felt the need to lie to a complete stranger.

"Well, you'd better wake him up and get down to the Pineapple Festival," Wifey insisted. "We just came from there, and it was awesome."

Laura glanced at the door, which was only a few feet away, trying to determine how she was going to extricate herself from this conversation.

"They have the most amazing grilled pineapple you've ever had in your life," Wifey continued. "I posted a pic on my Insta." She pulled out her phone.

"The internet's back?" Laura asked, shocked.

"Just came back a little while ago, thank God. Being off my socials sent me into a panic. My hubby can vouch." Wifey nodded at Hubs. Hubs smiled and rolled his eyes at Laura, then resumed reading the menu.

Laura pulled out her phone and checked her email, and sure enough, her inbox was filled with unread messages. A wave of relief washed over her body. It was as though she had been adrift at sea and the internet were a giant passing ship that had rescued her.

Normally, she swatted at spam emails like unwanted flies, but now she luxuriated in the stream of promotional ads that flooded her inbox. To be bombarded by data traveling at invisibly high speeds reminded her of being in New York, and she felt a pang of homesickness. But as she scrolled, she found no emails from Dave. She'd assumed he would touch base when he got back to New York, but there were no missed calls or texts from him either. Was he avoiding her? She felt a flash of anger then and checked his social media. He hadn't posted anything since they'd left New York. In fact, there was no evidence on the internet that he'd even gone on a trip with her. It was weird. What was he trying to hide?

She flicked to her own Facebook page and saw the photo Diana had taken of her on the limestone cliff. She was smiling, hands on her hips, the Caribbean Sea unfurling behind her. It was surreal looking at the photo now, in that it was a snapshot of a reality that was no longer her reality. Nothing she'd had in the moment that photo was taken was hers any longer. Everything—her job, her boyfriend, her place in the world, Diana—was gone, and she felt bereft. Even the pristine beauty of the island captured in the photo had been muddied by the storm. All of it was a lie.

"Found it," Wifey said cheerily and held up her phone.

Laura politely took Wifey's phone in her hand. In the photo, Wifey was smiling and holding up a spear of grilled pineapple.

"Doesn't that look amazing?" Wifey asked.

Laura nodded absently, and then something caught her eye. In the photo, a woman was standing in the background. She was looking off camera, unaware that her photo was being taken. A shiver ran down Laura's spine. The woman had wavy brown hair cut to her chin, and she was wearing denim cutoffs over a black bathing suit.

CHAPTER TWELVE

Diana was alive. She was here on the island. This information played over and over in Laura's head like a drumbeat. Diana was alive, which meant she hadn't fallen off the limestone cliff and drowned. Diana was alive, which meant she hadn't been abducted by the hikers or killed in some conspiracy orchestrated by Marcus Lowry. Diana was at the Pineapple Festival, which meant Laura was no longer a suspect in her potential murder. Sweet relief washed over her, both for Diana and for herself because she was no longer under suspicion. She couldn't wait to see Diana with her own eyes, to verify that she was, indeed, OK. But the more she thought about her sudden reappearance, the stranger it seemed. What had happened to her? Where had she gone? Why had her bracelet been abandoned on the cliff? Whatever the truth was, Laura was determined to track her down and confront her face-to-face.

The photo on Wifey's Instagram page had only been taken an hour ago, which meant there was a chance Diana was still at the Pineapple Festival.

"Where is this place?" she asked, handing Wifey back her phone.

"The fairgrounds are just south of Gregory Town. You can't miss it."

"Thanks," Laura said and headed outside.

"Have fun!" Wifey said.

Laura ran back to her room and wheeled the bike outside. She climbed on and pedaled across the parking lot and turned left, heading south. She saw evidence of the storm as she biked down Queen's Highway, workers fixing downed power lines, uprooted trees with their gnarled roots exposed, but the road had dried overnight, and the muddy water had evaporated from all the potholes. There were no cars on the road; the sea was her only companion. The waves glittered in the sunlight, almost too bright to look at, rising, then falling away.

When the sign for Gregory Town appeared, she turned onto the narrower, crumbling road she had walked two days before. She passed the candy-colored houses and the single-pump gas station and the small general store. When she passed the police station, she felt a flash of fear, but then she remembered that Diana was alive, which meant Laura was no longer a suspect in her disappearance. The surge of adrenaline she felt then pushed her up out of the saddle, and she pedaled as fast as she could.

People were milling in the street, all walking in the same direction. The aroma of grilling meat signaled to Laura that she was getting close, and after she crested a hill, she came upon a large field filled with white tents. Cars were parked on either side of the road, and throngs of people were milling around an open gate, over which a banner was strung that said *Eleuthera Pineapple Festival*. Two large cardboard pineapples smiling and wearing sunglasses were hoisted on either side of the banner.

Laura jogged the bike through the gate and onto the fairgrounds, scanning the faces in the crowd. Locals and tourists, young and old, were talking and laughing and standing in line for barbecue. Children ran past her, shrieking and squirting water guns. She spotted Javarro and a few of the other staff members from the Pink Sands drinking beer by a large stage, where a band was setting up.

Laura made a lap of the grounds, scouring every tent, but the longer she searched, the more she felt a growing sense of dread that Diana had, once again, slipped out of her grasp. She finally spotted the tent from Wifey's photo, where three women were grilling spears of pineapple on a barbecue.

"Excuse me," Laura said, approaching.

"Would you like to try?" One of the women held out a plate of samples.

Laura accepted a piece and bit into it. It was warm and sweet and slightly smoky.

"Thank you," she said, and pulling the newspaper out of her back pocket, she showed the woman the photo of Diana. "I'm looking for my friend. Have you seen her?"

The woman studied the photo, then shook her head. "No. But they might be able to help you."

She gestured at a group of police officers who were clustered around a grill station, eating barbecue chicken. Laura recognized Officer Solomon right away because he was the tallest of the group. He was decked out in formal police regalia and wearing the hat he had been carrying the day before, the black-and-white one with the red band.

"Officer Solomon?"

He turned and smiled when he saw Laura. "Good afternoon, Laura. I've been looking for you."

"Diana's here. At the festival. At least, she was earlier today."

Officer Solomon set down his plate and wiped his fingers on a paper napkin. "I was trying to find you," he said, "but when I went by the Pink Sands this morning, Priscilla said you were no longer staying there."

"They were fully booked, so I had to find another place."

"Where are you staying now?"

The band on the stage started playing Junkanoo music, and Laura had to raise her voice to be heard over the drumming.

"Conchy Joe's Motel," she said.

"Ah." Officer Solomon laughed to himself. "I'm sure it is quite different from what you were used to at the Pink Sands. How are you liking it?"

Laura didn't know why Officer Solomon was being so calm and chatty. She had just told him that Diana was very much alive and very likely close by.

"It's fine. And apparently, so is Diana," she said.

"That is why I have been trying to reach you," Officer Solomon said. "The current was fixed earlier today, and I was able to get in touch with Diana. She got back to the island last night."

Laura tried to absorb what Officer Solomon was saying, but his words didn't make any sense. *When she got back to the island?* When had she left the island? The drumming intensified then, and people started migrating toward the stage.

"What happened?" she asked. "Where was she?"

"My understanding is that she went to Abaco but got waylaid because of the storm."

"Abaco?" Laura felt her right eye begin to twitch, which was something that happened right before a headache set in. What did Abaco have to do with Diana's broken bracelet? Or the hikers?

"It's one of our neighboring islands. They lost power before we did, so she couldn't be reached by phone."

Laura suddenly recalled Diana standing on the edge of the limestone cliff, pointing at an island on the horizon: *You can even see Abaco from here.* Laura supposed it was conceivable that Diana had left Eleuthera and gotten marooned on Abaco during the storm. It made some sense, but there was a gap in the timeline: Officer Solomon's explanation didn't account for why Diana had disappeared during their hike. What Laura needed was information from the source. She needed to track Diana down and put it to her directly and extract the truth.

"Where is she now?" Laura asked.

"It's my understanding that she left this morning on a flight back to the US."

"I thought all the flights were canceled."

"I believe they are back in service now."

Laura stared at Officer Solomon. Was Diana really gone? She hadn't put on any sunscreen, and it felt like the hot sun was boring a hole in the top of her head. Her right eye was twitching, and her forehead throbbed. A bad headache was coming on. She glanced at all the people milling around the fairgrounds, laughing and dancing and eating grilled pineapple. She swallowed hard, nauseated suddenly.

"I'm grateful that you agreed to extend your stay, but since Diana is now accounted for, the case is closed and you are free to go home," Officer Solomon said. He nodded at Laura's bike. "Priscilla told me that you borrowed one of the bicycles from the Pink Sands. I am sure she would appreciate if you returned it before you leave the island."

Laura nodded, embarrassed, but said nothing. Her search had proved futile, and now she wouldn't even get any closure. She would have to live the rest of her life never knowing why Diana had chosen to abandon her at the top of the limestone cliff. Dejected, she climbed back onto the bike and pedaled away.

When she arrived at the Pink Sands, the white gate was open, and the security guard was talking to a taxi driver, who was leaning against his cab. Laura climbed off the bike and deposited it back on the white bike rack. She caught the security guard's eye and nodded politely. It took him a moment to recognize her, but when he did, his gaze turned suspicious. Only when he registered that the bike had been returned to its proper place did he resume talking to the cabbie.

Priscilla was at her post in the white gazebo, checking in a young couple on her computer. They were visibly in love, touching each other constantly and chatting delightedly about their vacation that was about to unfold. Laura could barely look at them. Priscilla's hair was back in its pristine bun, her silk blouse looked fresh and unwrinkled, and there was no trace of sweat on her brow. Laura watched as she unfolded a map of the resort and circled the gym, the spa, and the Wi-Fi password before handing the couple a set of cabin keys.

"Hi, Priscilla," she said after the couple left.

"Laura." Priscilla looked surprised to see her. "What can I do for you?" she asked, wary.

"I just wanted to let you know I brought back the bike." Laura gestured vaguely in the direction of the main gate.

"Thank you. I appreciate that," Priscilla said. "Did Officer Solomon find you?"

"He did. I heard the good news about Diana."

"Yes, it's good news, indeed," Priscilla said. She went back to her computer, then paused and looked at Laura. "She left for the airport a little while ago."

Laura stared at Priscilla, thinking that perhaps she had misheard. "Officer Solomon said she flew out this morning."

Priscilla shook her head and punched some keys on her computer. "No, she was scheduled to leave this morning, but her flight was delayed. It's now due to depart at noon." She looked at Laura intently. "There's a taxi outside. If you hurry, you might still catch her."

Priscilla had been chilly with her all week, so Laura didn't know why she was being helpful now. She checked the time on her phone. 11:12 a.m.

"Thank you," she said and bounded down the gazebo steps.

"Make sure to tell the driver to go to Governor's Harbour Airport, not North Eleuthera Airport or Rock Sound!" Priscilla called after her.

"OK!" Laura shouted over her shoulder. Why a tiny island like Eleuthera had three airports was beyond the scope of Laura's understanding, but she ran to the cabbie, who was still chatting with the security guard, and asked him to take her to Governor's Harbour Airport.

"No bags?" the driver asked.

"No bags," Laura said as she scrambled into the back seat. She'd left her carry-on at Conchy Joe's.

The driver slid into the front seat, and they drove through the open gate. As they sped down Queen's Highway, Laura mapped the airport on her phone. It would be a thirty-five-minute drive. That would still give her a few minutes to find Diana before her flight took off.

But as they neared Gregory Town, they hit traffic, and the taxi slowed to a snail's pace. Laura stared at the line of cars in front of them, honking and blasting Junkanoo music.

"I'm in a rush," she said. "Can you take another route?"

"This is the only road to the airport, miss," the driver said.

"Can you go any faster then? Please? It's important."

"I'm afraid not, miss. It's a jam-up because of the Pineapple Festival. Have you been?"

"I was there this morning," Laura said, squeezing her phone like a stress ball.

"Good eats and good tunes," the driver said, nodding his head to the music that wafted from the other cars through his open window.

Laura checked the time again. 11:32 a.m. "I really can't be late. Is there anything you can do?"

"Relax, miss. You're on Bahamian time." The driver smiled at her in the rearview mirror, but Laura did not smile back. She was sick of being told to relax. She was sick of being on Bahamian time. This was her last chance to find Diana, and the stupid Pineapple Festival traffic was going to blow it for her. She glared out the window at the cars blasting music, at the people walking down the highway, all heading in the direction of the festival. They looked so goddamn happy. She hated them all.

When they finally arrived at the airport, Laura paid the driver and raced into the tiny terminal, straight into a crush of tourists in Hawaiian shirts. She checked her phone. 12:04 p.m. It was too late. She had come all this way only to miss Diana by four minutes.

The tourists brushed past, jostling her with their bulky suitcases, and she felt a roiling anger build inside her. She wanted to scream. She hated all the stupid tourists with their stupid fedoras and boxes of Caribbean rum. She hated all the souvenir stores with their tacky key chains and bags of beef jerky. Her right eye was twitching very badly now, and her throbbing headache was exacerbated by the annoying yellow light flashing on a TV monitor that was suspended from the ceiling.

She squinted up at the screen. It listed all the day's flights. One was departing for Fort Lauderdale at 2:40 p.m. from gate two, and another was departing for Atlanta at 3:15 p.m. from gate three. Yet another had been scheduled to depart for Miami at 12:00 p.m. from gate one, but it was flashing yellow. Laura swallowed hard. The flight to Miami was the only flight that had been scheduled to depart at noon. It had to be Diana's flight.

Laura ran up to a woman who was wearing what looked like an official airport uniform.

"What does the yellow flashing light mean?" she asked, pointing up at the TV screen.

"It means the plane was leg short," the woman said.

"Leg short?" Laura asked.

"It arrived late from its previous destination."

"Does that mean the flight to Miami is delayed?"

"No, it's on time."

Laura stared at the woman, confused. "How is it on time?"

"It's on *Bahamian* time," the woman said and laughed.

Laura ran to the door with the number one painted above it on the far side of the terminal, thankful for once to be on Bahamian time. The door led out to a tarmac, where a small propeller plane was being loaded with suitcases. The door of the plane was open, and a mobile stairway was being rolled beneath it. There was a bench to one side where a handful of people sat waiting, and behind them another group of people stood, also waiting. Some of them were wearing hats, others carried boxes of rum, and almost all of them had sunburns. A woman was standing off to the side, alone.

"Diana!"

Laura ran to her, but Diana was wearing earbuds and couldn't hear her. It was only when Laura stepped directly in her sight line and waved that Diana pulled out her earbuds.

"Oh. Hey." She sounded more confused than surprised. "Are you on this flight?"

"No," Laura said, catching her breath.

It was surreal to see her. Alive. In the flesh.

"Are you OK?" Laura asked.

"What? Yeah. I'm fine."

Laura watched Diana slip her earbuds into their small white case and put the case in her pocket. It was strange how calm she seemed, considering the series of events that had transpired.

"I'm so glad I found you," Laura said. "I thought you were kidnapped or, I don't know, dead."

Diana's brow knitted in disturbed confusion. "Why would you think I was dead?"

"You know the police were looking for you, right?" Laura said.

"I heard," Diana said. "I've never been reported missing before, so that was new."

The tinge of sarcasm in her voice confused Laura. This was not the reaction she had expected.

"I didn't know what else to do when you disappeared," Laura said.

"Wait—*you're* the one who reported me missing?" Diana asked, surprised. "They said someone from the resort went into my cabin, but . . ." She looked at Laura curiously. "That was you, wasn't it?"

Laura fidgeted, growing defensive. "I was worried about you. I mean, on our hike, I went to pee, and when I came back, you were gone. Where did you go?"

Diana shouldered her backpack. "I left."

"You . . . left?" Laura asked.

Diana nodded. As if it were no big deal. As if it were the most natural thing in the world.

It was the simplest explanation for her disappearance, but it had seemed too cruel for Laura to consider seriously. Yet there it was: the truth. Diana hadn't drowned or been kidnapped or murdered in any kind of lurid way worthy of a cover story in *People* magazine. She had simply abandoned Laura on a cliff in the middle of nowhere.

"But what about this?" Laura asked, digging the bracelet out of her pocket.

Diana's eyes lit up. "Where did you find it?" she asked, taking the bracelet.

"On the trail, by the edge of the cliff."

"Thank you so much." Diana smiled, softening. "Seriously," she said and touched Laura's arm.

"The clasp's broken," Laura said. "I thought something bad happened."

Diana fiddled with the clasp. "Yeah, I've been meaning to get it fixed."

"So it just fell off?"

"I guess so. I thought I lost it."

A voice came over the PA system, announcing that boarding would commence shortly. The travelers began forming a line.

Laura blinked repeatedly, as though there were dirt caught in her eye. "I don't understand. Why did you leave?"

Diana adjusted the straps of her backpack. "Look, I thought you were cool, so I invited you on a hike. But then you picked a fight with me. So I left."

Laura felt the urge to slap Diana across the face. "You could have said something, you know. Before you left me on that cliff."

"You're right. I should have. I'm sorry."

But Diana didn't seem sorry. She seemed impatient, ready to board her plane.

"I mean, you came here all alone, and then you just disappeared," Laura said. "And then I saw one of the hikers wearing that T-shirt you bought. What was I supposed to think?"

"Oh yeah, I passed those guys on the trail," Diana said. "They were really sunburned, so"—she shrugged—"I gave one of them the shirt."

"But you said that you had to get away," Laura said, scrambling for evidence. "You said you were being watched. Those were your words. I mean, who deletes their social media and then leaves the country a week later?"

Diana studied Laura, growing concerned. "You were really worried about me."

Embarrassed, Laura avoided Diana's eye and watched the two airport workers slam the cargo door shut and push the empty luggage cart away.

"I don't remember if I told you, but I'm a documentary filmmaker," Diana said.

"I know," Laura said. "I googled you."

If Diana was disturbed that Laura had googled her, she didn't let on. "OK, well, last week, I finished editing a doc about the NSA, and I was exhausted, and all I could think about was taking a vacation on a beach somewhere. And working nonstop for a year on a project about the surveillance state made me a little paranoid, so I deleted my socials."

A voice came over the PA system, inviting passengers to begin boarding. Diana moved to the back of the line.

"Why'd you go to Abaco?" Laura asked, following her. "The cop said you got stuck there because of the storm."

"Yeah, we lost power and had to cancel our fishing trip because the surf was too high."

"We?"

"Me and Aito."

"Aito?"

"Nakamura."

"The sushi chef?"

Diana nodded.

Laura stared at her, baffled. "You went on a fishing trip with the sushi chef from the resort?"

"He had a day off and was going fishing off Abaco, and when I told him I always wanted to spear a bluefin, he invited me to come along and catch my own dinner."

Laura recalled Diana's words then: *I hear it's a great spot for bluefin.*

"What did you talk about with my boyfriend?" Laura asked.

"Your boyfriend?" Diana pulled her boarding pass out of her pocket and flattened it against her leg.

"The guy I was with. He said you had a conversation. What did you talk about?"

Diana shrugged. "Nothing. He bumped into me in the pool and thought I was you."

Laura felt so much anger in that moment, but there was nowhere to put it. The line inched forward.

"Look, I know you're pissed—"

"Yeah, I'm pissed. You ghosted me on a cliff."

"That's not what I mean," Diana said curtly. "I think you're angry that I came here alone."

"I'm not mad about that."

Diana opened her passport to the photo page and tucked her boarding pass inside. "Are you sure? Maybe you're mad that nothing bad happened to me."

"That's insane."

"Really? Because it sounds like it was easier to believe I was dead in a ditch, but apparently, the most radical thing in the world is that I, a woman on vacation alone, am fine. And now that you see that I'm fine, maybe you're angry that you were so afraid."

"I'm angry because you abandoned me!"

The voice came over the PA system, announcing a final boarding call.

"Well, forgive me if I wanted a week to myself where I didn't have to deal with someone else's trauma," Diana said, moving toward the gate agent.

"What trauma?" Laura said, following her.

"You and your friend. That girl you grew up with."

"What does any of this have to do with Chloe?"

Diana turned and stared at Laura. "Can I ask you something? In all the years since you last saw her, you never reached out to her, right?"

Laura shook her head.

"And yet you spent your entire vacation running around the island trying to find me, someone you barely know. Do you see how fucked up that is?"

Laura didn't know what to say.

"Why didn't you ever call her?" Diana asked.

"I don't know," Laura said.

Diana handed her passport and boarding pass to the gate agent.

"Well, if you don't know, I guess you'll never understand why I did what I did."

"What does that mean?" Laura asked.

"Have a nice life, Laura," Diana said.

Laura watched Diana walk across the tarmac and up the mobile stairway and onto the plane. *You'll never understand why I did what I did?* What the hell did that mean? Part of her wanted to board the plane and punch Diana in the face. But another part of her never wanted to see Diana again. How much better things would have been had they never met. She had upended her entire life for a woman she barely knew, and for what? Diana had never been a victim. It was Laura whose life had been stripped away. It was Laura who'd been the victim all along.

The plane door was shut and the mobile stairway rolled away, but Laura didn't stay to watch the plane taxi down the runway. As the propellers roared to life, she turned and walked through the gate and across the tiny terminal and outside. She hailed a cab and told the driver to take her back to Conchy Joe's.

As she sat in the back seat, she leaned her head against the headrest. What was wrong with her? How had she misread Diana so badly? How could she have been so wrong about Dave? Normal people didn't lose their jobs and boyfriends and initiate missing persons investigations. Maybe her mother was right all along. Maybe Laura had bad judgment and trusted the wrong people.

Strangely, though, she hadn't really given much thought to her job, and she didn't miss Dave at all. In fact, she didn't even miss her old life that much either. Truthfully, it had never really felt like her life to begin with. Even when she had first started dating Dave and it seemed like the pieces of her life were starting to fall into place, she had felt like a spectator watching it happen, as though all the trappings associated with it belonged to someone else. And now, seeing how easily it could all fall apart and yet how little she missed it, she felt overcome by a new feeling, a sense of meaninglessness that seemed to hang over everything like a fog. She was free to leave now, but she didn't feel like she had a home to go back to. She had an apartment, but it seemed far away and not at all like a home.

She stared out the window at the passing coastline. It occurred to her that she could stay on the island and live a quiet, monastic life. By day, she could take long walks along the cliffs, and at night she could sleep under the stars. People back home might ask what had happened to that promising young lawyer, but time would pass, and people would forget, and life would move on. Gradually, stories would develop about the mysterious woman who lived on the island alone, and over time those stories would turn into legend and eventually into myth.

The taxi arrived at Conchy Joe's. When she got out of the car, she saw a throng of people gathered on the wraparound porch and on either side of the road, waving and cheering at a caravan of pickup trucks that was rolling slowly in her direction. It looked like some kind of parade. As it drew nearer, Laura observed that in the bed of each truck, a teenage girl was standing in a ball gown, smiling and waving at the crowd. The girls looked about fifteen, and they all had their hair and nails and makeup done, and they were all wearing sashes across their chests that said *Junior Miss Pineapple Pageant*. It was then that Laura recognized the driver of one of the trucks—it was Freddie. He had one arm bent out the open window and was smiling proudly, his yellow teeth shining in the sunlight. It disturbed her that the flatbed of Freddie's truck could showcase stacks of T-shirts for sale one day but display his daughter the next. Laura felt a sudden urge to scoop up all the girls and drive away, as far as they could get.

And yet the way the girls were standing there in their billowing gowns, they resembled something classic and eternal, like ancient Greek statuary. They seemed to glide down the road fearlessly, with innate confidence, and this reminded Laura of both Chloe and Diana. These girls didn't know what was to become of their lives, but they didn't need to know, and this liberated them, allowing them to walk their paths blindly, as was meant to be.

Laura headed into her motel room and shut the door. She sat down on the lime-green bed and opened her laptop and rebooked her flight to New York. Then she went into the bathroom, turned on the shower, and stood under the hot water until her fingertips pruned. Afterward, she dried her hair and packed her things. The bed had been neatly made in her absence, and it felt nice to pull back the coverlet and slide between the cool sheets. She called room service and ordered conch fritters and a Diet Coke, and when her meal arrived, she ate it in bed, her damp hair making a wet spot on the pillow. When she was finished, she set an alarm on her phone and went to sleep.

The next morning, she awoke before her alarm. She showered and dressed, carried her bag out of the room, and locked the door behind her. She returned the key to the waitress, who was in the restaurant setting the tables for breakfast. She ordered a cup of coffee and called a taxi, and she drank the coffee while she waited. When the taxi arrived, she placed her carry-on bag on the seat next to her and sat in silence for the duration of the ride.

As the cab sped north along Queen's Highway, Laura barely registered the Great Bahama Bank out her window, but at one point, the island narrowed into an isthmus that was barely thirty feet across, and while the turquoise shallows remained visible out her left window, the dark-blue waters of the Atlantic Ocean became visible out her right window as well.

"Can you stop, please?" Laura asked the driver.

The cabbie nodded and pulled over. Laura climbed out and walked along the narrow strip of road, which seemed to be the only thing keeping the two massive bodies of water from spilling into each other and blending their colors like paint. Laura realized she was standing on the Glass Window Bridge, the Narrowest Place on Earth.

Besides the taxi, there were no other cars or buildings or people visible in either direction, and the lack of civilization on either side of the bridge evoked in Laura a sense of timelessness, as though her view were the same view that Winslow Homer had seen almost 150 years ago when he had rendered the bridge in his famous painting. The only difference was that the natural stone arch depicted in Homer's work had been destroyed in a hurricane some decades earlier and had been replaced by a land bridge made of reinforced concrete. Some years later, that bridge had also been destroyed in a hurricane and had been rebuilt again and destroyed again and rebuilt again. The existing concrete bridge was not as elegant or whimsical as the original stone arch, but there was something beautiful about the fact that every time the bridge had been destroyed, the islanders had rebuilt it. The effort seemed so Sisyphean, so futile, and yet the islanders did it anyway and would continue to do it for years to come, in order to keep the two parts of the island connected, so that they wouldn't lose touch and drift apart.

When Laura arrived at the airport, she carried her bag to her gate and then onto the plane. When the plane took off, she watched the island of Eleuthera grow smaller and smaller through her porthole window, until it looked tiny and abstract, like an angular fishhook wedged between the Atlantic Ocean and the Caribbean Sea. She gazed at it until it disappeared beneath a sea of white clouds.

It was raining when she landed in New York. The chaotic street noise was amplified by the sound of cars splashing through puddles. After becoming accustomed to the serenity of the island, the speed and energy of the city jangled her nerves. She felt as though she'd been swept into a cold, fast-moving current.

She took a Lyft to her building, and when she stepped inside her apartment, she closed the door and locked it, and for the first time since leaving the island, she was enveloped once again in silence. The only sound was the rain, which streaked across the living room windows and drummed quietly on the balcony railing. She set her carry-on bag on the floor and poured herself a glass of water and moved through her apartment cautiously, as though she were a guest in someone else's home. Her apartment was decorated with beautiful things that she had carefully selected to reflect her taste and sensibility, but they seemed alien and generic to her now, like props on a film set that had been chosen by someone else.

Laura felt a sudden urge to go back to the life she had been living before, the one in which she had a job and a boyfriend, the one in which she was moving forward along a specific upward trajectory, the one in which everything made a certain kind of sense. She suddenly missed Jasmine's Lady Hangs. Friendship was better that way, when it was light and superficial, scheduled once a month between the hours of 7:00 and 10:00 p.m. But she couldn't go back to that life now, and even if she tried, she knew she wouldn't fit into it anymore. Perhaps she never had. So perhaps she was better off. Perhaps she was more self-sufficient than she gave herself credit for. She had, after all, been stranded on a remote island in a tropical storm and survived. Perhaps she was actually fine. Perhaps she didn't need people. Perhaps people were the source of all her pain.

This conclusion seemed to satisfy her, so she hoisted her carry-on bag onto the sofa and started to unpack her things, but she stopped when she felt a sudden ache in her gut. She didn't know what the source of this ache was. It didn't feel like sadness or grief but like something else altogether, some kind of profound yearning she could not name. Her chest felt tight and it suddenly became difficult to breathe, so she yanked open the sliding glass door and stepped out onto her balcony.

The night air felt cool on her face, and the rain was so light now it was more of a mist. On the streets below, the endless parade of cars splashed through neon-pink and blue puddles, and the streetlights cast everything in a soft, lambent glow. Laura walked over to the little bistro set, the one she had purchased at IKEA because it had looked cute, even though it had proved to be uncomfortable. She pulled back the chair, making an ugly scraping sound against the concrete, wiped away the raindrops that covered the seat like tiny silver globes, and sat down. She felt the residual wetness of the raindrops seeping through her pants, and she was starting to feel cold, but she didn't care.

On the island, she had grown accustomed to seeing the stars overhead every night, but there were no stars visible now, just the glowing lights of the city. She took a few deep breaths and waited for her heartbeat to slow. It was soothing to listen to the rain and the din of traffic below and to look out at the sea of buildings that surrounded her, all lit up. It was comforting to think that every one of those little square windows of light contained a person, and that there were millions of people all around her living in apartments just like hers, all of them silently yearning for things they could not name.

She pulled her phone out of her pocket and checked her email. Now that she was home, she would have to go to the Apple Store to get her phone fixed. The cracked screen glowed white in the darkness and forced her to squint. A notification in her inbox informed her that she had just received a new Facebook message. She tapped through to the message, and what she read next made her inhale sharply through her nose. The message was from Chloe.

I'm in NYC next weekend and I need to talk to you. Can we meet for coffee?

The words were difficult to make out on the cracked screen, so Laura read the message again to make sure she had read it right. She didn't know why Chloe had reached out to her now, after all these years, but instead of analyzing the meaning of the message, she wrote back simply,

Yes.

CHAPTER THIRTEEN

Laura awoke with a start. She didn't know where she was, but as her eyes adjusted to the darkness, she recognized the contours of the books on her nightstand and remembered that she was home. It was Monday morning. There was no sound of ocean waves out her window, just the muffled din of morning traffic. She climbed out of bed and made a cup of coffee and drank it slowly, waiting for her senses to sharpen from the caffeine. She looked out her balcony door at the tiny cars rushing on the street below. It had stopped raining in the night, and everything looked bright and crisp. Usually, she didn't have time to stare out her balcony door while she drank her morning coffee, but now that she was unemployed, time seemed to unspool in front of her, vague and featureless.

There was only one thing on her to-do list. Donald Reinhart had agreed to pay out her contract if she signed a nondisclosure agreement, which she had agreed to do in person, but now she cringed at the thought of going back to the office. She eyed Dave's maroon hoodie, which was draped over the back of a chair. She still hadn't heard from him. Did he expect her to get in touch with him now that she was back in town? Because that was not going to happen. And if he wanted his maroon hoodie back, that was too bad. As far as she was concerned, it was asshole tax. He had been an asshole, and losing his hoodie was the tax. She finished her coffee, placed her mug in the sink, and headed into the bathroom.

She turned on the faucet and let the hot water drum on her back. She had forgotten how good the water pressure was in her apartment, how plush her towels, and how familiar the scent of her shampoo. When she was finished, she toweled off and rooted through her makeup bag for her face cream, where she found Diana's travel-size bottle of perfume. The memory of Diana's abandonment washed over her anew, and she closed her fist around the tiny bottle and squeezed. She felt a sudden urge to rid herself of all evidence of Diana's existence, so she opened her fist and dropped the bottle in the trash.

Laura poured herself a bowl of cereal and ate it standing up in her kitchen. It occurred to her that it was early morning on the island, too, the time of day when the water was the calmest, a placid reflection of the sky. Javarro had probably already raked the beach and was most likely opening the white umbrellas. Even though Eleuthera was a thousand miles away, it felt vivid and close by, but by the time Laura got dressed and left her apartment and slipped into the rushing current of pedestrians on the sidewalk, her time on the island started to feel distant and remote, like a strange dream she'd had that was already starting to fade.

Since she was no longer an employee of Reinhart, Mader & Stern, she decided to wear jeans to the office instead of a business suit, hoping it would convey a sense of freedom or even defiance. She felt confident when she emerged from the subway onto Sixth Avenue, but when the familiar building came into view, she felt a tightness grip her chest. She knew, as she pushed through the rotating glass door and made her way across the marble lobby, that her absence from the office had likely been noticed by her colleagues and that they had probably asked Dave where she was. Dave had probably told everyone what had transpired with Marcus Lowry—from his point of view, of course, no doubt insinuating that the debacle had been her fault. And she knew, as she stepped into the mahogany elevator, that any attempt to counter his narrative with her own perspective would only make her look defensive. It was too late. People's minds had been made up. Dave's version of events was the one that would be believed by everyone, not least of all because, between the two of them, he was the only one who still had a job at the firm.

The elevator doors opened on the twenty-sixth floor, and Laura held her breath as she stepped into the bustling bullpen. The associates were all clustered by the coffee bar, relaying their stories of the weekend, and the paralegals flitted between the offices, their hands busy with paperwork. As Laura moved along a row of cubicles, the chatter fell silent and all eyes drifted to her. She felt like she was back in high school again, walking down the main hall as rumors swirled about the girl who'd broken Chloe Shipman's wrist. Laura kept her gaze fixed on the door at the far end of the bullpen that led to Donald Reinhart's office.

Only when she passed Dave's office did she allow herself a brief glance in his direction.

He was sitting at his desk on the phone, and he was looking at her through his open door. As angry as she was with him, she couldn't help but notice how good he looked. His hair was stylishly tousled, and he was wearing her favorite blue button-down shirt, which offset his new tan nicely. His face was contorted in a strange expression that looked equal parts surprised, embarrassed, and remorseful. But what did she know? She no longer presumed to read him with any degree of accuracy. Maybe he'd had a bad breakfast burrito and was struggling with a bout of gas.

Laura knocked on Donald Reinhart's office door, and when she heard him say, "Come in," she opened the door and stepped inside.

Donald Reinhart was sitting at his wide oak desk, writing something on a legal pad. It was only the second time she had ever been inside his office, and it was exactly as she remembered it from her first day at the firm, the same legal tomes on the same built-in bookshelves, the same bar cart in the corner.

"Yes?" he asked and looked at her blankly.

It took a moment for Laura to realize that he didn't recognize her. They hadn't had many one-on-one interactions, but considering everything that had transpired, she thought he would at least remember what she looked like. The fact that he didn't was humiliating.

"Laura. I'm here to sign the NDA," she said, waiting for him to make the connection.

"Oh, right." Recognition washed over his face, and he pushed a button on his phone. "Cynthia, can you bring in the nondisclosure agreement for Laura Phillips to sign."

He gestured at the two empty chairs across from his desk. "She'll be right in. Please have a seat."

With the muscle memory of a Good Girl, Laura perched on the very edge of the nearest chair, but when she remembered that Donald Reinhart was no longer her boss, she forced herself to sit deeper in the chair, so that its stiff wooden back touched her own.

"I'm glad you made it home safe and sound," Donald Reinhart said. "I understand the police found that woman."

"Yes, it all worked out."

"That's good to hear."

She waited for him to say something more, but he didn't. They sat awkwardly in silence until the door opened and Cynthia entered with three copies of the NDA, each one marked with yellow tabs indicating where Laura was meant to sign. As she looked over the paperwork, it occurred to her that she could refuse to sign and instead sue the firm for wrongful termination. She would have to forfeit her severance package and endure a lengthy legal battle, but it was possible that she could win. Still, the thought of having to deal with these people repulsed her, so she signed the forms in triplicate.

Donald Reinhart countersigned, and Cynthia slipped one set of pages into a folder embossed with the firm's logo and handed it to Laura.

"For your records," she said. "Also, I have a box of things from your office."

"Oh, OK," Laura said and stood up.

Donald Reinhart stood up, too, and extended his hand. "Best of luck."

They shook hands politely, as though they were friendly colleagues, as though he hadn't fired her four days before. Then he sat back down and resumed writing on his legal pad.

She followed Cynthia down the hall to her old office. Her firing had been so fast, so draconian, she assumed they would have already lined up her replacement, but she was pleased to find her office empty. She thought of all the unfinished contracts that were waiting for her. She supposed they were someone else's problem now.

Cynthia pulled a Bankers Box out from under the desk. In it, Laura recognized her black cardigan with the tortoiseshell buttons; her business cards, useless now; her framed diplomas; and the stuffed bulldog her mother had given to her at her college graduation. It was sort of sad how all her belongings fit inside a single box. She had never put much effort into decorating her office, unlike Jasmine, who had brought in a Moroccan area rug to "soften the space," two scented candles, and a framed photo of her and her boyfriend on their zip-lining trip to Costa Rica. Laura had always been envious that Jasmine had the confidence to decorate her office as though she would never leave. But now that Laura was being forced to vacate, she was grateful that she'd kept her workspace sparse because it allowed her to make her exit discreetly, with a single box under her arm.

"For what it's worth, I think you did the right thing reporting that woman to the police."

Cynthia said this quietly, as though she was fearful of being overheard. Laura didn't know Cynthia very well, largely because the executive assistants ate lunch separately from the associates, but she felt a rush of gratitude toward her in that moment.

"Thanks for that," Laura said as she accepted the box.

She headed back through the bullpen the way she'd come and made a point of not looking at Dave when she passed his office. If he wanted to talk, he would have to come to her. But he didn't move.

It was a relief when she reached the elevators, and she pressed the down button multiple times, anxiously adjusting the box under her arm. She couldn't wait to get out of there. The bell dinged, the doors opened, and two women emerged, engrossed in conversation. It was only when Laura stepped inside the elevator and turned around that she recognized one of the women was Jasmine. Jasmine recognized Laura, too, and her eyes widened with surprise.

"Laura, you're back. How *are* you?" Jasmine asked in a sympathetic, even pitying tone, as though Laura had returned to the office after a long illness rather than a beach vacation.

Without waiting for Laura's reply, Jasmine mouthed the words *We should talk* and held her hand up to her ear like it was a phone. Then she flashed the smile she reserved for new clients, all white teeth, pink lip gloss, and professional distance. Laura recognized this smile and knew the false promises it contained. She knew that Jasmine's invitation to talk was not real and that her chummy tone was just for show. She knew she would never be invited to another Lady Hang at Jasmine's condo, and she knew that as soon as the elevator doors closed, their friendship would cease to exist. She knew this because in the adult world, women didn't unfriend each other dramatically the way they did in high school. There would be no blowout fight, no crying, no theatrical ultimatum. In the adult world, friend breakups were gift wrapped in promises of future social engagements that never came to pass. Part of her wanted to call Jasmine out for her phoniness, but since this was not high school, she just smiled and nodded, signaling that she was receptive to a future gossip session, even though she knew she would probably never see Jasmine Chaudhry again.

When the doors closed and the elevator began its descent, Laura felt as though she were sinking into a morass of humiliation and defeat. Reinhart hadn't recognized her, Dave hadn't even attempted to say hello, and the interaction with Jasmine had left her feeling hollow and a bit ill. But when she stepped out of the elevator and walked across the lobby and emerged into the afternoon, a peculiar thing happened. Maybe it was the crisp spring air or the bustle of people and falafel carts on the street, or maybe it was the view of Rockefeller Center to her left or the glimpse of Central Park to her right, but the heaviness she was feeling was suddenly replaced with a buoyant lightness. She'd never realized how beautiful Sixth Avenue was, how wide and grand, and how sunlight seemed to glint off everything.

Over the next few days, Laura and Chloe exchanged a few more Facebook messages, firming up a time and place to meet. Since Chloe didn't know the city very well, they decided to meet on Saturday afternoon at a coffee shop near her SoHo hotel.

As the weekend approached, Laura went about her business, laundering her clothes and buying groceries. Ordinarily, she would have refreshed her résumé and sent out feelers for potential new jobs, but she didn't reach out to anyone. She didn't even tell her mother she was unemployed. She figured she could live off her severance for a few months and take her time figuring out her next step. She wouldn't be able to sit through a job interview now, anyway. If they asked her where she saw herself in five years, she wouldn't know what to say. She didn't even know where she saw herself in five days. She took long walks instead, around her neighborhood and to the Apple Store to get her phone fixed. She tried not to think about her and Chloe's impending reunion, but she couldn't help looking at Chloe's Facebook photos of her and her son at the farmers' market, even though she had already seen them countless times before.

When she awoke on Saturday morning, she felt anxious and slightly nauseated and spent an inordinate amount of time selecting her outfit. In high school, Chloe had always dressed so fashionably, and even though Laura hadn't seen her in years, she felt the need to impress her now. She decided on her nicest pair of jeans and a flattering V-neck top, one that she didn't wear very often but that she thought Chloe would approve of, and she washed her hair and blow-dried it straight and then used a curling iron to create loose waves around her face.

Laura was the first to arrive at the café, so she ordered a latte and sat at a table in the back corner, where she had some privacy but could also keep an eye on the door. Normally, when she waited for someone, she checked her email on her phone, but she was too nervous to concentrate, so she just observed the people at the other tables and listened to the bossa nova music that was playing over the speakers. At one point, a woman with dark hair and sunglasses entered, and Laura tensed and half stood up, but when the woman removed her sunglasses, Laura saw that it was not Chloe, so she sat back down, embarrassed.

Chloe arrived fifteen minutes later. Laura's palms instantly became moist when she saw her, and she had to wipe them on her jeans. Chloe didn't immediately spot Laura, but instead of waving to get her attention, Laura studied her quietly. Chloe was walking swiftly, in a cloud of frantic energy. She was wearing a blazer over a T-shirt and jeans. Her dark hair was still long, but her slim teenage body had been replaced with the curvier body of a woman. Only her eyes were the same. They were as luminous as ever, fringed by thick, dark lashes. Laura waved, and when Chloe spotted her, she smiled with relief and walked over to her table.

"Sorry I'm late," Chloe said when they hugged. "I had a meeting and got turned around in the subway."

"No problem."

Chloe glanced at the menu, which was handwritten in chalk on the wall. "I'm dying for a coffee. Can I get you anything?"

"I'm good," Laura said, gesturing at her latte.

"OK, I'll be right back."

Laura watched Chloe walk over to the barista and place her order. When she returned with a cappuccino and a blueberry muffin, they smiled at each other and busied themselves with their coffees, neither of them sure how to proceed. So much time had passed and so many things had happened, but here they were, sitting across a table from each other, mere inches apart. It amazed Laura how, after all these years, the space between them had narrowed so suddenly. In fact, it felt like the narrowest place on earth. And yet an unknowable chasm still existed between them that seemed impossible to cross. So they avoided talking about the past and focused instead on the banalities of the present.

"How long are you in town for?" Laura asked.

"I go home tomorrow," Chloe said.

"Short trip, then."

"Yeah. I wish I could stay longer, but Jake's had Patrick for the whole weekend, so." It was strange for Laura to hear Chloe refer to Jake Hollinger simply as Jake. He had always been Jake Hollinger to Laura, but she supposed it would be weird if Chloe called her own husband by his full name.

"You look exactly the same," Chloe said and smiled.

"I doubt that." Laura looked down at her latte, uncomfortable suddenly. Chloe's smile was friendly, but she felt to Laura like a stranger. A nice stranger, but a stranger nonetheless, and Laura wondered if they had ever actually had anything in common, or if all these years, she had built up their friendship into something it never actually was. She was starting to feel that maybe this reunion was a mistake.

"It's true. You haven't changed at all. Or maybe you have, but I'm just used to seeing your Facebook pictures," Chloe said.

Laura looked up, surprised. It was strange to think that after all her years of passively observing Chloe's life on social media, Chloe had been passively observing hers too.

"You don't post that much, though. You should post more," Chloe said.

"I'm more of a lurker."

"I did see a pic of you somewhere fabulous looking, recently."

Laura thought of Diana then, taking the photo of her on the limestone cliff.

"I just got back from the Bahamas, actually."

"That sounds amazing. You look like you got some sun. Which island?"

"Eleuthera."

"Never heard of it," Chloe said, a crease forming between her eyebrows.

When Laura thought of Chloe, the image that always came to mind was of a teenage girl coasting on her bike in the full bloom of youth, so it was odd to see her now as a full-grown woman whose face showed subtle signs of aging. "It was pretty remote," Laura said.

"Who'd you go with?"

"My boyfriend."

Laura felt embarrassed then for not telling Chloe the truth, that she and Dave had broken up, but it felt important in that moment that Chloe think she was living a particular kind of life endowed with a particular kind of status. After all, Chloe had never known Laura to have a boyfriend. During the entirety of their friendship, she had always been single, and she wanted Chloe to think of her as someone who was capable of being in a relationship.

Chloe leaned closer. "I didn't know you were seeing someone. What's his name?" Her dark eyes lit up, and Laura felt an old, familiar pull.

"Dave."

"I'm assuming from that picture you and Dave did a lot of hiking?"

"Actually, Diana took that shot."

"Who's Diana?"

"This woman I met at the resort."

Laura didn't know why she felt the need to mention Diana now. She felt her hands trembling slightly, so she slid them under her thighs to keep them still.

"You met a woman named Diana on the island of Eleuthera?" Chloe smiled to herself.

"Yeah, why? What's funny?" Laura asked.

"Nothing, it's just, remember when we were kids and I was obsessed with the Greek gods?"

"Sure."

"Artemis was my favorite."

Laura nodded. "She never got married and traveled the world alone."

"Right." Chloe smiled, seemingly pleased that Laura had remembered this detail. "Anyway, her Roman name was Diana, and her epithet was Eleutheria. In Greek, it means 'freedom.'"

This gave Laura pause. "Weird."

"Did this Diana perform any acts of divine intervention in your life?"

Laura laughed and sipped her latte. "Not exactly."

Chloe peeled the paper liner off the bottom of her muffin. "So what does your boyfriend do?"

"He's a lawyer too."

As the words left her mouth, it suddenly felt strange to carry on this pretense with Chloe. A week ago, she would have lied out of fear of judgment, but now she had nothing left to lose, and this was freeing in its own way.

"But we're not together anymore."

"Oh. Sorry to hear that."

"It's OK. Wasn't meant to be."

"I know what that's like," Chloe said cryptically and took a bite of her muffin. As she chewed, her face darkened, and she looked at something out the window.

"Is everything OK?" Laura asked.

"Not really. That's kind of what I wanted to talk to you about."

"What happened?"

"Jake and I are splitting up."

Everything in the café seemed to fall silent then, and all Laura could hear was an acute ringing in her ears.

"Why?" she asked finally.

Chloe took another sip of her cappuccino and told Laura how she had spotted Jake on the street with his spin instructor three weeks prior and followed them to a hotel. She confronted him about it later, and he didn't deny that he had been having an affair. He moved out shortly after that and was staying at a hotel while they sorted out their separation. Laura struggled to absorb the news, but it was almost too much to take in. Chloe and Jake Hollinger were getting a divorce? Jake Hollinger had cheated on Chloe with his spin instructor? Jake Hollinger went to spin class?

"I'm so sorry," Laura said. "That must have been a shock."

"It was, but on some level, I had a feeling something like this might happen one day."

Laura thought of the summer after college when she and Jake Hollinger had slept together, how even then, when he'd been in a relationship with his future wife, he was already cheating on her. She considered telling Chloe this but decided that if she didn't already know, it was not a detail she needed to hear right now.

"I knew about you guys, you know," Chloe said.

Laura swallowed a sip of her latte too quickly, and it burned the roof of her mouth. "What do you mean?" she managed.

"Jake told me about those long phone calls you guys had back in high school."

"Why didn't you ever say anything?" Laura asked.

"What was I supposed to say? I was jealous. He never talked to me back then the way he talked to you."

"Well, you're the one he ended up with."

"And look how that turned out."

Chloe checked the time on her phone and then looked at the photo of her son that she had chosen as her lock screen.

"I guess it wasn't all bad." She held up the photo for Laura to see. "I wouldn't trade my Patty-Cake for anything."

"He's really cute," Laura said.

Chloe showed Laura a dozen other photos of Patrick, and as she flicked through them, she smiled so brightly it made Laura wonder if her smiles in all the photos she had posted over the years hadn't been performative. Maybe her son really did make Chloe that ecstatically happy.

"How's he taking it?" Laura asked.

"The divorce? It's pretty tough on him. Anyway, that's what I wanted to talk to you about. I need a lawyer." Chloe's forehead crinkled with anxiety. "I met with one this morning—that's why I was late—but everything he said . . . it's just all so overwhelming. I was wondering if you could help me."

Laura wasn't sure what to say.

"I know we haven't talked in a long time, but I really need a lawyer who knows me," Chloe said.

Laura nodded, but something about Chloe's request felt discordant, and she didn't want to agree to anything until she had the truth spelled out. "I guess I'm just a bit confused. I thought you wanted nothing to do with me."

Chloe tensed at this. "Laura, that was a million years ago."

"I know, and I get it. We had a fight, and I broke your wrist, and you stopped talking to me."

Chloe curled the edge of her muffin liner. "That's not why I stopped talking to you."

Laura looked at her imploringly. "Then why did you?"

Chloe was quiet for a long time. "Honestly? It was that stupid contract. I never should have signed it," she said finally. "It gave Jake this weird power over me."

Laura stared at Chloe, trying to make sense of her admission. "Why did the contract make you stop talking to me?"

"Because every time I looked at you, it made me think of it, and I felt ashamed. And then you went off to Yale and everything. I thought that you thought you were better than me."

"I didn't think that. I missed you."

"I missed you too. There were so many times I wanted to call you."

"Why didn't you?"

"I don't know. I assumed you had new friends and were off living this fabulous life."

"My life is hardly fabulous."

"Your life looks pretty together, Laura."

Laura shrugged. Chloe played with her phone.

"When did you and Jake get back together?" Laura asked finally, feigning ignorance.

"I bumped into him the summer after we graduated. I was lonely and he was different. He'd grown up a bit. We never really talked about the contract, not even as a joke, but still, I think it made him feel like he could get away with anything. And I guess he did."

Hearing Chloe recount her version of the events felt jarring to Laura, as though she were seeing herself in an old photo she didn't remember being taken. How easy it was to misunderstand someone and to be misunderstood, and how easily those misunderstandings could evolve into mythologies that felt real and true. How easily, had they not met up, they both would have gone on living their respective lives in eternal parallel.

Perhaps that was what true friendship was: being touched so deeply by another person so as to sustain an indelible wound that altered the course of one's life.

Laura didn't want there to be any more misunderstandings between them, no more lies of omission.

"There's something you should know," she said. Chloe looked at her expectantly. "The summer after we graduated from college, I slept with Jake. A couple times. But I didn't know you guys were together."

Laura watched Chloe absorb the news and braced herself for impact. But Chloe didn't get angry; she just uttered a strange, unfathomable sound.

"I should be shocked, but I'm not," she said. "I assumed he started sleeping around after we got married, but I guess he couldn't wait. Which means there were probably others."

She shook her head and crumbled what was left of her muffin into tiny pieces. "Why didn't you ever say anything?" Chloe asked.

"I don't know. I thought you hated me," Laura said.

"I never hated you. But it's just like you to assume the worst. Remember the summer we found that spot by the river?"

Laura nodded, surprised that Chloe remembered.

"Remember when it got trashed? You thought someone got murdered there," Chloe said.

Laura had no memory of this. "No, I didn't."

"You totally did. You said we had to leave and never tell anyone we'd been there or else we'd become suspects."

"Come to think of it, that does sound like something I'd say."

"Ya think?"

Chloe laughed out loud then, her deep, throaty man laugh, and hearing it triggered in Laura a kind of Pavlovian response, and she started laughing too. Suddenly, it was as if no time had passed and they were back in high school again, cackling away, their heads pulled together by their own gravity. In that moment, the vast chasm that separated them vanished, and the magic Laura had assumed was gone forever felt vibrant and palpable, coursing in the narrow space between them. She was overcome then by a feeling she had been desperately yearning for: the intimacy born of a shared secret, a sense of oneness with her old friend.

Laura looked up and saw that all the people who had been in the café earlier had been replaced with different people.

"I can help you with your divorce, but you should probably get someone who specializes in family law."

"I want you."

It felt good to Laura to hear Chloe say that out loud.

"OK, but there's something else you should know. I'm not with my old firm anymore."

Chloe absorbed this, the crease reappearing between her eyebrows. "But you're still a lawyer, right?"

Laura hadn't considered this earlier, but it was true. Though she was no longer an associate at Reinhart, Mader & Stern, she was still a lawyer. Technically, her specialty was contract law, not family law, but she was licensed in the state of New York, and since Chloe lived in Syracuse, representing her was within Laura's jurisdiction.

She nodded.

"Good," Chloe said and stretched. "I guess we're both on our own now."

She was right. Strangely, they were two single women once again. Laura glanced out the window. The sun was setting and the streetlights had come on. She was getting hungry for dinner.

"Can I get a picture of us?" Chloe asked. Laura nodded, and Chloe held her phone aloft.

They both looked up at the screen, and when the angle was just so, Chloe tapped the round button. In the photo, both of them were looking into the camera lens, unsmiling but happy.

"I'll post it and tag you."

Chloe pocketed her phone and asked what the next steps were, and as they stood up and shouldered their bags, Laura told her that she would follow up in the coming days with details about the divorce proceedings.

Outside, the sun had set, and everything was cast in a blue light. The air was cool, and the wind blew their hair around their faces.

"I'm sorry you're going through this, but I'm really glad you reached out," Laura said.

Chloe shrugged. "When I got your Facebook message, I took it as a sign."

Laura scanned Chloe's face, confused. "What Facebook message?"

"The message you wrote to me."

"I was just responding to your message."

"No," Chloe said slowly. "I was responding to yours."

Laura felt a strange tension fill the space between them suddenly. She was certain that she hadn't sent Chloe a Facebook message before receiving the one from her. After all this, was Chloe seriously not going to admit that she had been the one who reached out first?

"I never sent you a message, Chloe."

"Yes, you did."

Laura felt herself bracing for conflict. Perhaps it had been a mistake to reunite with Chloe, to open her heart again, even a little bit, to her old friend. She unlocked her phone, pulled up Facebook, and reread the original message she had received from Chloe the week before:

I'm in NYC next weekend and I need to talk to you. Can we meet for coffee?

Then she read her response:

Yes.

She showed both messages to Chloe.

"But you wrote to me before that," Chloe said, "right after you posted that picture on the cliff."

Chloe looked so sure of herself, so convinced that she was right, that Laura decided, for once, not to catastrophize and to instead give Chloe the benefit of the doubt. She scrolled up on her phone, and an earlier message did indeed appear.

Hey. Long time no see. If you're ever in NYC, I would love to catch up.

Chloe was right. Apparently, Laura had reached out first, except Laura had no recollection of ever sending Chloe that message. She read it again and noticed a time stamp above the message in a faint gray font:

June 5, 1:26 PM

Laura looked up at Chloe. She recalled that June 5 was the day she'd gone for a hike, the day Diana had disappeared. It hit her like a jolt. She'd never written that message to Chloe, but there was one other person who'd handled her phone that day. It was the same person who'd taken her photo on the limestone cliff. The wind picked up then, and

Laura felt tears forming in the corners of her eyes. She didn't know if her tears were the result of the wind or the kindness of Diana's anonymous act. She didn't know what she was feeling exactly, but it felt strange and painful and warm all at once. All she knew was that something had been done to her, something she couldn't quite explain, except to say that it felt a little bit divine.

ACKNOWLEDGMENTS

A huge thank-you to my agent Emily Westcott for taking on a first-time author and working tirelessly to find this book the right home, and massive thanks to my agent Abby Walters for bringing the book across the finish line and for guiding me through the wilderness of book publishing.

I'm tremendously grateful to my acquisitions editor, Dan Ehrenhaft, for his unwavering support, for understanding my vision, and for staying true to it. Dan, you will always be OG Dan from *Gossip Girl* to me. Big thanks also goes out to the rest of the Blackstone team, especially Josie Woodbridge.

I have immeasurable gratitude to my editor, Celia Johnson, for her incredible master class in suspense storytelling. Celia, I had so much fun editing this book with you. Thank you for not only being an enthusiastic champion but also being a fierce guardian of its intent.

Many thanks to my eagle-eyed copy editor Riam Griswold, for their painstaking attention to detail and logic, which saved me from embarrassment and made me look good. Thank you to my fantastic publicists, Tatiana Radujkovic and Brittani Hilles, and marketing whiz Bri Jones for shouting about my book from the rooftops. And thank you to Alta Tseng for designing such a fancy website.

I am deeply grateful to my manager, Craig Brody, and his coordinator,

Mia Flint, for always being in my corner, and to my agents at CAA, Ann Blanchard and Katie Laner, for being incredibly supportive advocates. At CAA, thanks also to Allie Cohen and Chris Licata for your encouragement. I would also like to thank my wonderful lawyer, Chris Abramson, for his support.

Thank you to the early readers of this book for their friendship and thoughtful feedback: Sydney Calvert, Sam Godfrey, Anusree Roy, Ria Tobaccowala, and Emma Bernstein. Thank you also to Liz Tuccillo and Amy Chua for contributing the dreamiest of dream blurbs. And big thanks to my high school English teacher Mr. Hodgson for encouraging me to keep writing my little stories. Your passion and enthusiasm have stayed with me since OAC English composition class.

Of course, much love and gratitude to my family—Mom, Luiza, Charlie, Will, and Peter—for your love and encouragement through this process. Dad: Because you wrote a novel, you made me think I could write one too. I miss you very much. And to baby Sloane: You were my sidekick on the inside for part of this journey. I love you very much. Last but not least, thank you to Jeff Alpern, my first reader and champion. Thank you for encouraging me to start writing this book in the dark days of the pandemic, but more importantly, thank you for urging me not to give up and to just goddamn finish it already. Thank you also for your story editing and for digging this book's title out of a pile of my prose.